M000235092

# AN IDLE KING

## ANDREW PATERSON

Copyright © 2021 by Andrew Paterson

ISBN        book: 978-1-7779345-0-7
            e-book: 978-1-7779345-1-4

Set in Adobe Garamond Pro

Design and typeset by Matthew Revert

This is a work of fiction. Names, characters, businesses, organizations, places, events, and incidents either are the product of the author's imagination or are used fictitiously. Any resemblance to actual persons, living or dead, events, or locales is entirely coincidental.

I am Odysseus. I suffered terribly and I was lost. But after twenty years, I have come home.

— *The Odyssey*

# CONTENTS

7     **PROLOGUE**

9     **PART I:** Why Does It Always Rain in April?

47    **PART II:** Offer, Acceptance, and Consideration

97    **PART III:** Green on Blue

127   **PART IV:** Louis Armstrong Is Dead

151   **PART V:** How to Console a Crying Baby

193   **PART VI:** War Is a Chisel

225   **PART VII:** *Inter Arma Silent Leges*

265   **PART VIII:** The Thane of Crumbs

287   **PART IX:** Eulogy Virtues

# PROLOGUE

"Callum, it's Dev. Give me a buzz. I've got a job for us."

Until that voice mail, Callum hadn't heard from Devon in over a year, not since the day after their court martial when he found Devon passed out naked on his bathroom floor, cradling an empty bottle of rye and a loaded shotgun, looking like a lean cut of steak slapped on the asphalt a few too may times and left in the sun to bake.

After that, Devon became a ghost. No matter what Callum tried, he couldn't get hold of him. Phone calls, voice mails, text messages, emails. He even went around to his house every day for weeks. Whenever he did, Devon's wife, Chloe, would be there but wouldn't know where Devon was or where her husband had gone or how to find him.

That was how it went for a whole year. Nothing. Until that voice mail.

As soon as he got the message, Callum punched out the number, but the robot voice on the other end said it had been disconnected. Then he hopped in his truck and drove to Devon's place as fast as he could. Chloe said she hadn't seen Devon for months.

After two more weeks of radio silence, Callum was ready to let it go.

Until the contract showed up in his mailbox.

# PART I

# WHY DOES IT ALWAYS RAIN IN APRIL?

# CHAPTER ONE

"I'm going back," Callum says.

"Can you take Timmy to school?" Penny asks, not even flinching.

"Did you hear me?"

"I'm not doing this right now."

Penny slams the door and leaves Callum alone in the foyer. That conversation was about twice as long as any other they had in the past year. Progress.

Callum pours a cup of coffee out of the pot on the counter. Kicks off his slippers and walks barefoot outside into the snow into the little backyard that looks out over the highway where the din from the early-morning traffic washes over every other sound. He stands like that while his feet turn numb from the cold, watching a murmur of starlings twist and turn over the back field, silver wings like a thousand shards of a mirror bound to the wind.

"Dad, can you take me to school now?" Timmy hollers from inside their house.

Callum dumps the full cup of coffee into the snow and turns to go back inside. He steps over laundry piled knee-high in a basket at the back door and gently closes the door behind him, so as not to wake the dog lying still on a pillow underneath the window. Not that it would matter.

He kneels next to the dog, buries his face deep in the pet's fur, and breathes in the animal's sickness, holding his breath as long as he can. Callum imagines the dog as he was, a time when they were both freer than they are now. Was that ever the way things were? Or is that how he wants to remember them?

The dog doesn't move or make a sound.

Callum grabs a towel from the pile of laundry and wraps it around the dog, tight as he can, careful to ensure nothing spills onto the ground, as if he were picking up a bag of sand. He carries the dog to the car parked in the driveway, sets the animal down in the back seat, walks around to the driver's seat, and gets inside.

Timmy comes out of the house and climbs in the passenger side of the car. They pull away from the house and drive in silence for a couple of blocks, away from their perfectly adequate little home through their perfectly adequate little neighbourhood. The only home Timmy has ever known. The neighbourhood where Timmy grew up. Where they tried to build a life for their son. And a family.

"Is Argus going to be okay?" Timmy asks.

Callum checks the rearview mirror to see the dog lying motionless in the back seat. "I don't know."

"Mom said you're going to take him to the vet again."

"I'm heading there after I drop you off."

"Didn't you take him yesterday?"

"That was to a different place."

"What about the place before that?"

"He's sick. He needs a doctor."

"Okay."

Callum glances at the boy. Light and inscrutable in the seat next to him. Timmy was a child once. But now he's something else. A half-child maybe. Something else he can't describe even though Callum was once the same. The impermanence of it all squeezes at him.

Timmy continues to gaze out the window at the cars passing in the opposite direction. "Dad ..."

"Yeah."

"I think I'm a pacifist."

"What does that mean?"

"It means I don't believe in war."

"What do you mean, you don't believe in war?"

"I don't believe in it."

"It's not the fucking tooth fairy."

Timmy pauses for a beat as he stares up at his father. "Mom says you swear too much."

"What else does Mom say?"

"About you?"

"Yeah."

"Not much really."

They pull up in front of Timmy's school, austere against the departed light of late winter. Children play in the surrounding fields, separated by age and size in no-go zones, restricted areas, and attack positions. A forward operating base dominates the basketball court across from a combat outpost erected along the back fence. The older kids occupy key terrain by the smoking pit while the main approach routes to the school entrance serve as vital ground. Jungle gym warfare.

Callum parks the car but leaves it idling. "All right. I'll see you at your game tonight."

"You're going back, aren't you?"

"Going back where?"

"I don't know. For work or something."

"Who told you that?"

"I heard you tell Mom this morning."

"Well, your mother and I still need to talk about it."

"I don't think you should go. We don't need the money. Mom's doing well at work now."

"It's not that easy, bud."

"Okay."

"We'll talk about it later. You're gonna be late."

Timmy doesn't say anything but reaches into the back seat and runs his hand through the threadbare mane still clinging to the dog's face. The boy gets out of the car and dashes into the school with his backpack jostling behind him, past a group of boys his age who don't acknowledge him.

Callum watches Timmy race off and fights the urge to chase him. For most of their lives, it was the other way around: Timmy standing on a rain-soaked tarmac holding Penny's hand, waving goodbye as his father boarded a waiting plane; Timmy as a small child, so small that Callum could hold him in two hands. And countless and unforgivable other times in between.

Now Callum is going to leave again.

Callum waits to drive away until Timmy disappears into the school. He shifts out of park, turns out of the school parking lot, and makes his way toward the veterinarian clinic.

The clinic is nestled between a European hair salon and a shawarma joint in a suburban strip mall. Unremarkable except for a giant sign placed over the entrance with a picture of a grinning Labrador retriever on its face. He parks the car in an empty spot outside the clinic and carries Argus inside.

Three even rows of hard plastic chairs face the reception, located at the far end of the waiting room. He bypasses a computer monitor emitting elevator music, fixed atop a pedestal in front of the reception counter, to speak directly with the receptionist. She doesn't look up when he approaches and continues to scroll past pictures on her phone.

"Excuse me," he says through the plastic screen in front of him. "I'm here for an appointment for my dog."

"Could you please sign in, sir?" She nods toward the monitor behind him before returning to her phone.

He's about to ask what she's doing here but doesn't and turns to face the monitor. Cradling Argus in one arm, he taps the screen with his unoccupied hand to bring the monitor to life and proceeds to answer a series of tombstone questions about Argus. When was Argus born? Where was Argus born? What is his breed? Favourite food? Favourite colour? Health concerns? Would Argus provide his consent to have his personal information disclosed to unknown third parties?

At the conclusion of the questionnaire, the monitor spits out a little ticket with a number printed on it. The life of Argus reduced to a barcode. Callum turns and slides the ticket under the glass to the indifferent receptionist.

"Thank you, sir. Please have a seat. The veterinarian will be right with you."

"Do you need to know my name?"

"We know who you are, sir. Please have a seat."

A ribald old lady sits front and centre before the reception, peering over the top of a crate, observing the entire exchange with the receptionist. "That's a lovely dog you have there."

"Thank you." He tries to glimpse whatever it is that's in the crate, big enough that the lady could fit inside. "That's a nice cat."

"It's a ferret."

"Oh …"

"I'm getting him fixed."

"Right."

"He gets a little frisky sometimes."

"Sorry to hear that."

"Oh, it's quite all right." She runs her tongue over her teeth, stained purple with lipstick.

Callum smiles politely while backing away to take the farthest seat at the end of the row. Argus, sprawled on his lap, tries to shift into a more comfortable position. But Argus can only manage to raise his nose for a moment before stoically settling his head back down. The two of them sit like that for some time, waiting to be called in by the receptionist.

To pass the time, he considers getting up to pace around the room but resists the temptation when he hears the old woman whispering into her crate and glancing back at them. On the verge of leaving, the receptionist finally says, "Sir, the vet's ready for you."

Moving briskly past the woman, he enters a door next to the reception counter, which opens into a short hallway with a second door at the end. Inside the second door is a plain room smelling of doggie treats and cat litter. Posters of animals with ailments, maladies, and disorders adorn the walls. The logos of various pharmaceutical companies imprinted conspicuously next to reams of fine print. Consult your vet today.

He sets Argus down on the examining table and slides over a stool so he can remain by the dog's side.

Although Argus doesn't betray any impatience, Callum can't sit still and wait any longer. At first, he starts by examining the posters on the wall. Once they've all been read, he wanders around the room. When he tires of that, he resigns himself to waiting on the stool next to Argus.

Eventually, the vet strolls in with his arms crossed and sits on a stool next to the table. "The results have come in."

"And?"

"I'm sorry. There's nothing else we can do."

"What does that mean?"

"It means we've done everything we can."

"But you're a doctor."

"Technically, I'm a veterinarian."

"Then do your job."

"I have, sir."

"No, you haven't. Just do your job. You said on the phone that maybe there were some treatments …"

"I know. And I'm sorry. But it's too late."

"It's not too late. He's right there."

"If you go to the front desk, we can make the necessary arrangements."

Callum slams his fists on the table. The vet recoils while Argus barely lifts his head. "Necessary arrangements. What the fuck does that mean?"

"Please, sir, you're going to have to calm down."

"My dog's sick, he's dying, and I can't help him. Do you understand that?"

"Yes, I understand."

"He's going to die and I can't help him."

"I'm going to have to ask you to leave."

"Fuck you!" He picks Argus off the table, who immediately voids his bladder, as if from a garden hose, all over the veterinarian. The vet, unperturbed, allows the urine to dribble down his chest and splash in a puddle on the floor before scribbling some notes on a chart hanging on the door.

As soon as Argus finishes, Callum says, "I'm not making any necessary arrangements."

"Please leave."

"I'm sorry about that. C'mon, Argus, let's go home." Before they're out of earshot, he whispers to Argus, "Good boy."

Callum ignores the receptionist and the ferret lady and storms outside, straight to his car, where he places Argus in the back seat. He gets in the front and stares at his hands gripping the steering wheel, squeezing until his hands stop shaking.

He can't look back at the seat behind him. He doesn't know what to say. What are you supposed to say to someone who's dying?

The last time he had that conversation was with his mom. It was breast cancer. And then it was something else. The last thing she asked him was whether any stars were out. He said, "No, Ma. I don't think there are." Then the drugs got hold of her and she never said anything again.

The first time was with one of his corporals who stepped on an IED outside some shitty patrol base. He doesn't remember what he said that time. Maybe "Hang in there." Or "You'll be okay." Most likely he didn't say anything at all. It didn't matter because the corporal bled out in thirty-two minutes before the medevac could get there.

Those were the things he said then. But he doesn't know what to say now. He glances back, anyway. Argus lifts his head to return Callum's gaze. Callum wants him to know in ways Callum never could.

Finally, he says to the dog, "I'm sorry you're going to die. And I'm sorry I couldn't save you. But I hope you had a good life."

Callum releases his breath and lets go of the steering wheel. He starts the car, and they drive away from the clinic without looking back.

# CHAPTER TWO

Callum parks the car in a narrow lot between a dilapidated church and a gleaming condominium tower. He gathers Argus from the car's back seat and carries him across the lot where the ice cleaves at the cracked asphalt. A heavy chain bars the church's main door, forcing him to stomp through knee-high drifts of snow around the side of the building in search of another way in. Callum comes to a side entrance down nine crooked steps. He descends to the bottom with Argus draped in his arms, fumbling with the handle before managing to open the door.

Every time he comes here, he likes to imagine the door leads to a bare-knuckle boxing gym or an illicit sex club instead of a veteran support group in a musty church basement. A man's reach should exceed his grasp.

Tattered curtains shield a dark stage at one end of the basement hall. Faded posters of smiling children form a collage on the wall. Metal folding chairs are arranged in a circle next to a collapsible metal table, half askew on one gimpy leg. Eight men mill about, speaking in low voices and sipping coffee from Styrofoam cups. One or two new faces. Otherwise, he recognizes the rest. Not the most they've ever had but not the least, either.

He makes his way to the table first and offers a head nod or handshake to the familiar people. A pilfered box of doughnuts are shunted toward the edge of the table. He picks up a coffee urn with his free hand while holding Argus in his other arm and attempts to unscrew the cap on top of the urn. But the urn slips from his hand, spilling the remaining coffee all over the table. One of the new faces, just a kid, rushes over to help him sop up the mess with a pile of napkins. After throwing the wet napkins in the garbage and wiping his damp hand on his pants, he mumbles thanks to the kid and takes a seat on one of the chairs.

Callum has been coming to the meetings off and on for the past year. No one knows when these get-togethers began or who started them. There are a few regulars, guys who are there every meeting. Most often, though, he would see someone show up for a couple of weeks and then miss a week here or there before disappearing completely. The membership didn't matter, though. They weren't all the same. But everyone told the same stories over and over again. Still, people kept showing up.

"All right, fellas, let's get started," Callum says. He isn't the group's leader. Not exactly. But they usually look to him to begin things and keep them moving. It ended up that way somewhere along the line. He's not sure when, though, or why. But it came naturally. So why not?

They each take a seat in the circle. "Thanks for coming out," Callum tells them. "I already know most of you guys, but my name's Callum. And this is Argus." He gently pats the dog's flank. "I see we've got some new faces here. Let's go around the circle and introduce ourselves. Maybe tell us something about how your week's going."

The man on Callum's right raises a hand. "Name's Patrick." He tugs on his white T-shirt, drawn tight over a belly shaped like a milk bag. "This week I walked in on my wife getting stove-piped by the guy who sold us our minivan."

"What did you do?" someone asks.

"There was something wrong with the brakes, so I took it back."

"Not with the van. What about your wife?"

"We're cool."

"Yeah."

"Yeah. I was kind of into it."

"That's messed up."

"I know."

"All right then," Callum says. "Anyone else?"

The kid who helped Callum mop up the coffee raises a hand, as if he knows the problem to a complicated math problem and wants to impress his teacher. "Hi, I'm Habs."

"Like the hockey team?" Patrick asks.

"No. As in, hard as b-b-baby shit," Habs stutters. "That's what it stands for. It's what they used to call me back in the battalion." Drawing a couple of puzzled glances, he continues. "Anyway, I figured out this morning walking over here, that I only want two things out of life." He waits for someone to ask him what they are, but no one does. "Have you guys ever been at a restaurant and some guy orders a bottle of wine and when the waiter pours the wine and the guy does that thing where he swishes it around on the table and then gargles it?"

Patrick nods.

"Well, I want to be able to s-s-smash the glass out of the guy's hand. And then the guy gets up and walks out of the restaurant and the rest of us get on with our lives."

More heads in the circle nod.

"I want to have enough power in my life to be able to do that," says Habs.

"What's the second thing?" Callum asks.

"You know in movies like *Star Wars* when the rebels blow up the Death Star and there's a scene with a bunch of wogs giving high-fives in the command centre?"

No one nods.

"Well, I want to be one of those guys ... not like in real life. I know there isn't a Death Star. At least not yet, I don't think. But like as an extra in a movie. Like that."

"That's great." Patrick nods and leans forward, elbows resting on his knees. "I've told some of you guys this before, but my thing is that I want to build a cabin someday."

"C'mon, man, you're about as handy as a fluffer at the Houston 500," says a man directly across the circle from Patrick, wearing a black toque pulled down low over thick brushy eyebrows that join at their edges with a bushy black beard.

"Thanks, Jax," Patrick says. "Always appreciate your input, bud."

"No sweat, bud."

"How about you?" Callum asks the other new guy at the meeting.

"I'm Theo." He raises his hand to acknowledge the group before brushing his leg with the back of his hand, as if it's covered in dust. "Did two tours in Afghanistan. First one with

Patrick there. That's how we know each other." Theo sends a quick nod in Patrick's direction. "He thought it would be good for me to come to one of these."

"Thanks for coming out," Callum says.

"How does this work then? Do I just talk about whatever?"

"Whatever you want. You can tell us about your tours. Or what's going on in your life. It's up to you."

"All right then. Well, I guess I'll start with tour stuff." Theo sweeps absentmindedly at the imaginary dust on his clothes. "On my second tour, we were leaving some shithole patrol base for some shithole village. Every day on patrol, this kid would follow us, and like clockwork, we got lit up every time. We'd tell this kid to piss off, but there he'd be every day. One day I said fuck it and gave him my iPod. He didn't know what it was and nearly shit himself when I put it on him. After he figured it out, though, he had this big shit-eating grin." Theo pauses for a second to tuck his greasy shoulder-length hair behind his ears. "But the next day, he wasn't there. First time in two weeks we weren't ambushed. We didn't see him the next day, either. And then on the third day we found his body in a ditch, five hundred metres from the patrol base. Every bone in his face was broken. The only way we could tell it was him was because the iPod was on his chest. After that, I didn't talk to the kids very much."

"All right," Callum says.

Theo draws in a deep breath before continuing. "And then, when I got home from my second tour, I started seeing this dude everywhere I went. I didn't know him. Didn't know who he was. But I saw him everywhere. The grocery store. The bus.

I thought he was following me. Like a narc. Then I saw him on TV. And then the dreams started. The next thing I knew, I woke up in cells. They said I broke into someone's house. Tried to blow it up by putting hairspray in the microwave. The fucked-up thing is, I don't remember any of it. Couldn't even tell you what the dude looked like. Guess I wigged out. They gave me a medical discharge. And that shit don't look too good on a résumé. So here I am."

"That's okay," Callum says. "Let me ask you this. Did you ever hurt yourself before? Your back? Your knee? Anything like that?"

"Yeah, I hurt my back."

"What did you do?"

"Went to the doctor."

"Right. You got help."

"I guess so."

"Ever been sick before? Had the flu or anything like that?"

"Of course."

"So what did you do? You got help, right? You got meds."

"Yeah."

"That's all this is, man. A place for you to get help. Just a different kind of help. It's a place to tell your stories. And we'll all listen."

"I did that. I went for help. And they sent me to a shrink who said I have a flat affectation, whatever that means. Then he gave me a prescription for a bunch of pills that I couldn't pronounce." Theo picks up an empty Styrofoam cup at his feet and tears thumbnail-size bits from it, flicking them onto the floor. "There's this constant ... pressure inside me. Like someone's standing on my chest. And the only thing that ever made it go away was when some asshole was shooting at me. Now they want me to take some pills to make all that go away."

"Bunch of fucking pussies," Jax growls. "I don't know why I come to these fucking meetings."

Callum shakes his head. "Easy ..."

"No, fuck that! I'm sick of all this victimhood bullshit. *Wah, wah, wah*. And look at you, man." Jax points a finger at Callum. "You're the biggest phony here. You used to be a fucking legend man. Now look at you. You're a washed-up, self-righteous prick feeding all these losers a bunch of fake-ass, self-actualize-yourself, Tony Robbins bullshit."

"It's not your fault."

"Fuck you, Good Will Hunting." Jax shoots to his feet, kicking the chair out from beneath him. Jaw and fists clenched. Three rifle lengths away from Callum. Maybe less.

Not much Callum can do in that position. Especially with Argus on his lap. He locks eyes with Jax. Breathes in through his nose until he can feel his pulse thumping in his temples. Slowly exhales through his mouth. Waits for the black to fade.

"Fuck this!" Jax flips over the coffee table on his way out. Sending the empty coffee urn skittering along the floor and the doughnut box spinning end over end into a dark corner of the church basement.

Callum has known Jax for a while. Not as far back as their army days. They know a lot of the same people, though. It's a small army. Everybody knows, or knew, everybody else. If not personally, then by reputation. Which is everything in a family like that.

Callum helped Jax through some shit. Is helping him through some shit. So none of this should have been a surprise. But it is. Not just Jax. Callum's reaction, too. A bit delayed. A bit slow. But the instincts are still there. The focus. The adrenaline. It's all still there. It's been a while. But it feels good. Really good.

Time to wrap the meeting up.

"Don't listen to him, man," Patrick says to Theo. "He's an asshole. No one's calling you a victim. You oughta be proud of what you did. You're a warrior." Patrick slides his chair over in front of Theo and reaches across to grab him by the shoulder. "You know when Apache warriors would come home from war, they'd go through the Sun Ritual and pierce wooden skewers through the skin of their chests tied to long leather straps. And the straps would be attached to a pole they'd dance around to the beat of a drum honouring their ancestors."

"I think I'd rather go to Vegas," Habs says.

Patrick and Theo both turn and stare at Habs, neither sure of how to respond.

"All right, fellas, let's end it there for the week," says Callum. "Thanks for coming out. Hopefully, we'll see you guys again. If you want to meet up before then, give me a buzz."

After the group files out in ones and twos, Habs approaches Callum. "Hey, man, what's with the dog?"

"He's sick."

"Poor guy," says Habs as he pets Argus on the head. "You kept your cool in there. I thought you were going to dust him."

"I don't believe in violence."

"Well, that's some serious Jedi shit you pulled on him." Habs stands there awkwardly, unsure what to say next. "Cool.

Well, I heard you're going to join one of those private military groups, outfits, whatever you call them."

Callum hasn't told anyone about the contract, so how does this kid know about it? "Where did you hear that?"

"From Devon."

Callum almost drops Argus. "When did he tell you that? How do you know Dev?"

Habs laughs nervously. "I knew him from back in the battalion. He was my duty NCO once. I knew about you, too, but didn't, like, actually know you. Everybody knew you. They fucked you guys over, man."

"That's a long time ago. But what about Devon? When did you last talk to him?"

"I don't know. A couple of weeks ago maybe. I hadn't heard from him in a long time. And then he reached out to me. He must have heard I was looking for work. Then he offered me a job."

"Did he tell you about me?"

"Yeah. He said I could find you here. That I should come and talk to you."

Callum hasn't heard from the bastard in two weeks and then this kid shows up out of nowhere. Why would Devon get this kid mixed up in all of this? That didn't make any sense. "Where's Devon now?"

Habs shrugs. "I don't know. I think he already went over. He told me I could go over with you."

Callum sits on one of the chairs. He needs to think. Figure this all out.

"So are we going?" Habs presses.

"Going where?"

"To Afghanistan."

"With you? Definitely not."

"Why not?" When Callum doesn't respond, Habs asks, "You're going, right?"

"I don't know. I haven't decided yet."

"All right, cool." Habs pulls up a chair next to Callum. "Here's the thing, though. Devon said you'd talk to the company on my behalf. Like a reference or something."

"Look, kid, this isn't a recruiting centre. I don't even know you." Habs can't be much older than Timmy. Just a kid. But he's definitely got something Timmy doesn't have. Something Callum's seen many times before. Maybe even something he himself once had. "Why don't you become a cop? They're hiring. And the benefits are better."

"Probably the same reason you d-d- didn't become a cop." Habs pauses and stares up at the church ceiling. "I've never been good at anything else. Wearing that uniform gave me something I never had before."

"Then you should have stayed in the army."

"That wasn't gonna happen." Habs tries to hide the embarrassment on his face by examining the cracks on the ground. But Callum sees right through it. "I got in some shit and they kicked me out. It wasn't my fault, though. And it didn't have anything to do with being a soldier."

"That's not much of a reference, is it?"

"No, I guess not." Habs perks up. "But I'm a checked-out troop."

Callum doesn't say anything. Keeps looking at the kid. Trying to think of something to say to get him to walk away. But knows there's probably nothing he can do or say to change Habs's mind. The kid will go somewhere else, anyway. Maybe some place worse.

"I need this," Habs insists. "I've got nothing else."

"Here, take down this number," Callum says.

Without hesitation, Habs enters the number in his phone.

"I need to talk to Devon and figure this out," Callum says. "Give me a call in the next couple of days."

"Awesome. All right, I'll give you a call."

"Okay."

"Thanks, man." Habs turns to leave. "And I hope your dog gets better."

After the kid leaves, Callum sits alone for a while with Argus still on his lap, gazing at the upturned table. His mind decided, he gets up and places the old table back on its rickety legs, turns off the light in the basement wall, and carries Argus out of the abandoned church into a late-winter afternoon.

# CHAPTER THREE

Callum drives away from the church along busy streets that quiet and turn white with snow the colour of asphodel, heading into the country through bleak fields ranged beneath grey skies. He turns onto a side road and slowly passes a barn askew on its frame, then goes down a narrow lane shrouded with trees. Parking the car next to an empty field, he lumbers through the snow holding Argus tightly to his body.

A lone oak tree stands guard in the middle of the field, void of leaves and bent low under the weight of the winter sky. Callum sits and rests with his back against the tree. Snow covers the ground, but he doesn't notice the cold. Argus rests on his lap and doesn't move.

A branch from the tree lies within arm's length. Careful not to disturb Argus, Callum leans over and draws the branch toward him. Longer than his arm and almost as thick, it's covered in rough bark all the way to the sharp end where it broke away from the tree. He holds the branch at the rough end, pointing it straight up at the sky, to weigh its balance and heft. In one motion, he flips the branch in his hand and grasps it toward the middle as if it were a javelin. With a slight heave, he launches the branch into the air and watches it sail away until it crashes to the frozen ground, skids and comes to a stop a short distance away.

Callum wills Argus to jump from his lap and sprint after the branch the way he's done a thousand times before. But when Argus doesn't move, Callum returns his hand to the dog's side. Where once there was muscle, now there's just bones and skin made weak by time and fate.

Shifting his weight after his legs have fallen numb, Callum is reminded of his other obligations by the lump of the cellphone in his back pocket. As he slides the phone free, the screen flashes to life with the icon of a single unread email message beaming from the lower right corner, bright as the lit stub of a cigarette in the middle of a patrol base.

The email came in late last night. He hasn't opened it yet but knows what it says.

After he got the contract, a company rep followed up with a phone call to explain the situation. At first, Callum didn't give a shit about the contract or anything to do with the company. He just wanted to know where Devon was. Callum hung up on the rep when the man couldn't give a straight answer.

They were persistent, though.

The next day another rep called Callum. This time he said Devon was busy getting their team together but would get in touch as soon as he could. In the meantime, they were "super-stoked" to have Callum on board. The rep said that Devon kept telling everyone Callum was the best, that they couldn't find a better man for the job. "So why don't you look over the contract?" the rep asked.

Callum did. But even after wading through all the legalese, the details in the contract were still a little hazy. Something about security work for a company bidding on an infrastructure project in Kandahar, or something like that. Apparently, Devon would give Callum the full download once he signed on.

And then he got a call from the company's lawyer on the third day to walk through the contract. "Industry standard," the lawyer said. "Boiler-plate stuff. But you should have a lawyer review it before you sign it. You know, because of liability issues. If you don't have any questions, just email us a scanned copy. There's even programs now that'll sign it for you electronically." Like the lawyer was getting paid by the word.

That was almost enough to make Callum eat his chunk.

But then there was another voicemail from Devon. "Sorry, man, been busy getting the band together and I want you to be a part of it. So hear them out, okay? Besides, what else are you going to do?"

Devon was right. What was he going to do?

Callum wrestled with that question for the past year. At first, he thought about going back to school but couldn't figure out what he wanted to study. He ended up taking a handful of online courses instead, which turned out to be as useful as a pair of Gucci gloves on a ruck march. After that he signed on with one of those executive leadership consulting groups run by a bunch of veterans that were popping up all over the place. The corporate-suit types ate that shit up. Callum hated it.

And then this came along. Callum never saw himself doing work for a private security company, let alone one doing something back in Afghanistan. At one point, they couldn't have paid him enough to return. But that was then. And now there could be a lot of zeros at the end of a paycheque.

It isn't about the money, though. He thought he buried the guilt with Devon and everything that happened in his past life, figured he moved beyond it all. If not into something better, then at least into some kind of middle zone stuck halfway between the past and the future. At least it was somewhere and not there.

Devon was one of his soldiers. But more than that Devon was a friend and a brother, too. Devon was his responsibility. Maybe still is. Perhaps Callum owes something to Devon even after all this time. If nothing else, then maybe he owes it to Devon to tag along, to make sure his friend doesn't mess everything up again.

Callum desperately wants to ask Penny for her advice. Tried to bring it up with her many times. Maybe not many times. Perhaps a couple of times. But the longer he waited, the easier it became not to say anything at all — until it spilled out this morning, probably not at the best time.

He closes his eyes for a moment and tries to imagine Penny stomping through the field toward him, yelling at him to get on with it, to stop being so sentimental. There might have been a time when that would have happened, when she'd have said those things. But that would have been a long time ago now, if there was ever a time like that at all.

With his eyes still closed, he pictures Penny standing on the far side of a distant green hill, in the same way he always dreamed of her when he was away. No matter how far he runs or how fast in the vision, she's always gone when he gets to the other side. Still, he knows she'll always be there — until he opens his eyes and she isn't.

Penny would understand. She always did. Especially when she finds out the reason for leaving is to find Devon.

But not Timmy. What will he say to his son?

The court martial was hard on Timmy. He didn't understand what was going on, why they were doing this to Callum when his father could do no wrong in his eyes. It probably didn't help that Callum disappeared for a while after the court martial.

Although they never did talk about what happened, things were getting better between them recently. Callum was getting more involved in Timmy's life. Going to basketball games. PTA meetings. Neighbourhood barbecues with all the other dads. Stuff he never thought he'd do.

He should stay for Timmy, unless his son doesn't want him to. Maybe Timmy wants him to leave. Do what he's supposed to do.

Callum's father will know what he should do. The man had to do it enough times with Callum, though Callum doesn't ever remember them talking about it. Maybe all Callum ever got was a pat on the back or a handshake, shoulders back, head up, eyes forward. But things were different then.

At least Callum will have someone to talk to.


Callum's father lives in a seniors' home a short drive back toward the city, outside the downtown core and beyond the sprawl of glass government buildings, tucked away down a quiet suburban street.

After Callum signs the visitors' book, he walks down a hallway to a solarium in the rear of the building. At least that's what his dad calls it — the solarium — when, really, the room is more like a school cafeteria reeking of burnt margarine and disinfectant. Molten teacups spill over in the sink. Yellowed newspapers and magazines are stacked knee-high on side tables, bookshelves, and cabinets. A black-and-white movie blasts from a TV in the corner while the inmates — that's what his dad calls them, the inmates — shuffle around with their canes and walkers, oblivious to the noise.

His father sits alone in the corner, moving back and forth on a squeaky rocking chair as he stares out the window. As if he's waiting for the past to walk in and sit beside him.

"Hi, Dad."

"Hello, boy," his father, Larry, responds without looking up.

Callum pulls over a folding chair and places it next to his father. "It's your birthday this weekend."

Larry expels a dismissive grunt.

Callum ignores the noise. "I was hoping you'd come over for supper."

"There are only three times in a man's life when he should have a celebration in honour of himself — his wedding, his retirement, and his death."

"So, are you coming over?"

"We have bingo nights on Saturdays."

"You hate bingo."

"No shit." Larry leans forward, resting his arms on his knees, and look Callum right in the eyes. "You know what would help, though?"

"What?"

"Can you get me some of that weed?"

"Weed?"

"Marijuana. Pot. A j-bone. Whatever you kids call it." Larry mimes rolling a joint between his fingers before pretending to smoke a pipe.

Callum sighs. "Yeah, I know what weed is."

"Can you get me some?"

"I don't know if they'll let you use that stuff here."

Larry rolls his eyes and flops back in his chair. "I bet you get invited to all the parties."

"No, not really."

"Well, fuck 'em. You'll pass them many times on their long march through the wide grey middle."

Two of the inmates draw Callum's attention. Each is the colour of aged cheese, the kind kept behind glass in a grocery store. They're cantilevered up at a Formica table with various implements. One of them appears to be asleep, while the other spoons at a tepid bowl of soup.

The old man with the soup places his spoon beside the bowl and pulls his T-shirt over his head. The sleeping man's head snaps upward as he snorts, "Bernie, what the hell? Put your shirt back on." The old man with the soup puts his shirt back on and returns to slurping the soup. After the other man's head bobs down on his chest, Bernie proceeds to remove his shirt again. The sleeping man's head snaps up as he yells, "Bernie, what the hell? Put your shirt back on." Around and around they go. Ever after.

"I got a job offer," Callum says to his father.

"Doing what?"

"A job back in Afghanistan."

Larry's eyebrows dart up while the corners of his mouth turn down. "With who?"

"A private security company."

"Mercenaries."

"I don't think they call themselves that, but yeah."

Larry lets loose a gob of spit that splatters on the carpet. "You're not going to take it, are you?"

"I don't know. Haven't decided yet." Callum pauses. "It's with Devon. He asked me to go with him."

"You mean that knucklehead who got you court-martialled?"

Callum releases a deep sigh. "We've been over this, Dad. It wasn't all his fault."

"Jesus, I never understood why you fell on your sword for that cowboy."

Callum wonders about that himself, as well. He would have made the same decision again one hundred times out of one hundred, but then he wonders what his life would have been like if he hadn't.

"What does Penny think?" Larry asks.

"We haven't really talked about it, but I don't think she's going to be too impressed."

"No, I wouldn't expect she'd be." Larry returns his attention to the window. "Strongest person I ever met, your Penny. She'd have made one hell of a soldier."

"I can't see Penny carrying a rifle."

"There's a lot more to being a soldier than carrying a rife, as you know." When Callum doesn't say anything, Larry adds, "You're going, aren't you?"

"I think so … yeah."

"So you didn't come here for my advice, did you?"

"I wanted to hear what you had to say."

Larry wipes the spittle from the corner of his mouth with the back of a sleeve. "You were always a clever boy, but sometimes I think all that nonsense you keep in that head of yours, duty, honour —" Larry pokes a bony finger into his temple "— was always going to be your downfall."

"I learned that stuff from you, Dad."

"And look where it got you."

Callum can't argue with that.

"Okay." Larry leans back in his chair and gazes out the window. "You tell Penny I'll be there for supper on Saturday. Five sharp. And tell her not to make any of that hippie three-bean shit. She knows I hate it but always makes it, anyway."

"I'll tell her. I've got to go now, though. Timmy's got a basketball game tonight."

"All right." The old man extends his gnarled hand to his son, holds on as if he might fall from a cliff if he lets go.

Callum releases his father's hand and leaves him alone at the window.

When Callum arrives at Timmy's school, the parking lot is already full. So he parks on the street a couple of blocks away, finding a spot beneath a lamppost unmoored from the ground. With Argus slung over his shoulder, he walks the short distance and enters the school through a side door into the gymnasium. Cheering streams outside; the game has already begun.

He pauses inside the door, allowing winter air to flood inside, provoking sideway glances from the spectators on either side of the door who expect him to come inside or close the door.

The crowd spills out around the court and the stands are mostly full. Callum spies space up on the back row of one of the bleachers where most of the parents reside, leaving the front rows for students. He offers a curt apology to the other parents before stumbling over and around the tangle of bodies and collapsing into an open seat.

Callum recognizes a few faces of other parents in the crowd but none he knows that well. Penny isn't there, either. She never misses a game. She's always there cheering the loudest of anyone. Sometimes she goes back to the office after the game, but she's always there to see it.

Turning his attention back to the game, he sees that the score isn't close. Timmy is on the bench. It doesn't look as if he's seen much action if the dry towel slung around his shoulders is any indication. His coach puts him in for a couple of minutes toward the end of the game. Callum might have to have words with the coach afterward. What does that guy know?

After the game is finished, he waits in the stands for Timmy to come out of the locker room. Most of the crowd has already emptied out of the gym. A few of the other parents give him a nod or hello, but that's it.

Per usual, Timmy is one of the last to emerge from the locker room. Most of the rest of the gym has already emptied out, but a couple of younger kids kick a ball around. They're too small to throw it in the net.

"Good game, bud," he says to Timmy as his son makes his way toward the exit.

"We got smoked."

"I thought you had a good game."

"Yeah."

"You played some tough defence at the end there."

"Okay."

They walk out of the gym through the nearly vacant parking lot. The cold mist of their breath hangs in the air between them. Timmy wears only a hoodie. Penny probably would have asked him to put on a jacket, but Callum decides to let it go.

When they get into the car and drive off, he asks Timmy, "Who was that girl you were talking to after the game?"

"No one."

"Do you want to invite her over for supper on Saturday?"

"Not a chance."

Probably a mistake to ask that one, so he goes in a different direction. "I went to see your grandfather."

Timmy pauses for a second, then glances at his dad before responding, "Yeah ..."

"You should go see him sometime."

"I do." Timmy turns his attention to his cellphone. "He's kinda crazy."

"We're all on the spectrum, bud."

"He wants me to call him Larry."

"That's his name."

"He asked me to buy him drugs the last time I saw him."

"That's not good. Don't buy your grandfather drugs."

"I'll do my best."

He looks over at Timmy. People always say they grow up too fast, but when does the growing up happen? Callum can't remember any of that. Only Timmy when he was so small. And now this. Not a boy. Definitely not a man. Something else.

It's Timmy who breaks the silence. "Dad."

"Yeah, bud?"

"Do you still love her?"

"Who?"

"Mom."

Callum draws in a deep breath before saying, "That was never our problem."

Timmy doesn't ask any more questions and lets the subject go as they pull up to their modest home looming at the end of the street beyond the car's headlights.

It's the first home he and Penny ever bought together. The only home they've ever known. The plan, at first, was to stay for a couple of years. Save up some money and then move into another neighbourhood closer to downtown. Maybe someplace with a little restaurant on the corner where they knew the bartender and always sat at the same window. Then Timmy came along and none of that ever happened. So they stayed year after year. Redid the basement and had a powder room put in on the main floor. Got to know some of the neighbours. And it became their home. At least for Penny and Timmy.

The house is mostly dark except for a solitary light shining from the living room window. Timmy rushes from the car and into the house as soon as they come to a stop. Callum cuts the engine and drags Argus from the back seat. When he enters the house, he places his keys in a bowl by the door and hangs his jacket in the closet. He hears Penny call after Timmy, "Did you guys win?"

"Nope," Timmy replies.

"How did you play?"

"Fine."

Penny sits in the dark at the dining room table. Light from the monitor of her laptop, bookended on either side by an empty wineglass and a full plate of food, illuminates her face. She closes the laptop and watches Callum sit down on a couch in the living room as Argus splays out on his lap. She gets up and pours herself a glass of wine from a bottle in the kitchen before sitting down in a chair across from him.

"How's my boy?" Penny asks.

Callum doesn't say anything, doesn't need to.

She can see by the look on his face. "Does Timmy know?"

"About Argus?"

"About you leaving."

He doesn't say anything at first, then manages, "Yeah, I think so. How did you know?"

After a deep sip of wine, Penny says, "Devon called me."

"When?"

"About a week ago."

"What did he say?"

"He had a job he wanted you to do with him back in Afghanistan, and wanted my permission before you went."

"Like a wedding proposal." When Penny doesn't react to the joke, Callum asks, "What did you tell him?"

"That you never needed my permission."

"Of course, I do." Callum casts his eyes downward, away from hers, and runs a hand along Argus's side. He wants to ask her more. Wants her to ask him to stay. But doesn't know how. Instead, he asks, "Do you remember that festival in Corniglia in Italy?"

"In Cinque Terre."

"The choir singing Bowie's 'Starman'? You in that red dress?"

"That was a good dress." She swirls the wine in her glass before taking another sip.

Callum closes his eyes. "That kid who slept on our couch in the villa?"

"What was his name?"

"I don't remember."

"Why are you thinking about that?"

"That's what I think about when I don't want to think about anything else."

She nods and stares in silence at her husband for a moment. "You have to tell Timmy."

"I know."

"When are you leaving?"

"Next week."

She inhales sharply before catching herself. "Okay."

"This is who I am, Penny."

"I know."

Cold presses in from outside, but Callum can't feel it. "What else would I do? Become an accountant?"

"Be a father. Would that be so crazy?"

"Going away doesn't change that."

"Tell that to Timmy."

"Then I'll stay. Tell me to stay."

"I'm not going to do that. I'm not going to become some kind of cliché." Wine splashes over the edge of her glass as she sets it indelicately on the table. "When was the last time you saw Chloe? You know she can't get out of bed anymore without a handful of pills. That's not gonna be me."

"No, I can't see that happening."

"You can go and come back. Or not. That's not up to me anymore. It never was, though, was it?" Penny downs the last of her wine. "You don't owe Devon anything, Callum."

She leaves him sitting alone with his dying dog and sad memories. Although he knows she probably won't sleep tonight, he waits as long as he can before putting Argus in his bed by the back door, then walks into the basement to pack his bag.

# PART II

# OFFER, ACCEPTANCE, AND CONSIDERATION

# CHAPTER FOUR

Callum startles awake to a loud bang on the door. "Sir, they want you in the tactical operations centre" comes a voice from the other side. Sleep fades at the edges. Still dark outside. He reaches over to the nightstand to check his watch but can't see the time.

"Sir?"

"On my way."

He throws on a T-shirt and some shorts hanging on the back of a chair. Grabs his rifle from the rack and loops the sling around his shoulder, then steps into the hallway where his escort, illuminated red by the exit sign at the far end, stands ready to take him to the TOC. Outside, the early-morning air swelters and hums with the sound of a nearby generator.

Less than twenty-four hours ago, he was decked out in a winter parka and some Canadian lingerie. Now his nuts are swimming around in the bottom of his gitch like a couple of swamp guppies. At least that part hasn't changed.

He expected to see Devon at the airport, ready for him to explain what the hell's going on. Instead, someone from the company who introduced herself as Tina was there to pick him up. Sporting aviator sunglasses and grey body armour, she led Callum through a series of checkpoints before arriving at a jeep outside the main terminal, waiting for them with a driver already at the steering wheel. Before climbing inside, she handed Callum a rifle and told him to throw his kit in the back.

As soon as they pulled away from the airfield, Callum asked about Devon. Tina said they'd link up with him later when they got to the base. Other than that, she was pretty sparse with the conversation and spent most of the drive firing off messages on her phone, leaving Callum to take stock of his situation.

He kept her in the corner of his eye during the drive but couldn't get a solid read on her. There were a lot of questions he wanted to ask but got the impression she wouldn't say much. Once they approached a security gate at the base, she finally glanced up from her phone and explained that the base had mostly been abandoned by the Afghans except for some isolated pockets she pointed out as they drove along. Security consultants and conflict entrepreneurs had overtaken the remaining spaces, she said, transforming the camp into another corporate caravanserai along China's twenty-first century Silk Road economic belt.

After a meandering trip through the sprawling camp, she dropped Callum off at his barracks and told him she'd send someone to pick him up in the morning. Good thing she did, since there's no way he'd find his way around the camp on his own.

Now, he follows the escort down a long row of oblong Quonset huts, each one indistinguishable from the last, before stopping at a hut marked by an array of antennas pierced its roof. The escort swipes a security card through a reader on the door and motions Callum to enter when the light blinks green.

Inside, a bank of TV monitors fixed on the wall flash satellite images, drone feeds, and maps. Icons in blue, green, white, and red mark units, outposts, no-go zones. The escort joins another subbie absorbed in a shooter video game projected on the main screen, the kind Timmy used to play.

Callum tries to pour coffee into a Styrofoam cup from an urn on the table, but the urn is empty. "Fellas, you're out of coffee." When neither responds, he considers telling them to bring their heels together and sort it out. Maybe in a past life. Instead, he places the cup upside down on the table and steps into a windowless side room.

Pallid light radiates from a fluorescent bulb running the length of the ceiling, and the screen of a laptop projects onto the near wall. Tina sits facing the door while a man has his back to Callum as Callum enters the room. She says, "Callum, this is Alex Burnes."

Burnes's face is cut from a block of gunmetal with a tumour-size lump of tobacco nestled in his lower lip. While shaking Burnes's hand, Callum asks, "Where's Devon?"

With a Scottish accent, Burnes says, "I sent him away."

"What do you mean, you sent him away?" Callum glances at Tina.

Burnes responds instead. "I sent him south. Advance party." Burnes slaps Callum on the shoulder and gestures for him to sit in an empty chair. "Don't worry. We'll meet up with him shortly. In the meantime, we've got some things to talk about."

As Callum eases into the chair, Burnes clicks a thumb drive into the open laptop and finger-pecks a short password on the keyboard. "I've got a meet-up with these two gentlemen." He spins the laptop so Callum can see two photographs on the screen, even though their faces are projected on the wall. "Dognuts Number One and Dognuts Number Two."

Pointing to the first image, Burnes continues. "Dognuts Number One is Ramzi Khan, the nephew of the governor of Kandahar Province. His father fought with the mujahedeen against the Soviets back in the 1980s, but he grew up over the border in Pakistan. Earned an engineering degree at the University of Islamabad. Spent some time in Dubai working for a big construction company. Came back to Kandahar after 9/11 and served in several positions in the new government. Doesn't matter what his title is, though. He also happens to own quite a bit of real estate in KC."

Burnes clicks to another photograph. "And Dognuts Number Two is Muhammed Taraki. As far as we can tell, he's affiliated with the Mahaz-e Milli, the National Islamic Front of Afghanistan. Or at least whatever remains of it. Make no mistake, though, this motherfucker's a true-believer."

"What do you mean?" Callum asks. "Taliban?"

"Where the fuck have you been? The Taliban folded faster than a Frenchman defending Paris after the Chinese kicked them out. They're still lurking around but aren't too much of a force anymore." Burnes spits into a Styrofoam cup, leaving flecks of tobacco stuck to his chin. "Nope, Taraki and his crew are all about margins and opportunity cost. Armani and Mercedes. They bleed green. I mean, every now and then, Taraki makes his little jihadi videos to keep up the street cred, but in the final analysis, it's all about dollars and cents."

"All right."

"The problem is, we have to go through Khan to get to Taraki."

"Go through?"

"You don't need to worry about that." Burnes turns the laptop back around and closes the file. "You guys are there for personal security detail. That's grade-one, page-two shit. Get me to the meet, stay in your lane, and we shouldn't have any problems. Piece of piss."

"All right."

"Everything else you need to know is on that memory stick. Password is *kleos*." Burnes slides back from the table. "You have any questions, give me a buzz. Otherwise, we step off tomorrow at this time."

Callum glances at Tina, who keeps her eyes fixed on Burnes. "Tomorrow?" Callum says.

"Tomorrow, aye. Is that going to be a problem?"

Callum didn't expect that, didn't expect any of this. He knew they were going to Kandahar but thought he'd have at least a week on the ground to shake out and get to know the people he'd be working with. And have Devon here to make sure it all made sense.

Before Callum can respond with any objections, Tina says, "No problem. We're ready to go. Right, Callum?"

Callum shakes his head but says, "Yeah, sure."

"Good." Burnes raps his knuckles on the metallic table before shoving back his chair and leaving the room.

Tina finally returns Callum's gaze.

"What's all this?" he asks.

"It's the job. What did you expect?"

"I don't know. More time, I guess."

"More time for what? You thought there'd be a parade? A change-of-command ceremony or something? If that's what you want, we can do that. I can get all the troops formed up on the parade square, give you a chance to make a little speech." When Callum doesn't say anything, she adds, "Or you can do the job like the man asked."

"Where's Devon?"

"You heard Burnes. He'll meet up with you when you get to KC."

"And when were you going to tell me that?"

"We just did."

Callum turns his attention to the open file on the laptop. There's a separate intelligence report for Khan and Taraki. Basic tombstone data, date of birth, believed current location, aliases, a number of photographs. "Not much here."

Tina snorts. "What else is new?"

He leans back in his chair and crosses his arms. "How's this work? Is Burnes the client?"

"Yes."

"Then who does he work for?"

"Global Contingency Solutions. We looked into them but don't have the full picture. The company's registered in the British Virgin Islands, but that's about it."

"It's a shell corporation?"

"Yes. Burnes is legit, though. He's ex-SAS. Started up his own company in Iraq, but they got into a bit of trouble. He dropped out of the picture for a couple of years and ended up in Singapore working for a venture capital firm."

"And now we're working for him." Callum leans forward and moves the cursor over the eject button. A message flashes across the screen — *The thumb drive cannot be ejected at this time.* He yanks the drive out of the laptop, anyway, and slides it into his pocket. "If we don't know anything about the company he works for, I'm assuming we know even less about the company his company works for."

"You catch on quick."

"This is what I came back for then, is it?"

"You could've stayed home. Become a cop or something."

"I hear they have better benefits."

"But we pay better." A faint smile curls at the edge of her lips. "And this is more fun."

"I still don't get your role in all of this."

"I'm the mother wolf who keeps all her pups in line." She rests her elbows on the table, fingers steepled under her chin. "Look, I know this is all new to you and it's a lot to take in. But you're the best person for this job. I wouldn't have brought you here if you weren't." When Callum doesn't immediately respond, she says, "It's one short job. If it's not for you, you don't like it, anyone rubs you the wrong way, you can walk. It won't hurt my feelings. We'll send you home first-class on the next flight out of here with a nice little bonus in your bank account. But if you decide to stay —" she leans back in her chair, hands spread open in front of her "— I'll be frank with you. This contract's huge for us. If we can break into the market down south, there could be a lot of work coming our way."

"Can I think about it?"

"Sure. You've got about —" she checks her watch "— four hours."

"Four hours?"

"Devon's already put your team together. You're briefing them at 1430." She slides another thumb drive across the table. "You can find all of their bios on this."

"Brief them?" Callum says, incredulously. "I haven't even met them yet."

"You'll be great. They'll love you. Just be cool. Two days there and back. You can do this in your sleep."

"It's not exactly a Sunday morning drive, is it?"

He picks up the thumb drive from the table and turns it over in his hand before placing it in his pocket next to the other thumb drive.

As he gets up to leave, Tina says, "Have fun."

"Yes, ma'am."

When he returns to his room, he pours himself some day-old coffee from a thermos on his desk, then turns on his computer and clicks Burnes's thumb drive into a USB port on the side. Once it's on, he opens the single file and starts to read through it a second time. He turns away from his desk and pulls a locked barrack box out from under his bunk. A musty smell emanates from the box after he opens the lock with a key hanging around his neck on paracord. He digs around in the bottom of the box and grabs three laminated maps, each one folded and held in place with a binder clip. Choosing the most faded one, he tosses the rest back in the box. After he unfolds the map, he tapes it to a wall with four pieces of gun tape.

The map is unmarked except for grid lines indicating eastings and northings. God's control measures, as one of his old company commanders used to say. He sits down, studies the map, and estimates routes, times, and distances. Two days there and back, if everything goes according to plan. Better make it three, he decides.

As soon as he inserts the second thumb drive they gave him into the computer, it opens a folder containing ten documents, each labelled with a single name. The team Devon put together, obviously. For all Devon's many faults, he does have a talent for turning a bunch of mouth-breathing knuckleheads into checked-out troops. Callum figures he'll find out soon enough whether that's still true.

He opens the first document labelled "Murph." The one-pager has basic personal info along with highlights of her service record. He scans to the bottom where Devon has inserted a handful of notes. She's already done a few jobs with Devon and impressed him with her leadership abilities. Sharp as a sergeant major's bayonet, Devon writes, pegging her as Callum's second-in-command.

The next file up is Ash's. Apparently, he's an old buddy of Murph's, and she took him under her wing. Devon writes that his skills are squared away but that he's a real pain in the ass, a barrack-room-lawyer type. Devon and Ash had a run-in of some kind not long ago. The details are otherwise lacking, though Callum can fill in the blanks.

And then there's Habs, the kid Callum ran into back home. *Shit!* Callum didn't think the kid would go through with it, or that they'd bring him on board. In any case, it's probably too late to send him packing.

Other than that, the rest look like a real goon squad. No shortage of experience, that's for sure. Some have even done a stretch in Kandahar. There's JP, who served with the Canadian Van Doos. And Kamal, a Tajik from the north country, with connections in Kandahar. The rest definitely have literal question marks next to their names. That's what Callum's worried about. And he's not going to have enough time to figure all that out before they hit the ground.

Callum tries to remember all the times he was sent out the door with less information than he has now. His old CO once told him, "Your soldiers will give you the ninety-percent solution to every problem you'll ever encounter. But when things go wrong and they're all looking to you for answers, your job is to make up the difference. That's what I rely on you for." But this isn't the ninety-percent solution. Not even close. There are a lot of unknown unknowns, starting with the crew he's about to lead back into one of the most dangerous places on earth.

No time to worry about that now. He's got a job to do, and he'll have to trust Devon they've got the right people to get it done.

He delegates and assigns tasks to the people in the team. Murph will take care of their logistics and the resupply plan. Sung, their medic, can look after their medevac, if that's even going to be possible. Reno, a Māori from New Zealand, will get all their vehicles squared away, and JP can look after their comms gear. He'll see if Kamal can tap into his network and get them an updated intelligence report from down south. He types that up in a short warning order that he emails to the team.

After the warning order is sent, Callum closes the laptop and leans back in the chair. He debates going back to bed so he can stare at the ceiling for another two or three hours. Instead, he decides to go through the files again to make sure he hasn't missed anything.

# CHAPTER FIVE

It took Habs thirty-six hours to get from Toronto to Kabul. Three flights and two layovers. Toronto to Frankfurt. Frankfurt to Dubai. Dubai to Kabul. Ten thousand kilometres plus change.

He barely slept the whole time. Mostly because of the excitement and because he sat next to a fat Turkish dude on the flight from Frankfurt who draped his sweaty socks over the upright seat tray in front of him for the entire flight.

But things were somewhat anticlimactic when he finally hit the ground in Kabul. Not that he expected a hero's welcome or anything. But after six years in the army — it was actually five and a half, but he tells people six — where you needed approval from nine levels of the chain of command before taking a dump, he imagined there would be more structure, perhaps a little more guidance. Instead, his only instructions were to make his own way to the base as soon as he arrived.

After grabbing his luggage from a heap on the tarmac, he flags a cab outside the airport's main terminal, the first in a long line of taxis stretching down the block. The driver does a double take when Habs tells him where he's heading. After Habs repeats the location, the driver shrugs and sets off through the mad Kabul midday traffic.

Nearly an hour later, the driver drops Habs off at the front gate of Bagram Air Base. At least Habs assumes it's the front gate.

Sky-high blast walls stretch for kilometres on either side of the security gate, topped by spools of concertina wire, with no sign of any other way in. Before Habs gets out of the taxi, the driver clears his throat and points at the meter, displaying a number that wasn't there before. Habs doesn't feel like arguing with the guy, so he hands him a wad of bills, which the driver accepts graciously.

Once the cab peels away, Habs checks his phone to see if he has any new instructions. Sure enough, there's a message from someone named Murph telling him to meet up with someone named Reno at LV-426. And they have an O-group at 1430. He's sure that message wasn't there before. Maybe they're keeping track of him, after all.

His watch reads 0935. Almost five hours until the O-group. Should be plenty of time.

The security guards at the front gate don't even check Habs's papers and wave him through without a second glance. He pauses to ask for directions, but the guard who waved him through shrugs. Undaunted, Habs carries on into the camp but doesn't make it far before realizing he's completely lost.

The base is pure chaos, as if someone on an acid trip lit a controlled burn in a military-industrial wasteland. Armoured personnel carriers and light-armoured vehicles in various states of disrepair lie abandoned outside buildings and in the streets. T-walls and concrete barriers festooned in graffiti hive off sectors and zones and subdivisions, forcing Habs to double back and retrace his steps when he isn't able to climb over the barricades. He searches for LV-426 on the face of every building he passes, but when he finds any signs at all, they're mostly in languages Habs doesn't understand.

Whenever he asks for directions, no one wants to help. The first person he questions tells him to fuck off in what sounds like Polish. The second unleashes a pack of feral dogs after him. The third propositions him for a rusty trombone. At least that's what Habs thinks the man said, but he doesn't stick around long enough to find out.

He checks his phone for a satellite map to see if that'll give him an idea where to go. Once he finally manages to get a signal on his phone, the map is pixelated where the base is supposed to be.

It would have been nice if Murph sent him a map. Or provided someone to show him around. Unless this whole thing's a joke. Something someone cooked up back home to hurl him halfway around the world. Except no one back home cares enough about him to do something like that.

Tired and hungry, he gives up his search for LV-426, hoping to find someplace to eat. Eventually, he stumbles on a building advertising *nodels*, written on the window with a black Sharpie. Or maybe it spells *nudes*. Habs isn't sure. But a guy is passed out in front on top of a picnic table with an empty takeout container on his chest. Recognizing that as a sign, Habs heads inside the shop where he's greeted by the stench of boiled cabbage and stale soy sauce. He's so famished that the smell doesn't bother him, so he orders a large container of mystery noodles from the proprietor sitting behind a greasy countertop.

After scarfing down the noodles, Habs asks the proprietor if he knows where LV-426 is. The man grunts and points at a building across the street.

Habs says, "No shit. Thanks." He tosses the empty noodle container into an overflowing trash bin and walks across the street into LV-426.

Inside, a couple of swinging dicks play cards at a cheap table. One of them glances up briefly before returning his attention to the game. Distorted techno music blasts from a cellphone confined in a plastic beer cup on their table. The bar, made from sheets of warped plywood, leans precariously in the corner, rows of empty bottles of whiskey and tequila line shelves hanging from a wall.

"Are you Reno?" Habs asks the giant Māori folded over a sofa eating a protein bar, the trident tattooed on his throat stabbing up and down with each bite.

*"Kia ora,"* Reno says, his voice seeming to rise from the bottom of a mineshaft.

Habs pulls up a chair next to Reno. A rugby match is playing on a tiny TV in the corner, resting on top of a beer fridge. Or at least it looks like rugby. "I'm Habs. I got a message from someone named Murph that I was supposed to meet you here."

Nodding at the fridge, Reno says, "Grab me the hot sauce."

Without hesitating, Habs opens the fridge and picks out one of many bottles of hot sauce. He hands Reno a bottle and watches the Māori dribble a line of sauce on the protein bar. "You p-p-put hot sauce on that?"

"This shit tastes like dehydrated dog semen." Reno snaps off a piece of the bar and hands it to Habs. "Here, ram that down your guts."

Habs eyes it suspiciously before taking a nibble. "So ... is there anything I need to know?"

"Yeah, we've got two rules. Don't fuck your buddies. Don't step on your dick." While finishing his last bite, Reno adds, "And if someone points a gun at you, shoot him. You get those things right and you should be okay."

"Are those our rules of engagement?"

"ROEs, mate? You're not in the Boy Scouts anymore. This is the Wild West."

Before Habs can respond, he's interrupted by a burst of laughter from the card players. The largest one pounds the table and recites in Russian what might be a joke to his buddies, possibly at Habs's expense. The other two remain stone-faced with their attention fixed on their cards.

"Um ... that's cool." Turning back to Reno, Habs says, "The message also said we've got a brief at 1430."

"You have all your kit yet?"

"What do I need?"

Reno checks out the duffle bag at Habs's feet. "Go see the CQ and he'll get you squared away."

"Where's the CQ."

"I'll take you over there after the match."

Habs shuts up and tries to follow the game, but he doesn't know the rules and can't figure out what's going on.

When the TV cuts to a commercial, Reno asks, "You got any experience?"

"Six years in the army."

"That make you some kind of cowboy?"

"More like an astrosamurnaut."

"What's that?"

"Never mind." Habs scratches an itch on the back of his head. "What do we do for fun around here?" Habs's question sends the card players into a fresh bout of laughter. "Something funny over there," Habs asks them.

One of the laughing men says, "Yeah, bro." Pausing to wipe the tears from his eyes, "Olaf here asked what I'd rather have. Reno's head full of nickels or a million bucks." Doubled over with laughter, his head resting on the table, he reaches down for something on his other side that Habs can't see.

Habs begins to get up, but Reno puts up his hand and says, "Relax, mate, these guys are amateurs."

"What was that, bro?" Olaf snarls.

Reno folds the wrapper in half and places it on the table next to three other neatly folded wrappers. He picks up the TV remote, which is the size of a stick of gum in his hands, and tries to pause the game. Before he can, one of the card players charges, waving around a Bowie knife the length of an arm. Reno doesn't even get up but still manages to kick him in the leg, sending him to the ground in a howl of pain as his leg snaps backward at an awkward angle.

Olaf approaches Reno next in a low boxer's stance. More cautiously than his disabled friend. Olaf is a large man. But Reno easily towers over him when he stands up from the couch. Olaf throws a flurry of jabs at Reno. With unexpected quickness for a man of his size, Reno dodges all the blows. He grabs Olaf in a crushing bear hug and smashes the crown of his head into Olaf's nose, which erupts into a crimson fountain. Olaf's body goes limp in Reno's arms after a loud pop emanates from the attacker's back.

As Habs watches the melee unfold, he narrowly ducks a spinning bottle that smashes against the wall behind him. Habs launches himself at the culprit, still seated at the table, and tackles him into the flimsy bar. The plywood boards fly off in all directions as a dozen bottles crash around them. Seizing the opportunity, Habs grabs a hefty tequila bottle from the pile. It only takes three blows before the bottle shatters into a shower of pieces. Fortunately, that's all it takes before the man underneath Habs goes silent.

"Jesus Christ!" Habs cries, trying to catch his breath. "What the fuck was that all about?"

Reno surveys the carnage with indifference. "Russians." The first attacker still rolls around on the ground clutching his shattered leg. But the other two don't have very much to say anymore. "C'mon, let's go for a feed."

Gawkers crowd around the entrance to peer inside. When they see Reno emerge, they give him a reverential wide berth. Habs follows Reno, trying to make it clear to the throng that he's with the Māori.

After leaving the square and LV-426, Reno leads Habs on a meandering tour of the base. They pass along pathways and buildings that Habs didn't recognize from before, which he didn't think was possible. As Reno points out various landmarks, he offers Habs a breakdown of the camp.

"When the Americans left, they sold off bits and pieces to a bunch of big corporations. The rumour is that Chinese money bought up most of the camp, but no one was sure how much. In any case, their money employed mostly Western security firms staffed by veterans from the Afghan wars back in the good old days. The big players are a couple of American corporations, but there are some British, Aussie, and a South African company in there, as well. There's also a big Russian private military company occupying the northeastern section of the base. But no one likes the Russians, so we mostly leave them alone."

"Was that those guys?" Habs says, gesturing back in the direction they came from.

"That's them. And then there's a horde of subcontractors from all over the place who fight over whatever contracts they can get."

"That would be us?" Habs asks.

"That would be us. The Afghan government runs the camp. At least they like to think so. But they don't have much of a presence anymore. And even if they did, I'm not sure anyone would listen to them. Every now and then, the various factions get into a dust-up with one another. But for the most part, there's a natural order to things most of the time."

Eventually, they arrive at a massive hangar at the edge of the camp. "Here we are," Reno says as he walks inside with Habs in tow. Surplus military hardware occupies every spare centimetre of the cavernous hangar, like a doomsday prepper's wet dream. Equipment spills out of Sea Can containers stacked one on top of the other all the way to the ceiling. A Humvee that's been cannibalized for parts rests on cinder blocks. Even an M777 howitzer retires neglected in a dark corner. Habs follows Reno through the dense maze all the way to the back of the hangar.

Out back, a squat motherfucker with a murder beard stands hunched over an oil drum. Thick smoke with the aroma of mesquite chips and barbecued pork billows from a stovepipe, causing Habs to salivate, even as he feels radiating waves of heat from dozens of metres away. Reno yells out, "CQ," but gets no response.

The CQ lifts the lid on the drum and is briefly concealed by a plume of smoke and steam. When he emerges, he carries a boar skewered on a lance over to a workbench with custom-made supports on either end. Raising the welding mask that covers his face, he beams at Reno. "Look at that, lads. The trick is you need to get the heat right at the end to lock in the juices." He takes off his leather apron and places it on a hook next to the workbench along with gloves thick enough to handle radioactive meteorites. "Reno, my boy, what can I do for you?"

"Young lad here needs some kit," Reno says, pointing at Habs.

The CQ sizes Habs up and down before saying, "All right, fella, follow me." He sets off back into the hangar before yelling back at Reno, "Don't touch the bloody hog. It needs to breathe."

The CQ climbs a ladder fixed to one of the Sea Cans up onto a narrow shelf. With Habs joining him, the CQ rifles through a key chain attached to his belt before inserting a key into a lock on the Sea Can door. As they enter, a flood light hanging from the ceiling flickers to life, casting a pale green glow over the wares inside. Rifles and carbines with every possible modification are pinned from one end of the wall to the other. The CQ asks, "Any preferences?"

"I don't know. Something that will raise some pulses, I guess."

A wide grin emerges from the shaggy beard on the CQ's face. "I've got just the ticket."

# CHAPTER SIX

Callum is the last to arrive in the crowded briefing room. The rest of the team is already there crammed around a board table. Their conversations pause as they size him up, then resume.

He meant to get there earlier, make his introductions as the team filtered in. But he ended up lost on the way over and had to backtrack to make his way there.

Even if he showed up early, it wouldn't have been enough time. He would have preferred to meet them all one on one, spending as much time as they needed getting to know one another. There's only so much you can get from reading a bio. None of the important stuff is in there. Who they served with and when doesn't matter at this point. Why they ended up here in this room does. That's what he needs to know.

Callum would have liked to run them through a rehearsal of concept drill after orders. First, around the map table. And then a shakeout on the ground, marching through some glass-house drills. The company has a set of tactics, techniques, and procedures everyone was supposed to read up on before deploying. That doesn't mean shit, though, until you can rehearse it together.

There won't be enough time for any of that now. Instead, it's one-two-three-follow-me. Not for the first time in his career.

Scanning the room, he puts a few names to faces. The bios indicate he'd have a full section of ten. Plus Burnes and Burnes's interpreter makes twelve. They should all be here minus Burnes and his terp. But he only counts nine, including himself.

Sung scribbles notes on the whiteboard while Murph sets up a laptop, projecting maps and satellite images on the screen behind her. Habs, who perked up when Callum walked into the room, sits next to the biggest man Callum has ever seen. That must be Reno.

Callum doesn't recognize the other four.

He grabs a seat at the head of the table next to Murph. "We're all set," Murph says.

"What's going on with the AC?" Callum glances at the air-conditioning unit hanging from the wall in the back corner. A steady drip falls into a garbage bin positioned beneath the unit. Nearly full to the brim by the sound of the splash from each drip.

With a shrug, Murph says, "It hasn't been working since we got here."

"All right then, let's get started." All eyes turn to him. It's been a long time since he's had that happen. Every doubt, any ounce of uncertainty he might have had, disappears. He has a job to do. And they'll expect him to do it.

Callum won't earn their trust and respect in this moment. That only comes later, if at all, after months and months of following the stiff in front of them for reasons more important than the number of bars on a shoulder. Soldiers haven't changed since the time of Julius Caesar. They aren't looking for a friend and they don't want a hero. But they do expect someone to lead them. And that's something Callum knows how to do.

"My name's Callum. No need for formalities. You can call me Callum. Let's go around the table and introduce ourselves."

Murph is up first. "I already know all you perverts," she says. "But, hi, Callum, pleasure to meet you."

"Thanks, Murph."

"Sung," says their medic, the only one in the group without any army experience. According to his bio, he's a paramedic from Vancouver who figures he should have a little adventure before heading off to med school. Now here he is.

Habs jumps in. "Hi, sir."

"Please don't call me that," Callum says. "Do you want to introduce yourself to everyone?"

"Right. Hi, everyone. I'm Habs."

"Like the hockey team?" asks Sung.

"No, it's what people call me."

"And I'm Reno," says the giant Māori before anyone else can say anything.

"Good to have you on board," Callum tells Reno.

"Kamal," the Tajik from the north country offers. He spent some time in the Afghan army before leaving for better money in the international security sector. Taught himself English watching 1980s action movies, mostly flicks with Michael Biehn in them. Callum intends to lean on him heavily for his situational awareness. "And this is JP," Kamal adds, referring to the former Van Doo to Kamal's left, built like a Saguenay swamp donkey. JP's plan is to save up enough money to move to Las Vegas and join the UFC.

"Gents," Callum says, offering a slight bow of his head to Kamal and JP. "And you two fellas in the back?"

"Pope."

"And Squeeze."

Callum doesn't have much info on them. Two Ukrainians who might or might not be brothers. They sure don't look like brothers, though they share the same lupine set of eyes.

"Thanks. Pleased to meet everyone. I appreciate that the situation isn't ideal. But it never is. Fortunately, we aren't going to be storming the beaches of Normandy." That draws some mock laughter from Pope, echoed by Squeeze. His first test. "I don't know all of you and you don't know me. But everyone in this room is a professional, and I certainly expect nothing less from you." No one responds to that, so he lets that last part linger to get a sense of the temperature in the room. "You should already have the warning order I sent earlier. For those of you that I've already given some initial taskings to, good work. I've already seen some good initiative." That last part is a test for them. "Unless there are any questions, let's carry on." When no one says anything, Callum asks, "Kamal, you good for the sitrep?"

"Yeah, boss." Kamal gets up from the back of the room and makes his way to the front. "I've already emailed everyone a copy." He hands out a stack of stapled briefing notes. "But I know none of you are going to read it, so I'll run though the highlights."

Callum read it. Twice. It's sound. Kamal knows his shit. Being a Tajik means he won't have as many connections with the Pashtuns in Kandahar as he does up in Kabul. This being Afghanistan, though, there are only two branches on the family tree, so he probably has a cousin or three down there he called on.

Kamal continues. "The political situation stabilized a little after the Taliban got turfed." That bit draws a few cheers. "The new governor in Kandahar seems to be aligned with the central government, so that's managed to cool things off a bit, at least in Kandahar City. It's a different story in the badlands, though." He clicks on the laptop and flashes a map of Kandahar onto the screen. The city's broken down into sectors, each one coloured either green or yellow. Shades of red are interspersed between the greens and yellows around the city's periphery, which then becomes the dominant colour in the surrounding areas.

"After Abdul Raziq's assassination, Zhari-Panjwai reverted back to its usual shithole status." Kamal shifts the map to focus on an area west of Kandahar City where the Arghandab River slices from east to west through a narrow band of fertile farmlands and densely packed, built-up urban areas. "The government says they've launched a spring offensive. But everyone knows that's bullshit, which means that all the usual factions are fighting over territory out in the green belt."

With another click, a series of text boxes and images become embedded within the map. "The dominant group is the Quetta Shura, who are still backed by the Pakistanis, especially after the peace accords. The new player, probably since you all were down there, is the Khorasan Group. The Haqqani Network and HiG have somewhat of a presence, as well. Plus, there are some newer players in town, like these dudes." Kamal high-lights one of the text boxes on the screen. "The Mahaz-e Milli. They come from up north but apparently have migrated down to Kandahar. To be honest, I don't have much on them, but by the sound of things, they're the reason we're headed south."

As Kamal continues with the brief, Callum surveys the room. Most of the team follows along with Kamal attentively, except for Pope, who scratches an itch on his head while fiddling with his cellphone under the table.

"Excuse me," Callum says to him.

"Hmm," Pope murmurs.

"I'm assuming you've read Kamal's sitrep?"

"Yep, I'm good," he replies, still not looking up.

"All right then, why don't you come up here and finish it?"

Pope makes a great show of sliding the cellphone back into his pocket before crossing his arms and leaning back in the chair.

Callum holds Pope's gaze for a moment before turning to Kamal. "Sorry to interrupt. Please continue."

"All good, boss. I was pretty much done."

"Thanks for that. Good work." Callum slides a stack of briefing notes over to Sung and indicates they should be passed around. Nodding at the new package, Callum says, "There's your mission brief. As you now know, we're heading south. The task is a personal security detail for a new client, Alex Burnes. You'll have the pleasure of meeting him tomorrow. We're to escort him south for a link-up with a contact in KC. After that, we're heading out for a meet-up in the Panjwai. All the details are in there."

Callum places on the screen the two images of Khan and Taraki that Burnes showed him earlier. "We'll keep the scheme of manoeuvre real simple. Phase One is the road move down to KC. Phase Two is the link-up with Khan. Depending on timelines, I'm expecting we'll have to bed down in KC overnight.

Maybe in Khan's little hacienda if he likes us enough. The following day we'll head out to the Panjwai to find Taraki. Phase Three is the journey home."

He returns the screen to the map of Kandahar City that Kamal had up earlier. "Reno's already plotted our routes for us." Callum glances at the giant Māori. Reno nods in return. "There's just one road into KC and one road out to the Panjwai, so that should be straightforward. Things might get a little dicey in KC, though, so we might have to adjust. Reno's already uploaded all the main and secondary routes into your GPS but make sure you check them before we step off."

The final slide in his mission brief is a matrix that sets out everyone's tasks and responsibilities. "You already have your tasks, so thanks for jumping in. In terms of our groupings, we'll take three trucks down there. JP, Kamal, and Pope, you're with me in Alpha. Murph, you've got Reno, Squeeze, and Habs in Bravo. And Sung and Ash are riding with Burnes and his terp in Charlie." He scans the room, finally realizing who's missing. "Where's Ash?"

"I'll talk to him," Murph says.

They briefly exchange looks before Callum says, "All right then. Murph, you want to brief the sustainment plan?"

She stands to face the room, commanding everyone's attention. Even Pope straightens in his chair. "Plan to be self-sufficient for three days, so load your vehicles accordingly. Any resupply after that will have to be on the local economy. Shouldn't be a problem for consumables — water, food, fuel. Might be a problem though if we run out of bullets. If you have any special requests, give me your administrative reports before

1900 tonight and I'll see if the CQ can hook us up. Otherwise, you're on your own."

"Great, thanks," Callum says. "JP, you got comms."

"*Oui.*"

"English, mate," Reno interjects.

"*Cela n'a jamais été un problème pour ta mère,*" JP responds as a quizzical look passes over Reno's face.

"Okay, the comms plan is in the briefing package, too," Callum says. "Make sure your radios and sat phones are all good to go." He turns to Sung. "You got anything for medical?"

"I've already checked the med kits in each of the vehicles, so they're all squared away. Come see me, though, if you want anything extra for yourself. The company's still working out the contract with Phoenix Air, but I've talked to a couple of their people. If we need medevac, they might be able to pull us out."

"Well, that's encouraging. Reno, can you get Habs sorted out with our TTPs?"

"Shoot, move, communicate," Habs says.

"He'll be all right," Reno says, silencing the questioning expressions that appear on the faces of the others.

Callum surveys the room. "Okay, any questions?"

Pope raises one of his mitts. "What's going on with our contracts?"

"What do you mean?"

"I don't know. Something about our insurance policies not applying for this job. I can't understand any of that legal shit."

Callum saw that, too. He sent Tina a message about it, and she said the company was looking into it but probably wouldn't get it sorted before they left. According to the reactions from everyone else in the room, it looks as if they didn't read that part of the contract and probably skipped over that section to focus on the number of zeros at the end of their bonuses. "I brought that up with the company," Callum says. "They're going to look into it."

Pope rolls his eyes. "Not good enough, boss."

The air seeps out of the room as everyone holds their breath. Callum gestures toward the exit. "There's the door. I'm not going to take it personally."

Pope flares his nostrils while the rest of his face remains impassive. Pope slaps Squeeze on the back, "Fuck this. Let's beat it." Squeeze hesitates before following Pope out of the room.

"Anyone else?" Callum sees the doubt in at least a couple of faces. "I know this isn't the kind of mission you were looking for. But it gets you out of escorting a bunch of suits around Kabul. And I assume you've all seen the bonus structure in the contracts." A couple of heads perk up at that.

He continues. "You've all heard the sitrep, so you know the threat's there. It's been a while since any of us have been south, but I don't need to remind anyone of what we can expect. The good news, though, is that no one knows we're coming. So hopefully we can get in and out before anyone knows we're there. Keep it professional and we shouldn't have any problems."

He pauses briefly, then adds, "Again, it's up to you. Make your own decisions. I'll understand if you want to stay back. If not, I'll see you all first thing tomorrow morning. Go get some sleep. Orders end."

One by one they all filter out of the stuffy room. He looks each of them in the eye on the way out and knows the rest will be there tomorrow.

# CHAPTER SEVEN

Murph wants nothing more than to return to the shacks, stand under a hot shower, and wash off all the crap sticking to her like a second skin. Maybe eat something that doesn't come from a ration pack, preferably sitting down. And then sleep. That's all.

Instead, she leaves the TOC to look for Ash. She checked on him in his room before the briefing to make sure he'd come along, but he wasn't there, which was usually the case more and more these days. Not that she has any idea where he's spending his time lately. She figures she might as well start there.

"Ash, you in here?" Murph shoves open Ash's door and steps into a warren-like room. Plastic bottles, soiled rags, cigarette packs, and crumpled pieces of paper litter the floor. Two sets of rough-hewn bunk beds hang off one wall, a row of shelves on another. Ash lies on a wooden bench in the middle, staring blankly at the ceiling.

"You missed the brief." She kicks a piece of garbage out of the way and leans against the wall.

He turns toward her, the lines on his face drawn as tight as those on a chessboard, his eyes the two remaining black pieces in a field of white. "What did I miss?"

"You know we're stepping off in less than twelve hours."

"I know. I read the contract. Looks like the company wants to fuck us over again."

"I can't argue with that," Murph says.

Ash slides his feet off of the bench, leaving room for Murph to sit down. "How's the new guy?"

"Who? Devon's friend?"

"Yeah, him."

"I don't know. All right, I guess. Devon spoke highly of him."

"That's not saying much."

"Don't be an asshole."

"I'm working on it."

Murph presses the palms of her hands against her eye sockets in a vain attempt to ward off an incoming headache, possibly from dehydration or the heat. It could also be the room's dank smell. Most likely a combination of all three. "You need to take a shower, bud. You've gone feral."

Ash raises a hand to his forehead in a mock salute. Although they both joined the company about the same time, Murph has always been given more responsibility than him, a fact he consistently likes to remind her of. They still ended up forming some kind of weird bond, even though they have little in common aside from being two ex-soldiers too bored, broke, or broken to fit in anywhere else. Just like all the rest.

Letting her hands drop from her face, Murph examines him closely. He can only hold her stare for a moment before turning away. "You're not looking so good."

Ash frowns. "Did you come here to bust my balls?"

"Yes, I did. That's exactly why I came here." She sighs and crosses the floor to sit at his feet on the bench, to close the gap between them. "You're not taking that shit again, are you?"

"No, I'm good."

"Go see the doc."

"What doc?" A wan smile registers on his face as he rolls onto his side to gaze up at her. "Besides, I don't need a doc, Murph. I've got you."

"You need to sit this one out."

He draws a shallow breath into his chest and traces a line of sweat along his forehead with a finger. After exhaling, he says, "Sometimes when I wake up in the middle of the night to go for a piss, I stand in the dark for hours, holding my fid like it's a wounded bird, wondering what it would've been like to walk the halls of the Library of Alexandria. To know what they knew."

Murph shakes her head slowly. "Sometimes I have no fucking idea what you're talking about." She rests her hand lightly on his knee before getting up to leave. "Sleep this one off. We'll talk when I get back."

"Murph ..."

She pauses at the door to glance back at him.

"We're going down south, aren't we?"

She catches the brief flicker of haunting in his eyes. If she didn't know him better, she would have missed it. She heard the stories from others but not from him. Mostly bits and pieces, never the full picture. He was a corporal at the time, maybe a senior private, in a section manning a forsaken outpost at a blinking icon on the edge of some colonel's map. Almost overrun, it took the quick reaction force nearly eighteen hours to relieve them. By that point, the entire section had to be medevaced out of theatre, with injuries at varying stages of priority.

Tattoo sleeves adorn his arms all the way to his fingers, ending with AMOR tattooed on the knuckles of his right hand and FATI on the left. But the tattoos can't conceal the burn marks left over from that day, etched deep into his skin, as if someone inked tattoos over the rough bark of a tree.

"I'll be there," Ash says.

"Get some sleep. I'll see you when we get back."

She gently closes the door and steps out of his room. Instead of heading back to her hut, she spends some time wandering around, eventually making her way back to the bunkhouse where she finds a folding chair near a smoking pit. No one's there, so she takes a seat and sits there thinking, looking up at the stars.

With Pope and Squeeze likely gone, that puts their numbers down to ten. Without Ash, that would leave them with nine. Murph has no idea what to expect from Burnes and his terp. So, really, they're going to run with seven trigger pullers. Maybe a lighter footprint would be better in this situation, anyway.

Except Callum wasn't too happy about losing Pope and Squeeze. He asked Murph's opinion after the briefing, and she told him it would probably be for the best because those two guys could be toxic. Pope in particular. And whatever Pope says, Squeeze usually follows along behind.

Callum deferred to Murph on that, but Ash might be a different story. Murph isn't sure how much Devon told Callum about everyone, Ash, in particular. Devon and Ash briefly worked together before but didn't see eye to eye, which is probably an understatement. But they managed to work out an understanding in the end, based more on mutual respect than any kind of affinity for the other.

Murph appreciates that Callum isn't walking into the easiest of situations. Still, he came across a little too aloof, like other officers she'd served with back in her uniform days. But Devon said there's no one else he'd rather have leading them into the badlands. Murph would have to trust him on that point.

She's still not sure what to do about Ash. Murph can ask the other guys in the team if they know anyone who could step in as a replacement. Especially Kamal and Reno, who have been with the company the longest of anyone and who have the most connections with some of the other crews. But it's probably too late to find any replacements at this point.

She'll have to let Callum know sooner rather than later that they're going to be down one more. But she wants to come up with a solution first, or at least a couple of options.

Maybe Ash will be good to go. He's had his demons in the past but managed to get himself clean. That's what he told her the last time she asked. Not that it's her job to be his counsellor; she has enough of her own shit to deal with. Ash didn't look too hot just now. Getting out on a job might do him some good, though. If nothing else, it will give him a chance to dry out.

Adapt, improvise, and overcome.

The cellphone in her pocket buzzes to life, interrupting her planning. It's a message from Elise asking her to call. "Shit," she mutters, realizing she forgot to call Elise earlier. She goes into her room and turns on her laptop. It takes a minute for the connection to go through before Elise's face appears on the screen.

"Hey, is everything all right?" Murph asks.

"I can't see you" comes the disembodied voice from the other end.

"Oh, hang on." Murph removes the sticker she uses to block the camera on her laptop.

"There's my little weirdo." Elise's face beams onto the screen, sending a rush of endorphins tingling down Murph's neck. Same as always. Ever since the first time they met at a party, right after Murph joined up with the company. The party wasn't Murph's kind of scene. Too many bros drinking seasonal fruit beers. It did give her a kick when they found out she carried an assault rifle for a living.

But when Murph saw Elise, everything changed. That molten core of rage that ran through her for as long as she could remember went cold. For the first time in her life, there was something there in its place. With Elise, there isn't room for anything else.

They spent the whole night flirting. Actually, it was Elise who did all the flirting. She started off by making fun of Murph's cargo pants, asking what Murph was hiding in the pockets. Murph didn't have anything clever or witty to say. Truth be told, Murph had a Leatherman multi-tool and tourniquet in her pockets like a checked-out troop, but she didn't tell Elise that. So Murph stood there awkwardly while Elise told her about the latest juice cleanse she was trying and her last wellness retreat in Costa Rica, the kind of shit Murph used to make fun of other chicks for.

At first, Murph was a little embarrassed to tell Elise what she did for a living. After the truth came out, things had already progressed, and they soon ended up moving in together. By that point, Elise didn't care. Aside from the fact that Elise didn't want her gone as often as she was, it never made a difference.

"I wanted to chat before you head out," Elise now says. "You said you were going to be out of touch for a couple of days."

"We're heading out of town for a little bit."

"Were you going to say goodbye before leaving?"

"Of course. I've been running around getting everything ready."

"Babysitting, you mean."

"That's what it feels like sometimes."

"All of those boys would be lost without you, wouldn't they?"

"I think some of them already are." That reminds Murph of all the shit she needs to take care of before they leave. She scribbles down a list of tasks on Callum's briefing note while Elise continues talking. Murph still hasn't received any adreps. Typical. She'll have to head over to the CQ and make sure they're topped up with everything they need. She also wants to check in on Habs to make sure Reno or Kamal or one of the others hasn't completely freaked him out. And she still has to pack her own kit. The list runs down to the bottom of the page.

"Hello, are you still there?" Elise asks.

"Yeah, sorry." Murph glances back up at the screen while keeping her pen poised over the paper.

"So where are you guys going?"

"You know I can't talk about that."

"It's safe, though, right?"

"Of course."

"I know when you lie to me."

"I'm not lying."

"I want you to get your ass home."

"I know. I will. A couple of more weeks. This is good money, though. Maybe if you're nice, I'll take you out somewhere special when I get back."

"Like we talked about?"

Elise tried to talk Murph into moving back to the coast where Murph is from. She hadn't been back to Halifax since she left years ago. It didn't hold the best memories for her. But Elise had a thing for VW vans and talked about selling all their stuff so they could buy one. Drive out east with their two dogs in the back. Maybe buy a little shack on the water so Elise could open a yoga studio or coffee shop on a beach. Murph could open a gym next to the yoga studio or be a professional dog walker. It's all such a fucking cliché, but Murph loves every bit of it.

"How are our babies doing?" Murph asks.

"I'll go get them." Elise disappears off the screen and calls the names of their two dogs. One of them runs up to the computer and sticks his nose into the camera.

"Oh, there he is. There's my boy. Do you guys miss me?"

Elise nudges the dog's nose out of the way so that her face can come back on the screen. "All right now. Get out of the way. Of course, they do. And I miss you."

"I miss you, too. Look, I need to go get some sleep. We're up early tomorrow."

"Okay. Call me as soon as you get back."

"I will. I love you."

"I love you, too."

Murph closes the connection but leaves her laptop open for some time without looking at it. She only grants herself a moment to be back with Elise in her mind before turning back to the expanding list in front of her. With a sigh, she resigns herself to the realization that it's going to be a late night.

# CHAPTER EIGHT

Callum doesn't sleep that night. Nothing unusual about that. He doesn't sleep much most nights, especially since returning to this place.

He gets out of bed early to take a long shower, before the hot water runs out due to everyone else in the camp having the same idea. When he arrives at the shower hut, a line has already formed. "Only one of the shower stalls is working," says the guy standing in front of him in line. Callum considers returning to his room, but the line starts moving, so he figures he might as well wait it out. Could be his last shower for a while.

Fifteen minutes later, he stands underneath a gelded shower head that piddles into his cupped hands. He splashes enough water on his face to make the whole trip worthwhile, grabs the towel hanging on a hook, and returns to the shacks.

All his kit is already laid out on the floor. He sits on a chair by his desk to survey it one more time. Tactical vest and ballistic plates. Three-litre CamelBak, canteen and water purification tabs. Six magazines loaded with twenty-eight rounds each. A couple of pen flares and a smoke grenade. Satellite phone. Second-generation night-vision goggles because the company can't afford anything better. Spare batteries for the phone and the NVGs. Individual first-aid kit with compression bandages, tourniquets, and ranger candy aka extra-strength Tylenol.

Protein bars. Baby wipes. AeroPress and five hundred grams of Arrowhead coffee from home. Garmin GPS. Leatherman multi-tool. SureFire flashlight. Paracord, duct tape, and a tube of CLP gun lubricant. Two pairs of socks, two pairs of gitch, one extra T-shirt, a puffy jacket, and a toque all jammed into a compression sack. It should all fit in the patrol bag at the foot of his bed.

Plus his rifle, resting in a crude wooden stand by the door. An HK416 A5 5.56 x 45 mm with a long barrel. Nothing fancy. Not compared to some of the checked-out gear he's seen around camp. For as long as he can remember, people liked to yammer on about stopping power. But last time he checked, everyone here still speaks five-five-six.

All in, the loadout reaches twenty, maybe twenty-two kilos once he fills up the CamelBak and canteen with water. Pretty light compared to what he used to carry. In part because his knees aren't what they were ten years ago. But also, because he's planning to keep the humping to a minimum. The more time they spend inside their trucks, the better. Mech yourself before you wreck yourself.

His attention shifts to the small, smooth stone on the edge of his desk, drawing him into the stone's long-familiar tidal well. He knows the shape and feel of the stone by heart. The only memento he carries of Penny. The only thing he ever carried to remind him of her for as long as they've been together. He picks up the stone from the desk and lets it rest on the centre of his palm. Allows the memory to return of a long time ago when she pulled the stone from the ocean and handed it to him before skipping away.

He opens his laptop and checks his email, scrolls down to the draft folder to an email he's been staring at for days. The email begins: "To: Penny." That's as far as he ever made it.

The time back home would be about 1930. Penny's just gotten home from work or picking Timmy up from basketball practice. She's in the kitchen probably with a half-empty glass of wine on the counter and something boiling on the stove or baking in the oven. But she's already forgotten about the food and is checking her work. Music is playing. She always has music playing. Usually old soul at night. Etta James or Otis Redding or Marvin Gaye. She loves that stuff and can listen to it over and over again. She says it reminds her of growing up. He can see her standing there singing to herself. And he can see all the decisions that led him away from her.

Callum tries to write the email to say all the things he's never said before, all the things he's already said a hundred times. But maybe he hasn't said them the right way. Or maybe they wouldn't make a difference if he said them now.

He places the stone in his pocket, deletes the draft email, and closes the laptop, shutting down any regret he might have had. Cauterizes the sentiment with something deeper that he can't name, something that kept him alive after all this time. At least that's what he tells himself.

Turning back to his gear, he checks it again. Ballistic plates. Water. Ammo. Radio. Batteries. NVGs. Individual first-aid kit with compression bandages and tourniquets. Protein bars. Baby wipes. GPS. Knife. Flashlight. Flares. Rifle leaning against the wall below a tactical vest hung on a hook. His patrol bag resting at the foot of the bed with everything else. Three days there and back.

What he decides to bring is the only thing within his control. As soon as he steps outside that door, nothing else will be up to him. Fate. Chance. *Inshallah*. Take your pick. Any one is as good a reason for why shit happens as any other.

There's comfort in the process, so he runs through his kit over and over like a mantra or a prayer, playing out every possible scenario and contingency in his mind. How will he react? Will he make the right decision when they're all looking to him? The adrenaline's there humming beneath the surface like a ten-thousand-watt emergency generator waiting to be fired up. But right, now he needs to block out the noise and focus.

Callum packs all of his kit into his tac vest and throws it over his shoulder, then picks up his patrol bag and rifle and walks out of his room and down the hall. Stepping outside the shacks, he pauses to gaze at the still-dark sky where satellites of crimson and amber tumble in a continuous arc at 35,000 kilometres, blocking out all sound and light from the stars. He wonders if alien archaeologists will discover them in a thousand years. Post-historic sentinels orbiting a dead civilization from which they'll extract humanity's digital DNA to re-create something resembling humans. Maybe they'll design their own version of Jurassic Park and call it Anthropocene Park. What a fucking ride that would be.

His focus returns as the mechanical thrum of a helicopter passes overhead. When the echo fades, the only sound is from his boots crunching over the heavy gravel path as he walks toward the assembly area, out past the edge of the huts ringed in by high blast walls sealing off the camp from the outside.

The team's all there, checking the vehicles and their equipment under the glare of floodlights positioned around the yard. Tying down straps, loading ammo into their weapons, arranging rucksacks in the back of the trucks. The scene's a familiar one. Even a relief of sorts. As if he plucked a shard of glass from the bottom of his foot and can walk again without discomfort.

Callum searches for Murph, who's speaking into the handset connected to the radio in her truck. "How are we doing?"

"We've got some problems," she says.

"Of course, we do." Hefting his patrol sack onto his opposite shoulder, he adds, "Okay, lay it on me."

"Pope and Squeeze both showed up."

"I thought they weren't coming."

"They aren't."

"So what's the problem?"

"They tried to talk us into not going, like we should start a protest or strike or something."

Callum quickly checks around the vehicles but can't see any sign of them. "Where are they?"

"They left." When Callum raises his eyebrows, Murph says, "Actually, Reno almost threw both of them over the blast walls. They got the message after that."

At first, Callum wasn't too keen to be down two rifles, but he trusted Murph's instincts on this. Now he's glad he did. "We'll need to shift around our manifest."

"Already done. Kamal and JP are still with you. Reno and Habs are with me. Sung and Ash can ride with Burnes."

"Are you sure that's a good idea?"

"What?"

"Sticking Ash with Burnes."

Murph glances up for a moment to spy on Ash leaning against his truck with a smoke hanging from his lips. "He'll be good when we get out there."

Callum suspects there's more to the story but trusts that Murph has it under control. And he doesn't have time to deal with it now. "Okay. You said problems. Plural."

"You need to talk to Sung."

"Shit." It's got to be something to do with the medevac. He had a hunch that was going to happen. Are they going to have to shut down the mission? In the old days, they would have, when going outside the wire without medevac would have been number one on a very short no-go list. But this isn't the old days. "All right, I'll talk to him."

"Should we still get ready to go?"

"What do you think?"

"I don't know." She hesitates before responding. "I mean, we don't usually have it. But we're doing jobs around here. If anything happened, we could come back to the camp. But we haven't done anything like this before. If something happens to us down there, who's going to pull us out?"

He doesn't have an answer to that question. He brought it up with Tina. She said she'd look into it. Kind of like the insurance thing she didn't get back to him on, either. "Let everyone know what's going on. I'll try to get it sorted out." Most likely they already knew, which means he was the last one to find out. But if they're all still here, that might be a good sign. Or it might be a sign they're all bananas.

Ash doesn't acknowledge Callum as he passes by, keeps smoking, eyes drawn.

"Where's Sung?" Callum asks.

Ash points his thumb at the back of their truck where Sung is rummaging around in one of the kit bags he uses for first-aid supplies.

"How's our medevac?" Callum asks Sung.

Sung bangs his head on the roof of the trunk before extracting himself while rubbing the back of his head. "Sorry, boss. Phoenix bailed on us. Said they won't send anyone down south."

"No need to apologize. The company should have sorted this out, not you."

"Thanks. There's some South African outfit that'll lease out a helicopter, though. I talked to one of their guys. It could be an option."

"All right. Let me run it up higher. Do you have the details?"

Sung hands him a card with an email address and phone number scribbled on it. No other information.

"What's the name of the company?"

Somewhat sheepishly, Sung says, "I don't think they have one. This might be off the books, if you know what I mean."

"Okay, good work." As he makes his way back to the TOC to check in with Tina, he's intercepted by Burnes coming in the opposite direction. An Afghan man follows at Burnes's side. Once they join up, Burnes says, "This is Mohan Lal. You'll need to fit him in."

After shaking hands with Lal, Callum says, "We have a problem."

"And that's why we're paying you, isn't it, to sort out problems?"

"We don't have any medevac."

"Medevac. Oh, I'm sorry. I didn't realize we were going on a field trip to the zoo with a bunch of schoolchildren."

"We're not going without medevac."

Burnes steps forward and thrusts his hand into Callum's chest. "Listen to me, boyo. You have ten minutes to sort this out. And then we step off. If you're not ready to go by then, you're on the hook for the break fee in your contract, and I make sure no one ever hires your company again. Copy?"

"This is my team and I'm in command. We've got twenty-three minutes before departure. I'll get this sorted before then."

"Excellent. Then we understand each other. Where do we sit?"

Callum catches Ash's eye, who saw the entire thing. Nodding toward Ash, Callum says, "There's your driver. You're in great hands." Before Burnes can respond, Callum jogs over to the TOC. He knows Tina is unlikely to be there but figures he can leave her a message.

When he gets to the TOC, he's ignored by a new duty subbie playing the same video game on one of the monitors. But Tina isn't there. Not enough time to track her down now wherever she is. He types out a brief email to her on one of the laptops with the details that Sung provided.

Callum also takes a minute to fire off a sitrep to Devon with a subject line that reads "Where the Fuck Are You?" Not that he can be sure Devon will even see it. Or that Devon is even down in KC to meet them. It would probably take smoke signals to get the man's attention.

Back at the team, the vehicles are all marshalled and ready to go. He walks around to the lead vehicle to throw his gear in the back, but a punching bag occupies most of the space. "Fellas, what the fuck?" Callum says.

"It's JP's punching bag, boss," Kamal tells him.

"I can see that. Why are we bringing a punching bag?"

"JP's got a big fight coming up. Gotta get his training in."

Callum glances at JP, who says, *"Oui, c'est correct."*

Callum jams his kit into the last possible space available, then walks around and climbs into the passenger seat. "You guys are killing me," he mutters. Then, picking up the handset on the radio, he signals, "Zero, this is Three-Two, over."

Static hisses over the network.

"Zero, I say again, this is Three-Two. We're ready to depart, over."

"Three-Two, this is Zero. I read you loud and clear." After a brief pause, the radio follows up with "Your TIE fighter escorts are on station and at your command, over."

"Who are these clowns?" Callum asks.

"They're probably high from sniffing too many bicycle seats," says Kamal.

"All right then. Three-Two, roger out."

# PART III

# GREEN ON BLUE

# PART III

# GREEN ON BLUE

# CHAPTER NINE

Rust colours the sky and dust blows down from the hills into corrugated fields of poppies scored along the banks of the Arghandab where the desert yields to the sallow river basin.

Their convoy approaches the city from the north across a scorched hardpack road. When they crest a shallow ridge, the city emerges from the plain below. Callum signals over the radio, "Zero, this is Three-Two actual, entering Kandahar now, over."

"Zero, roger out."

Two faded signs mark the city's frontier. The first proclaims in English, WELCOME TO DISTRICT NINE OF KANDAHAR CITY. And the second, DRUG ABUSE IS BOTH MATERIAL AND SPIRITUAL LOOS FOR HUMAN BEINGS.

Kilometres of low mud walls extend from either side of the road into a wide patchwork of empty lots. Crooked figures labour in the untilled fields, though the early-morning heat is already tight as a drum. Wild goats and sheep roam the cracked earth.

The convoy accelerates deep into a city that isn't there, at least not in the present. Donkey-pulled carts laden with sacks of grain hasten to market while SUVs with dark-tinted windows shoulder past. Jingle trucks rumble along beneath rooftop billboards advertising smartphones. Walled compounds shelter behind ivory-tipped gates and vacant guard towers. Dense warrens of squat dwellings and shopfronts spill into the streets. Merchants sip tea, indifferent to the passing traffic. Everywhere there are melons and pomegranates piled in wooden bowls, flat breads stacked on tables, and signs for watches and computer parts next to grills burdened with sizzling slabs of meat. And everywhere people teem, shift, pulse.

The traffic intensifies the more they get into the city, the roads narrowing and turning in unexpected directions, folding back in upon themselves without warning while cars and trucks crowd them from every side. Callum tracks their progress through the GPS mounted on the dash, but the image on the screen bears little resemblance to the chaos in front of them.

To provide them with a little bit of anonymity, he swapped out the U.S. Army surplus Humvees the company used for most jobs around Kabul in favour of the three Land Cruisers that make up their convoy. It wasn't a popular decision to trade the armour and protection that most of the team was used to having up north. But they all came around in the end. His thinking was that he wanted to keep them as incognito as possible while they were in Kandahar.

Not that it makes any difference now.

Every imaginable vehicle swarms the streets: cars, transport trucks, and an old Soviet LuAZ with a bathtub bolted on the back; a motorcycle with a goat riding in the sidecar; a wood-panelled station wagon vibrating at the same frequency as a spaceship upon takeoff; and even the occasional U.S. Army surplus Humvee.

Callum, sitting shotgun, bangs on the dashboard. "I thought you guys got the AC fixed before we stepped off!" He has to yell over the sound of the air-conditioning fan belching condensed air at his face so thick he can chew it.

"We did, boss," replies Kamal.

"Then why isn't it working?"

"It is."

Callum glances back at JP crammed into the rear seat beside all their gear. The quiet French Canadian shrugs before turning to scan out the window. JP didn't say much on the drive down, letting Kamal do the talking, mostly about JP's upcoming fight as well as his last fight, which apparently didn't go too well. JP didn't seem too fussed about it either way.

The fight was in a Muay Thai gym outside Bangkok. JP trained there for a couple of weeks to work on his striking skills, as Kamal explained. It was an amateur fight, but promoters from Shanghai and Tokyo often showed up to scout new talent. Kamal flew down for the fight to act as JP's corner man. After a nasty elbow cut opened a gash above JP's right eye, which still hasn't fully healed, Kamal wanted to throw in the towel. But JP wouldn't let him. He put in another three rounds before the referee called it when the ring canvas turned slick with blood. JP still got in a couple of licks before it was all done, said Kamal.

"Where to now?" Kamal asks as he leads the convoy onto a broad, tree-lined boulevard, placing them nuts to butts in reams of traffic stacked in every direction. Callum isn't sure. He went over the maps a dozen times before they set off, checking each of the main in-routes plus a number of backups on their

GPS with Reno. But all the maps are obviously out of date because nothing makes sense. He can see the red dot of their objective blinking on the screen of the GPS, but it remains one or two blocks over no matter which way they turn.

Eventually, a turnoff opens, allowing them to slide out of the traffic onto a quieter side street. When they nearly reach the end, Callum points to a building, mostly obscured by high blast walls, looming ahead of them. "There it is," he says with relief. "Pull over at the gate."

"Roger," Kamal says.

Slabs of concrete bar the entrance to the compound. A single camera set above the gate tracks to observe the convoy, its red light blinking as they idle up to the entrance. They don't have to wait very long before the concrete entrance slides open, revealing a man in a grey suit and wraparound sunglasses, an AK-47 slung across his chest. He motions them to enter while his other hand remains fixed on the rifle. Stepping aside, the guard allows them to enter a cramped parking area where each truck turns in sequence and backs into the vanishing shade beneath the blast walls, all lined in a row.

Once his vehicle is parked, Callum steps down from the cab, pulls off his tac vest, and throws it onto the passenger seat before dumping a bottle of water over his head. The water evaporates as soon as it connects with his skin, granting him little respite from the heat. He tries to stretch some of the stiffness that settled into his lower back but that doesn't make much of a difference.

They set out before sunrise, taking nearly the full morning to get here. Despite the long journey, all his crews have already dismounted and settled into their familiar routine without the need of his supervision. They check their trucks and gear to make sure they'll be ready to step off when needed, not that they have any idea when that will be at this point.

"When you're finished up, you wanna do a recce for me?" Callum asks Kamal, indicating a shack in the corner where the guard who let them in has already vanished. Another has taken his place and stands leaning in the door frame, observing them for a moment before he, too, disappears. Although it's dark inside the sturdy hut, Callum can sense they're still being watched. If not from there, then certainly someplace else.

"Time spent in recce is seldom wasted," Kamal says.

"That's right," Callum agrees. "And the corollary is that time spent in recce is seldom."

"You got it, boss."

The rest of the compound appears to be otherwise deserted. Although the boulevard outside the gate hums with activity, no sound penetrates the thick walls surrounding them. A single building dominates the ground, rising over everything. Even with his head craned back, Callum can barely see to the top. It might have been an old office or apartment building at one point. Now it's impossible to tell. Great swaths of paint fleck away from the walls, as if a giant raked his fingernails across the building. Most of the windows are shattered. No light emanates from inside, so it's too dark to see into any of the rooms.

There's no sign of Devon anywhere. He must be up there with Taraki and Burnes, who already made his way over to the building before Callum even had a chance to dismount. There's little for him to do now, other than wait for them both to come down.

Murph has already given directions to the team, which she's more than capable of by the looks of it. He doesn't want to interfere or interrupt their work, but he figures he might as well check in on them, if for no other reason than to get to know them better, something that hasn't always come easy for him.

Being a platoon commander is the loneliest job in the world, but that never bothered Callum. He even kind of liked it. The solitude suited him. But this is different now. He doesn't have any rank to hide behind, and he needs them to trust him, which he'll never earn sitting by himself in the back of a truck.

He joins Murph, who's barking orders at their crew between bites of a protein bar. "How was the ride?" she asks him.

"Just like coming home."

"Think they remember us?" She takes off her ball cap to wipe sweat away from her forehead.

"Hope not."

"Doesn't look like things have changed much."

He nods in response. Kandahar's changed, though, in ways he didn't yet understand, probably never would. Afghanistan has always been an alien country to him even though he spent a couple of lifetimes here. But most of that was up north. There were days when Kabul felt like the dark side of the moon, but you could still get Starbucks there. Kandahar, however, is in a different universe.

"Where's Devon?" Murph asks.

Callum gestures toward the building, "Up there, I'm guessing. With Taraki and Burnes."

"Are you going up?"

"Nah, I'll let them do their thing." Now that he's here, Callum isn't sure what he's going to say to Devon. The extra time should help him figure that out. He grabs a water bottle from the cooler in the back of Murph's truck and downs it in three gulps. "How's the new guy doing?" he says, referring to Habs, who stands consumed in Reno's shadow.

"Kinda weird, but he's okay."

"Reno looks like he's solid."

"Yeah, Reno will sort him out." She glances over in Ash's direction. "Not too worried about them."

Callum follows her gaze. "Who? Ash?"

"Yep."

"What's the story between him and Devon?"

Murph releases a deep sigh. "They didn't exactly see eye to eye."

"I heard Devon tried to throw him through a window."

"That sounds about right."

"Devon isn't always the easiest guy to get along with."

"He can be a real prick."

Callum chuckles at that.

Murph says, "Devon and Ash sorted their shit out, though. They developed some kind of weird mutual respect for each other."

"Good to know. I'll go check on Reno and Habs first, then Ash after that."

"Sounds good."


Reno hunches over the hood of his Land Cruiser, mitts buried deep in the engine. His bulk occupies most of the front of the truck, leaving Habs with little space to peer around him to see what the Māori is doing.

"Captain," says Habs when he notices Callum standing across from them.

"Don't call me that."

"Then what do I call you?"

"Callum. Is Reno looking after you?"

"Yeah, him and Murph have been great. The drive down here has been a real bonding experience."

"I bet they loved that."

Reno plucks a part from the engine, which he holds up for observation as if it were a rare flower, before tossing the spare part over his shoulder and returning to digging around in the engine.

"So, ah, Callum," Habs begins, "me and Reno here were having a little bit of a debate."

"About what?"

"I asked him who he'd rather be. Batman or Superman."

"What did he say?"

"Batman. What about you?"

Callum glances at Reno, who hasn't looked up from the engine. "I don't know. Haven't given it much thought."

"What about James Bond or Indiana Jones?"

"Which Bond?"

"Doesn't matter."

"Indiana Jones."

"Tupac or Biggie."

"Sorry. That's not my thing."

"That's cool. What's your thing then?"

"Soft rock mostly."

"Like saxophones and shit?"

Reno slams down the hood of the truck and wipes his hands on his T-shirt. "Got that sorted." Then he says to Habs, "Give me a hand changing out one of our tires."

"Roger." Turning his attention back to Callum, he says, "I've got some more I'll hit you up with later."

Habs isn't much older than Callum was when he first came to Afghanistan. Not much older than Timmy is now, for that matter. He's seen a lot of kids like Habs over the years. Some were friends at one point. Friends who have moved on to other things by now. Got real jobs. Had families. All grown up. Not Callum. He's still here along with the ghosts of friends who ended up in neither place.

No point thinking about any of that now. It's probably as good a time as any to chat with Ash. No telling how much longer Devon and Burnes are going to take. Might as well make the most of the available time.

# CHAPTER TEN

Callum can't find Ash. He looked everywhere. Not that there's anywhere he could have gone, except inside the building. But why would he go in there?

Callum gazes up at the building and really notices it for the first time. Not the colour or the details or even the shape itself. Instead, he allows his eyes to soften until the building expands to fill his entire view, eclipsing everything else. Until the building takes on a new meaning. As if a massive, hanging scroll has been unspooled in front of him, with one end held up in the sky while the other reaches to the ground. Except the words on the scroll are written in an alien language he can't understand.

Still, he remains rooted there, trying to decipher the scroll's meaning as time passes, until a crackle on the radio from one of the trucks draws his attention. After one final glimpse at the building, he returns to his vehicle to check out the message.

Kamal and JP are racked out in the back seat with the air conditioner blasting. As Callum climbs inside, he says, "It's like an icebox in here."

"We got the AC working," Kamal says without opening his eyes.

"I can see that. Did somebody call in over the radio?"

"Nope. Haven't heard anything."

Callum checks the radio to make sure the volume's turned on, which it is. Even turned up all the way, it's unlikely he would have heard anything with the windows up and the AC on.

While he fiddles with the radio, Kamal asks, "How long are we gonna wait for, boss?"

"Your guess is as good as mine." Callum checks his watch. Burnes has been gone for hours. How is that possible? He wasn't standing in front of the building that long.

And where the hell's Devon? Callum came halfway around the world because Devon asked him to. And then nothing. No messages. No thanks for coming. Nothing.

Callum should have gone to find Devon earlier, probably when they first got here. But he didn't for some reason. Possibly because there's something about the building that feels off. Either way he intends to have a word or two with Devon, with his friend fully on receive. Better to wait, though, until Burnes and the others aren't around for that conversation.

He envies Kamal and JP and wants nothing more than to settle in for a kip. Wait it out until Burnes and Devon get back. But there's too much running through his mind, and he can't get that damn building out of his head.

While his attention is drawn back toward the building, Kamal taps him on the arm and says, "Looks like there's our answer."

Burnes is storming out of the building in their direction, Lal following in his wake. He rams his face through the open window before Callum can get it fully open. Shaking his head, Burnes yells, "Your boy fucked us!"

"Who? Devon?"

"Yeah, him."

"What do you mean? Where is he?"

Burnes reaches through the window and grabs a half-empty water bottle from a cup holder on the dash and dribbles a spindly rope of tobacco juice that trickles down the inside of the bottle. "I don't know. Khan won't tell me where he went."

"Let me talk to him."

"Talk to who?"

"Khan."

"What are you gonna say to him?"

"I'll be resourceful."

"Resourceful. We're not organizing a fucking bake sale." Burnes spits another stream of tobacco juice into the plastic bottle. "All right. Tell him we need someone to take us to Taraki. And if he won't give us that, tell him to tell us where we can find Taraki."

"Sure. Should I bring Kamal?"

"Nope. Khan speaks better English than you or me."

Callum isn't even fully sure why they're here, or why they need to talk to Khan in the first place. What does Khan have to do with any of this? Why can't they go directly to Taraki? But he doesn't care about that. He just wants to know where Devon is.

"Right then." Burnes slaps his hand on the dashboard twice before extracting himself from their truck with the same amount of grace with which he appeared.

"You need backup boss?" Kamal asks.

"No." Pausing halfway out the door, Callum reconsiders. "But if I'm not back in ten minutes, come and get me. Say there's an urgent call or something."

"You got it." Kamal slides his cap back over his eyes and resumes the position.

Having stared at the goddamn building for what turned out to be hours, Callum figures he should at least have an idea how to get inside. He still has to lap the building twice before stumbling on a glass door situated atop three concrete stairs halfway down from the corner. But when he tries the handle, the door won't budge.

He lifts onto the balls of his feet so he can press his face against a glass window, set high up on the door. His eyes take a minute to adjust to the darkness inside. Rubble carpets the floor and the ceiling has collapsed, obscuring his view beyond the entranceway. He bangs on the door and calls out for someone to open it. When no one responds, he continues in search of another way in.

A tangle of rusted-out cars and trucks occupy the space behind the building. He walked by here twice already but didn't see any way in. Picking his way through the maze, he arrives at a steel door partially slid to one side. With a heave, he manages to reef the sliding door open, revealing a cavernous garage inside.

The garage was once used as a mechanic's workshop. Dismembered pickup trucks are hoisted up on car lifts. Corroded engines lie abandoned on a workbench. Tools and spare parts spill out of overflowing crates. One corner of the garage is sealed off with the kind of heavy plastic dividers usually found in hospital operating rooms or the movie set of a snuff film.

The only light in the entire place emanates from a dim red bulb hanging in a service elevator at the back of the garage. Callum steps into the elevator and finds two buttons on the control panel. One going up, the other down. After pressing the up button, the elevator hesitates momentarily before lurching into motion. As the elevator grinds laboriously upward, a distant *ting* marks the passage of floor after floor. When the elevator finally comes to a halt, the doors remain shut, forcing him to pry his fingers into the crack so he can yank them open.

Light and colour flood his senses, leaving him momentarily disoriented. He steps forward out of the elevator while raising a hand to shield his eyes. After his eyes adjust to the brightness, he emerges into a shimmering garden. Graceful paths made of smooth white pebbles lead in every direction through groves of trees, all ripe with exotic fruit he's never seen before.

He continues down the central path deeper into the garden until he comes upon a man wearing a dark wool suit and blood-red tie with a knot the size of a hand grenade at his throat. A young boy sits cross-legged by his side. The man says, "Please come." He motions to a chair at an ornate wrought-iron table upon which there's a teapot and two empty cups. "This is the best part of the garden, a most beautiful sight when the oranges take colour."

After Callum takes a seat, the man says, "My name is Ramzi Khan."

"*As-salaam alaikum.*"

"*Wa-alaikum salaam.*" Khan pours them each a cup of tea. "Your colleague didn't seem impressed with the garden."

"He can be a little difficult."

"Yes, I got that impression. He reminds me of an American who lectured me once. That man said we Afghans have no institutions or assemblies for making laws. My understanding is that officer was eventually court-martialed for war crimes." He pauses to sip from the steaming cup. "What is your role in all of this? Are you here for business, as well, or are you just a band of roving pirates?"

"I'm looking for my friend."

"And who is that?"

"Devon Walker. He was here earlier."

"Ah, yes, we spoke."

"Do you know where he went?"

"He went to find a very dangerous man."

"Taraki?"

Khan cocks his head to the side and examines Callum for a minute. "I told your friend that he must not speak with this man. He is a warlord, violent and uneducated. He wants Afghanistan to stay in the past."

"Sounds pleasant," Callum says. "Can you help me find Devon?"

Khan hesitates for a moment, then asks, "How long have you been in our country?"

"Many years."

"Then you know something about Afghanistan."

"A little."

Peering through a clearing in the trees, Khan gestures to the city beyond. "Did you know there is a tribe of Nuristanis who live in the valleys north of Kabul? Even today their children are born with blond hair and speak the same language

Alexander the Great's army spoke thousands of years ago. And west of here you can still see Alexander's palace. But it is a ruin now." Khan turns back to Callum. "Your people have been coming here for thousands of years trying to conquer our country. You might as well throw sand against a mountain." Staring Khan in the eye is akin to facing the business end of a double-barrelled shotgun.

"That's not why I'm here."

"Then why are you here?"

"I told you. I want to find my friend."

Khan smiles and gazes fondly at the boy. "This is my son. He will go to school in China next year and study to become a quantum engineer." He says something to the boy in Pashto, who then runs off. "This building was a hotel once, in the 1970s before the wars. Politicians, businessmen, and professors used to stay here. We will rebuild it like we have rebuilt everything else. Without your help."

"Without our help, you'd still be in Dubai and this city would be a war zone. A lot of good people died trying to help your country."

"And were their sacrifices worth it?"

Callum has asked himself that question many times before, but never came up with an answer he'd ever admit to anyone, Khan least of all. And himself. "That's not my call."

"Then whose call is it?" When Callum doesn't respond immediately, Khan asks, "Do you know why you lost?"

"Who said we lost?"

"I will tell you why you lost. It is because you can only think in binary terms. East and west. Liberal and Conservative.

Democracy and the Taliban. That is a heuristic. A logical tool designed to make something complex simple. But that is the problem. The world is not simple. Afghanistan is not simple. That is why you lost."

Khan can't weigh more than one-sixty. Wouldn't take too much effort to launch him off the roof. But he wouldn't want Khan's boy to see that. Instead, Callum says, "That's a nice suit. What is it, Gucci?"

"Canali."

"I think my wife has the same one."

The bare hint of a smile traces the edges of Ramzi's face. "You are a clever man."

"That's what they tell me."

Khan gently places the teacup on the table. "My apologies. I must be going. And you must leave here. I have already told my men to escort you out of the city back from where you came."

"That's not gonna happen, pal."

Khan hesitates for a moment before saying, "There are many forces in this city whose interests do not align with mine and whose interests certainly do not align with yours. I cannot guarantee the city will be safe for you."

"You don't need to worry about me. I'm going to find my friend."

"And how are you going to do that? You don't have any power here. No one will help you. You are nobody." Khan ceremonially nods, then walks away on a different path than the one Callum came in on. As he does, the low whirl of a helicopter gathers force from the direction Khan went. The sound crescendos until a helicopter rises from beyond the garden's edge, hovering for an instant before pivoting and darting away. Callum walks over to the building's ledge and watches the helicopter fly away to the north.

Callum turns his attention away and gazes over the city below. Trucks of all sizes transport thick red clay to giant brick kilns. Their chimneys stab upward beneath a curtain of haze weighing down over the city. Tiny figures scatter about between the desiccated husks of palm trees, feeding the kilns with their offerings of earth and clay.

Most of his memories of this place have faded due to the dominion of time. But standing there, surveying the city below, the memories start seeping back. Slowly, at first, and then with ever-increasing clarity. His thoughts travel out through the labyrinth that unfurls before him, along the twisted paths and roads that lead into the killing fields of the Panjwai.

Devon's out there somewhere, for reasons Callum doesn't fully understand. But he's going to find him, anyway. He's not going to let him down again.

# CHAPTER ELEVEN

Callum hears the commotion before he hits the ground floor. Faint at first. Muffled by the elevator's tin walls. Then louder and louder, building as the elevator makes its plodding descent. Callum's grip on his rifle tightens as his thumb slides over to lean on the safety switch, unsure of what he's going to find on the other side.

The elevator shudders to a stop like an old man taking a piss in the middle of the night. Callum presses his ear to the elevator doors. Despite the noise, he can't tell if anyone is directly on the other side. While keeping one hand firmly on the rifle's pistol grip, he yanks on the elevator doors with his free hand, but they don't budge.

He releases the rifle, allowing it to dangle on its bungee sling, and jams his fingers into the crack between the elevator doors. Heaving on the doors, he grinds them open centimetre by centimetre along the rusted-out rail before he launches through the narrow space and lands in a heap.

Not exactly a textbook tactical entry drill.

Fortunately, the garage is empty, but the noise has come into sharper relief, allowing him to relax the grip on his rifle as he exits the garage and encounters dozens of scoobies kitted out with AK-47s, cheap suits, and more hair gel than a squad of buck privates ready to go out on a Friday night.

That escalated quickly. Before he left, there was only one or two guards in the little shack by the front gate. Now they're in the middle of a full-on scoobie squad convention. This complicates the situation.

One or two of them cast a sideways glance in his direction as he shoulders his way through the crowd. But for the most part they part and allow him to pass.

He stumbles onto Burnes halfway through the crowd, his trigger finger jammed into the chest of one of the scoobies. Lal remains impassively at Burnes's side, translating the vitriol spewing from his boss's mouth. Not that it has any effect on the subject in question, who wanders off into the crowd mid-sermon. Burnes doesn't know how to react for a moment before he spots Callum coming in his direction and roars, "What the fuck did you say to Khan?"

"He won't help us."

"No shit. He fucked us right in the chocolate hallway."

"He says the city isn't safe and he can't protect us."

"Protect us? Bless his kind heart. No, my son, that's what I'm paying you lot for."

"Then what do you want to do? It's your call."

"You're goddamn right it is." Burnes is already punching a number into a satellite phone. With the phone cradled to his ear, he says, "I'll find Taraki. You get us the fuck out of here." As Callum turns to walk away, Burnes yells after him, "You need to unfuck this!"

If Burnes can get them to Taraki, then Devon should be there, as well. But first Callum will have to figure a way to get them out of this mess without getting in a shootout with the scoobies.

Khan's man-on-the-mountain bullshit doesn't faze Callum. The helicopter from the rooftop was a nice touch, but otherwise, same shit different Tuesday. At the same time, no point in calling Khan's bluff. His scoobies are here for a reason. They don't seem too hostile at the moment but that could flip in an instant, especially with Burnes running around playing pokey-chest.

Callum needs to make sure that doesn't happen.

Back at his truck, Kamal is sitting on the hood with a bewildered expression on his face when Callum approaches. "What happened?"

"I don't know, boss." Kamal shrugs and waves at their new guests. "When you left, these dudes showed up."

"Did you talk to any of them?"

"Yeah, they said we have to leave the city and they're going to take us out of here."

"Did they say where?"

"Nope."

While Kamal and Callum are talking, Murph joins them. "What's the plan?"

"Khan wants us to leave," Callum tells her. "His dudes are here to escort us out of here, I think."

"I got that impression, too."

Callum pulls a map from a pocket in his pants. He shoves Kamal off the truck before unfolding the map over the hood. The three of them lean over while Callum starts to trace a series of routes with the tip of his pen. "My guess is they're going to take us north, back the way we came."

"That looks right to me," Murph says.

"Once we get out of the city, we're going to have to loop around to the north and then try to find someplace we can cross the Arghandab through one of these small villages." Callum circles a series of built-up areas northwest of Kandahar City.

"That's gonna take hours, boss," Kamal points out.

"Unless you wanna get in a shootout here, I don't think we have much choice."

"I don't know. Could be a blast."

They both glance at Murph, unsure if she's joking or not.

"I think we'll go with Plan A," Callum says. "Can you brief the crews?" he asks Murph.

"You got it. What about Burnes?"

"Let me handle him. Kamal, can you talk to whoever's in charge here? Let them know there won't be any issues with us?"

"No sweat, boss."

"How long do you need?"

"Two minutes Turkish."

Nothing ever takes two minutes. That's okay, though. Burnes isn't going to like the delay, but he's not going to have any choice. Unless he wants Plan B like Murph. Callum hopes it doesn't come to that.

He finds Burnes with his finger plugged into one ear, straining to listen into the sat phone with the other. He waves Callum away impatiently without bothering to look up. Before Callum can turn way, Burnes tells the person on the phone to hold as he cradles it to his chest. "What?"

"Did you find Taraki?"

"I'm working on it."

"We need to go."

"All right, we're coming." Burnes presses the phone back to his ear and turns away before Callum can say anything more.

No point telling him anything else then. He'll figure it out soon enough.

Murph already has the team marshalled at the front gate. Khan's crew is a different story. They're as organized as a gypsy flea market. A flash game of soccer-volleyball has broken out over a net fixed between two of their SUVs. Suit jackets neatly folded mark the court's four corners. One of Khan's men, wearing a red *shemagh* wrapped gracefully around his neck, gestures madly on the sidelines. When his exhortations fail to have the desired effect, he snags the ball and boots it over the compound's walls, setting off a squabble between the various factions. *Shemagh* versus Armani. Before the matter escalates any further, the man with the red *shemagh* rips off a few rounds into the air from his AK-47, sending the participants sulking back to their vehicles.

After they eventually all mount up, the convoy forms a snake that winds around the inner wall of the compound and out of sight behind the central building, Khan's men at the head and tail with Callum's crew trapped in the middle. Without warning, the convoy lurches into the boulevard outside the main gate. Instead of heading north, as Callum expected, they turn west, deeper into the city's maw.

Kamal glances over at Callum. "I thought they were gonna take us back up north."

"So did I."

"Should we peel off?"

"I don't think we can."

The traffic is suffocating once they blast onto the main thoroughfare. Cars, trucks, and lorries crowd in on every side. The SUV in front of them accelerates, forcing Kamal to follow suit. A gap opens between them. A car length at first and then two. As Kamal struggles to catch up, a yellow pickup truck swerves in front of them, filling the vacant space. Kamal zips forward, clipping the pickup in the corner of its rear fender, sending the vehicle spinning off the road and onto the sidewalk while Kamal manoeuvres their truck back in line with the SUV in front, matching its speed.

Callum checks behind them. He can barely make out Reno's face through the windshield as the Māori zooms forward to close the distance. "Keep it tight," Callum sends over the radio. Not that they need the incentive.

They continue west along the boulevard and then beetle south through Sardar Madad Khan Square into the city's own version of a financial district. They pass two banks facing each other across the street. All the windows of the bank on the western side have been blown out, leaving jagged shards of glass in the frames like the shattered teeth of a prizefighter who took a shot to the mouth. Across the street, a crowd lines up between even rows of security barricades that wind all the way down to the end of the block underneath an electronic ticker with stock prices streaming along its facade.

Past the duelling banks, a moped with a kid riding on the back sidles up next to Callum's truck. The kid leans over to peer into their window. He clutches a cellphone in one hand and hangs on to the back of the bike with the other, mouthing something into the cell before he speeds off.

"Homie's flexing on our whip," Kamal says.

"It's just a kid." Callum swivels his head to look behind him, making sure the rest of their trucks haven't accordioned too far. "JP, how're we doin' back there?"

JP has the muzzle of his rifle pressed into the door below the window. He glances forward, nodding at Callum before returning to scan out the window.

Kamal slams on the brakes as the convoy screeches to a halt. Callum braces his hands on the dashboard to stop from slamming through the windshield. Good to know the airbags aren't working, either.

Callum opens his door and steps up onto the door frame to scan ahead. The congestion extends forward at least twenty car lengths before opening onto a large square at the end of the line of traffic. Every vehicle in the line engages with all the others to see who can achieve horn dominance.

Afghan Police have set up a roadblock at the entrance to the square. Two green Ford Rangers are parked in a chevron, DShKs mounted on the back of each aimed squarely at the traffic in both directions.

Without warning, the tires on the escort vehicle in front of them screech as it rapidly backs toward their truck, narrowly avoiding a collision. It launches forward in a tight arc before speeding off in the opposite direction followed by the other vehicles that were also providing them with the escort.

"Should we follow them?" Kamal asks.

"No," says Callum. He checks over his shoulder to watch the escort leave. Where are they going? When he turns back around, he spots two of the Afghan policemen shuffling down the line of traffic in their direction, checking into the windows of each passing car before carrying on to the next.

"What the fuck's going on up there?" Burnes voice crackles over the radio.

"Our escort left and the police have blocked off the road ahead," Callum replies.

"I can fucking see that."

"We're going to turn around and take a detour."

"Run these motherfuckers over."

"Does this guy always talk like an asshole?" Kamal asks Callum.

Callum studies the GPS mounted on the dashboard. "There's a side road about a hundred metres back that should take us around Shaheedan Square and back to Highway One. Can you turn us around?"

"Yeah, boss." Tightly gripping the steering wheel, Kamal spins their truck around using the same manoeuvre as the escort that just left. Instead of carrying on in the opposite direction, he turns their truck down a constricted alley off the main thoroughfare, barely wider than their SUV. They quickly stall out thanks to the crush of pedestrians pulling carts, shopping at the surrounding market stalls, going about their daily business. They're mostly indifferent at first until the interruption becomes more than an inconvenience.

Their trucks are soon reduced to a crawl and can't turn back around, so Callum's mind races, searching for a solution. They can't go back, and the way forward is blocked. Stale air inside the truck makes it difficult to breathe. Strange faces peer in the windows all around.

An explosion erupts somewhere behind them, back in the direction they came, followed by the dull staccato of DShK reports. Glancing back, Callum sees a black plume of smoke rising above the buildings to their rear.

*We need to get the fuck out of here.*

Callum rolls down his window and snaps off a three-round burst from his rifle into the air. The locals scamper off the street in front of them, opening a space for them to pass. He says to Kamal, "Punch it, Chewie."

Picking up speed, they skid onto a busy open street, crashing into the oncoming traffic. Complete pandemonium prevails as vehicles and people scatter in every direction. Sirens from a cavalcade of police trucks cruise by, racing in the direction of the explosion. Snaking into the opening left by the wake of the police cruisers, Kamal darts through to the condensed road. Gradually, the stream of traffic recedes as they continue west toward the city's outskirts.

Callum lets out a deep exhale and claps Kamal on the shoulder. "Good driving back there."

"Thanks, boss."

"Let's hope we don't have to do that again."

# PART IV

# LOUIS ARMSTRONG IS DEAD

# CHAPTER TWELVE

It's late afternoon. A full-faced moon rises at the far end of the valley, night pressing down on day, snuffing all light from the sky. Still, the heat endures, even away from the stifling miasma of the city.

Callum rolls down the window to let fresh air into their truck, and to drone out Kamal who's been running a one-man hot wash ever since they were a grenade toss from the city limits. "Can you believe that shit? Did Khan sell us out? Do you think those cops were gonna arrest us? Would we have shot at them? We could have taken them." That last one, mostly a statement but partly a question, as well.

Even JP lobbed in the odd question.

It's like driving home from the movie theatre with a couple of eight-year-olds. But he didn't have the heart to tell them to shut up even though he needs some quiet to figure out what happened.

He knows it's been too long since he's been in a situation like that. He was sloppy and never should have let it happen. It could have ended up a lot worse than it did. That's all on him. He needs to do better. Will be better. But right now, he has to focus on the bigger picture and figure out what he's got himself into.

This whole time the only thing he's cared about is finding Devon. But Devon's nowhere to be found for reasons that don't make any sense. He left a message for Tina on his sat phone telling her he needs to talk to Devon ASAP. But still no word. He also sent up a sitrep over the radio but left out some details because he's not sure how secure their comms are.

He's unlikely to get any answers out of Burnes, either. But at least Burnes should be able to tell him what's going on and why they're looking for Taraki.

Without Devon around to explain everything, that might be the best Callum can do.

Kamal pokes him in the shoulder. "Boss." Kamal might have been calling his name for a couple of minutes.

"Yeah?"

"Do we know where we're going?"

Callum doesn't even know the answer to that question.

He didn't have a plan after leaving the roadblock other than to get clear in one piece. At least they were successful doing that. And they fortunately managed to exit the city on the west side instead of having to circle around from the north. Other than that, Burnes messaged him over the radio after leaving the city's outskirts to say he would pass on directions once he had a sense of where they're going.

Might as well ping Burnes now to see if he has any updates. "Charlie, this is Three-Two actual. Any instructions, over?"

The radio's dead on the other line. As Callum is about to replace the handset, Burnes's voice crackles back over the radio. "There's a goat track in five hundred metres that peels off to the south. Take that."

"Roger."

On cue, Kamal turns their truck onto the entrance of the track at the mouth of two projecting promontories facing each other. They rumble along the uneven track for nearly a kilometre before arriving at an opening beneath towering cliffs. Kamal stops the truck at a point too narrow to carry on. The other two vehicles pull in tightly behind, blocking anything else from following after them.

While each of the crews dismount from their trucks, Callum scrambles up on one of the cliffs to survey the surrounding area. Burnes hasn't given any indication where they're heading, but there's a village two hundred metres farther south, which seems a likely possibility.

He scans through the scope of his rifle into the fields surrounding the village before shifting his sights into the village itself, searching for any sign of activity through the dense mud walls that conceal whatever lies inside. Smoke rises from one of the dwellings in the village, but that's it. They're now well past the midday heat, so he expects to see more signs of life.

When Callum returns to their vehicles, Burnes and Lal have already left, not waiting for an escort. Callum considers letting them go but thinks better of it. "I'll take JP and Ash with me," he tells Murph. "Can you sort this out?" He points at their three trucks all bunched up, making an easy target.

"Already on it," she says.

They set off at a brisk pace down the narrow path that twists and turns away from the village. When they catch up to Burnes, he's stopped and checking his position on a GPS. He acknowledges Callum with a grunt and carries on along the path until they arrive at a fork in the trail. Burnes swears in a language none of them understand as he waves the GPS unit over his head.

Ash pulls a pack of cigarettes from his tac vest and slides one into the corner of his mouth, observing Burnes the whole time. "What are we doing here?" he asks Burnes.

"Looking for a fucking signal. What does it look like?"

"No, I mean the mission."

"You got the briefing."

"It was a little short on details."

Burnes smirks. "Endeavour at every opportunity to divide your enemies against themselves."

"Is that what this is about?"

"Something like that."

Sounds to Callum like Ash has some of the same questions he has. But the last thing he needs right now is Ash having a go at Burnes. Not that he wouldn't mind watching that happen under different circumstances. But Callum would prefer to have that conversation with Burnes in private, away from the others.

Callum then takes the lead, even though he has no idea where they're going. "It's this way." He doesn't stick around to see if they follow him. Sure enough, he recognizes Burnes's creative use of language behind him a long minute later.

At the edge of a field, a farmer squats on his heels, his twisted hand guarding his eyes from the sun while he moves the beads of a rosary in the other. The farmer watches them approach, muttering under his breath, as if he's been waiting for them to appear.

Callum asks Lal over his shoulder as they pass, "What's he saying?"

"He says a great king used to live here, but no one remembers the king's name."

"So why is he still sitting here?"

"Because he's waiting for the king to come back."

Probably not the most reliable source for directions. Callum presses on.

They pass through tall mud walls that line a narrow dirt path leading into the village. Overhanging pomegranate trees spill fruit onto the ground, leaving their fruit to rot in the dirt. A shallow ditch carved along the length of one of the walls is full of brackish water.

The water in the ditch flows into a wadi, dividing the village in half. In the late afternoon, the water is still and dark. Up along the path, a young boy races ahead of an old man pulling a donkey behind him. The boy turns and yells something to the old man, who doesn't respond. Stopping for a moment before crossing a footbridge, the boy disappears into one of the doors lining the wadi.

They come upon a square in the middle of the village surrounded by brick huts with straw-thatched roofs. Wooden tables sit empty in front of storefronts shuttered against the heat. In the centre of the square is a well beneath a gnarled willow tree. Sitting on the lip of the well is a girl watching over a goat drinking from a bucket. A broken watch hangs from her thin wrist as a bird perches on her finger.

Lal asks the girl, "Can you take us to your father?"

She points at JP.

"She wants your sunglasses," says Lal.

JP looks pleadingly at Callum.

Callum says, "It's your call, man."

"*Tabarnak!*" JP tosses the sunglasses to the girl, who snatches them out of the air. She studies them for a moment before placing them on her head, but the sunglasses are too big and slide down her nose. She slips them into her pocket before bounding off the well's lip and skipping down a side path from the square, leaving the goat with water dribbling from its chin.

They follow the girl through the winding streets before arriving at a wooden door hanging loosely from its hinges. The girl stops to gesture at the entrance before dashing off. Burnes knocks twice on the door, then enters with Lal behind him.

"You guys stay here," Callum tells Ash and JP.

Light from an open fire illuminates the room. A cast-iron pot hangs over the hearth. Thick smoke fills the room, masking some other pungent odour. A man leans over the fire, throwing pieces of dried dung into its centre. With a spark, they ignite, casting shadows over the man's face. A dead goat lies on a table, flies buzzing around its carcass.

After Lal says something to the man, he wipes his hands on his trousers and walks over to a desk in the corner. He opens a drawer and digs around inside before pulling out a pouch made of leather, drawn tight with a silver string. The man hands the bag to Burnes.

Burnes doesn't even look inside. "What the fuck is this?" When the man doesn't respond, Burnes says, "I don't have time for this shit." He empties the contents onto the ground and tosses the empty pouch into the fire, releasing a puff of smoke that swirls around the room before escaping through a chimney in the rear wall. Then he grabs the man by the arm. "Where the fuck is Taraki?"

The man shrugs free of Burnes's grasp and returns to crouch by the fire, poking around in the embers with a sharpened stick.

"Fuck this place!" Burnes storms out, yanking the door clean off its hinges.

Callum picks up the door from the ground and leans it against the frame. Maybe they have some tools back at the truck they can use to fix it. Callum turns to apologize to the old man, who gazes back at him with the same indifference reserved for the flies in the room.

How many other broken doors has this man seen in his life, put up with a man like Burnes crashing into his home uninvited, not a guest but an enemy? Was he ever angry or even afraid? Was he always this way?

A lifetime passes in that moment and then it's gone. With nothing left to say, Callum leaves the old man alone with the shattered door and his unwritten histories.

When he steps outside, he needs to adjust his eyes for a second to the light. JP crouches beside the door, but Burnes and Lal are nowhere to be seen. Neither is Ash. "Where's Ash?"

"He had to shit," JP replies.

"You let him go by himself?"

"Il m'a demandé d'attendre pour toi."

Shaking his head, Callum asks, "Where did he go?"

JP shrugs.

"All right, head back with Burnes. I'll find Ash."

Callum figures Ash would have gone in a different direction from the one they came in on, likely to get away from him and the others, Burnes most of all. Callum follows the path past the well and the tied-up goat, then along the wadi to a new place he doesn't recognize from before.

He comes upon a man in white holding a cage in each hand. A black fox sleeps inside the cage in his right hand, while a grey fox paces in the other. The man in white holds up the two cages, offering each one for sale, as if they're the most prized items on the planet.

Callum asks him if he's seen Ash, if he saw a man who looks like Callum. But the man in white doesn't understand, or pretends not to. But how clever are the foxes, the grey one in particular, he seems to indicate. Wouldn't Callum like to buy them?

The man in white follows Callum down the path with his two foxes, unwilling to give up the chase. Finally, Callum turns to the man and offers to pay him some money to make him go away. But the man in white becomes offended and walks off, leaving Callum with cash in hand. He continues down the path and finds Ash sitting on a wall smoking a cigarette while looking out over a field.

Callum walks up and rests his forearms on the wall. "You staying here?"

"There's a nice view. Thought I'd stay a minute."

"I bet the real estate is pretty cheap around here."

"Maybe I should buy myself something nice with the pay-cheque after we get through with this bullshit." Ash takes a long drag on the cigarette. "So that's who we've sold out to, is it?"

"Who? Burnes?"

"Yeah, Burnes. How have you rationalized it?"

"The paycheque helps."

Ash smirks at Callum as if to say he doesn't believe him. When he turns back to the view, he says, "You know, soldiers used to fight for their god. And then when their god stopped caring about them, they started fighting for their state. And when the state stopped giving a shit about them, they fought for each other. Now we fight for a paycheque. Not you, though. It's about something else with you, isn't it?"

"Maybe I just like fighting."

"Nope, that's not it, either." Ash takes a last draw on the cigarette and flicks it into the field. "And I know it's not your buddy Devon. That might be your cover, but that's not it, is it? I don't get you, man. Why are you even here?"

Callum hesitates before pointing east toward Kandahar City. "Last time I was here was in the back of a Chinook flying that way. Never thought I'd come back."

"They did you dirty, didn't they? Devon told me all about it. We were deep in a bottle of rye, though, so I don't remember all the details. But he's still steamed about it. What about you? You still mad?"

"Doesn't matter anymore. That's all in the past."

"Bullshit."

"Yeah, maybe." They share another moment in silence, watching the sun set on the horizon. As it does, Callum says, "C'mon, let's get back to the others."

# CHAPTER THIRTEEN

Ash and Callum return to find everyone mounted in their trucks, pointed back up the track they came in on. Callum passes Murph's truck first. She doesn't have to say anything. Her expression says enough. Somewhere between "I'm going to break something" and "I don't care anymore." He's getting to know that expression pretty well, which also serves as a solid bellwether for how everyone else is doing. As long as it leans more toward the former than the latter, they should be good.

Burnes sits shotgun in the second truck with the sat phone glued to his face, fully on receive, nodding meekly with whatever instructions emit from the other end. Callum would love to hear whatever's being said on speaker. Instead, he has to satisfy himself with the knowledge that Burnes appears to be eating a flaming pile of dogshit. When Burnes pulls the phone from his face, he hits the end button and tosses the phone at his feet. Callum doesn't wait for it to land before asking, "What's the plan?"

"Sounds like there might be someone else farther west who can help us find Taraki."

"Where?"

"I've uploaded the locstat to everyone's GPS. You should have it now."

"It's getting late."

"So what."

"We might want to think about bedding down for the night."

"You sleep when the job's done. We find Taraki first."

Callum knows he should push back, or smash Burnes's face through the windshield, but he lets it go instead. He'll allow Burnes to lead them around in the dark to make a point. And then, hopefully, find a cozy little grape hut to crash for the night.

Stepping back, Callum points to the GPS display in front of Murph in the truck behind them. She gives him the thumbs-up before he hops back into his own truck. "Looks like we have our new marching orders," he says to Kamal, pulling on his seat belt. Kamal starts the engine and rambles their truck down the track. When they reach the main supply route at the track's end, the convoy turns back onto the highway and drives west.

They share the road with other vehicles travelling in every direction: transport trucks heading out to Helmand and beyond, several generations of families packed into tiny cars driving into Kandahar City, uniformed soldiers clinging to the backs and sides of motorcycles. But the highway grows less busy as they drive farther west.

Pointing out the side window, Kamal says, "Boss, you see that?"

Callum's been tracking it for a while now. Hard to see in the near dark. A black speck distant but growing closer, hovering in the air. "Yeah, they've been following us for half a klick now."

"One of ours?"

"Doubtful. We can't afford that shit."

Callum signals over the radio, "Zero, this is Three-Two. Do we have a UAV on station? Over." He waits but doesn't hear any response. "We'll have to keep an eye on —"

Behind them, an explosion rips apart the air, the concussion blast washing over their truck. Kamal slams on the brakes as an RPG round skips off the ground in front of them. The round thunders into the slope on the other side of the road. Small-arms fire pours into their vehicle. The armour on their truck provides them with some protection, but the sound is deafening.

"Fuck, that was Charlie!" shouts Kamal. He's already started to manoeuvre their truck into the ditch to give them some cover from the incoming gunfire.

Callum glances behind them. An inferno has engulfed Burnes's vehicle. He tries again to raise Zero over the net. "Zero, this is Three-Two. Contact. Wait out."

JP dismounts and takes up a firing position in the ditch. He returns fire into a walled compound a football field away to their south.

"Keep suppressing them," Callum says to Kamal.

Kamal fires rounds through a crack in the window. "Where the fuck are they?" he yells back.

Callum scuttles down the ditch, bent over at his waist. Rounds sail over his head and snap at the earth in front of him.

When he gets to Murph's truck, it's already backed up and providing cover for Burnes's shattered vehicle. Reno and Habs take potshots out of their windows. "Where's Murph?"

"Taking care of the casualties!" Reno hollers back between firing off rounds.

Callum squints at the wreckage through the smoke. The RPG round exploded in the back of the truck, completely blowing off the rear tire and most of the trunk. Lal took the worst of the blast. He's mostly covered in soot except for the red mulch where his left arm used to be. His head flops on his chest like a gutted fish. Murph is trying to pull Sung out of the rear passenger seat.

Moving around to check the front seat, Callum finds Ash unconscious. Burnes mutters something unintelligible through slurred words. Callum shouts at him, "Are you hit?"

He can barely hear Burnes say, "We need to get out of here."

"You've been hit with an RPG round and we're taking small-arms fire. Do you understand me?"

"Yeah."

"Murph's going to get you into her vehicle. Can you move?"

"Yeah ... yeah."

Callum glances back at Murph doing chest compressions on Sung. The entire side of his body has been ripped to shreds, as if someone raked shears across his body. "We need to cross-load them into your vehicle," he tells Murph.

She nods but keeps working on Sung.

"Move now!"

Murph picks up Sung from the ground, throws him over her shoulder, and fireman-carries him back to her truck. Burnes has already unstrapped Ash from the driver's seat and is hauling him through the passenger door, but he isn't able to pull him clear of the vehicle.

Callum snatches a tourniquet from his vest and applies it below Lal's shoulder, who responds with a grunt when the tourniquet is tightened. There's not much else he can do for the terp at this point, so he drags him from the passenger seat and humps him over to Murph's truck, propping him against it.

Rounds reverberate against the other side. He reaches up and grabs the radio. "Alpha, this is Three-Two actual. Charlie's truck is down. We're cross-loading their crew onto Bravo. Do you have eyes on? Over."

"Alpha, negative."

"Stay firm. I'm moving now to a grape hut one hundred metres south of our position. Once I'm set, move down to Bravo's location and cross-load the other casualties."

"Roger."

He says to Murph, who's trying to shove Sung into their back seat, "Go get Ash and Burnes. I'm taking Habs." She nods to acknowledge before getting Sung secure in the back, then turns and dashes back to the other vehicle.

Habs snaps off rounds into the distance in cover behind the truck's engine block. Callum shouts at him, "Hey, come with me." Before stepping off, he turns and adds, "I'll take point. Don't fucking shoot me."

Habs's eyes are the size of claymores, but he nods in agreement.

They sprint toward a walled compound as rounds crack into a nearby wall. Pausing for an instant at the entrance, they circle around the corner with their rifles at the ready. The compound is empty except for a lone hut sitting in the corner. Callum stalks toward the hut, his rifle pointed at the entrance, motioning for Habs to keep his eyes on the rooftop. Finding nothing inside the hut, Callum says, "Boost me up." Once on top, he reaches down to pull up Habs.

Sighting down his rifle, Callum scans the nearby compounds for any activity. His breathing hasn't steadied yet, so he struggles to control his sight picture. He signals over the radio, "Alpha, Three-Two. I'm set now. Move to link up with Bravo."

"Alpha roger. We have eyes on some scoobies moving down a wadi line approximately one-fifty metres west of your position."

"Do they have weapons?"

"Not that we can see."

He scans down his sight, tracing along the wadi line, but can't see anything except dense foliage. There hasn't been any return fire since they took up their position. Maybe the scoobies have bugged out. No sign of the UAV, either.

"I'll stay in place and cover your exfil. Go link up with Bravo," Callum calls over the radio.

"Do you want us to pick you up?"

"Negative. Get off the X. We'll RV with you down the road. Once you're secure in a new location, send me the locstat and we'll meet you there."

"Roger. Moving now, out."

"Habs, how're you holding up?"

"I'm all right."

Callum doesn't look over at him but can hear the jumpiness in his voice. Or maybe that's the sound of his own heart beating in his chest. "We're going to post up here for a minute. Give the others a chance to get the casualties out of here."

"Okay." Habs pauses for a moment before saying, "Looks like we outpunted our coverage."

"Huh?"

"They've vanished."

"They tend to do that."

They both continue to search along the wadi lines but don't have any success picking up anything. It's possible they're clear. He wants to make sure they stay in overwatch long enough to give everyone time to get out of the ambush.

"Are they going to be okay?" Hab asks.

"Who? Sung?"

"Yeah."

Callum glances up from his sight. "I don't know."

Habs doesn't say anything else and otherwise remains quiet except for his heavy breathing.

Callum asks, "You ever been in a donnybrook before?"

"This is my first time."

"You did all right."

"I think I shit myself."

"It happens."

"Three-Two, this is Bravo," the radio crackles. "We've cross-loaded the casualties and are moving now to RV, over."

"Have you sent a casrep to Zero? Over."

"Negative. We can't get hold of them."

"Fuck! All right. We're moving now. Going to blow Charlie's vehicle, then we'll link up with you. Keep trying Zero."

"Roger out."

"Okay, bud," Callum tells Habs. "Just you and me now. We

have to go blow up our truck and then beetle down to link up with the others. Can you handle that?"

"Hoo-rah!"

"Please don't say that."

"Why?"

"Because that's the sound of a man's brain shutting off."

"Oh …"

The two move in turns off the hut's roof, then make their way over to the burned-out vehicle. Pieces of the truck litter the highway. Callum can't see the rear tire anywhere.

Habs stays in the ditch to give Callum cover while Callum roots around in what's left of the back. He spots Burnes's satellite phone on the floor by Burnes's seat and stuffs it into one of his empty mag pouches. Next, he fires two rounds into the radio, throws one grenade into the front seat and one into the back, then dives beside Habs in the ditch. Seconds later the vehicle flashes with a bang and sags, leaving nothing to be pillaged.

The two of them move to the far side of the road. They stay in cover from anything that might be watching from the south, unless that UAV is still tracking them, and shuffle for a kilometre down the road until they meet up with the others.

Kamal has secured a location off the highway. The two remaining trucks are hidden behind a brick wall in an abandoned compound. JP waits at the entrance to wave them in. Murph has triaged the casualties inside.

Ash and Burnes are both conscious and sitting up. Reno kneels over Lal, who isn't moving. Murph is still working on Sung. Callum asks Murph, "How's it look?"

She doesn't glance up. "We need medevac for Sung. I've pumped him full of morphine, but he still might go into shock. He won't last more than a couple of hours if we don't get him out of here."

"Get everyone mounted up."

"What the fuck? He's gonna bleed out."

"I know, but we can't medevac them here."

"No one's fucking coming for us."

"I've got Burnes's phone. I'll get us a helicopter."

Once they're all mounted in their vehicles, Kamal asks, "Where are we going, boss?"

"There's an old Afghan army outpost a couple of klicks down the road. Just get us there."

"You got it."

Kamal pulls out from behind the wall and turns right down the deserted highway. Callum pulls Burnes's phone from his vest and enters a number from memory, then hits send. Waits for the line to ring. Once. Twice. He feels relief when he hears the voice at the other end.

"How did you get this number?" Tina asks.

"It's Callum. We need a helicopter."

"When?"

"Now."

"It's going to take some time."

"We're going to lose Sung."

There's a pause at the other end. "Okay, where?"

"I'll send you the coordinates."

"Close this line and delete it from his phone. I'll raise you on the net."

The line goes dead. He deletes the call history, closes the phone, and prays she comes through for them.

They pass across some kind of frontier where light bends to the dark. The combat outpost appears abandoned. It's nestled into the volcanic crook of the surrounding foothills like an ancient fortress carved from some dim memory.

The two trucks pull into an open space beside the fort's blast walls. Manning separate cardinal points, they're in darkness now. Callum slips his NVGs over his face before sending over the radio, "Zero, this is Three-Two. Secure in the LZ now, over."

"Zero roger. Call sign Dust-Off is inbound now, over."

A moment later, Callum hears from their medevac. "Three-two, this is Dust-Off. I'm tracking your situation. Will be in your location in figures twenty, out."

Callum walks a hundred metres away from his truck, pulls a glow stick from his tac vest, and shakes it up before cracking it and tossing it onto the ground. He paces out a hundred metres perpendicular to the trucks and performs the same ritual. Then does that again two more times, marking a square on the ground only visible to someone wearing NVGs.

Sung and Lal lie on stretchers behind Murph's truck. She kneels next to them, offering quiet words of solace, checking their bandages, doing what she can, even though she knows it's not enough. The others provide security outside the vehicles.

Burnes sits in the back of a truck wrapped in a blanket. Callum tells him they have a helicopter coming in to pick them up.

"No fucking chance. I'm staying."

"Me, too," says Ash from the back, barely audible.

Callum sees no point in fighting them. They can make their own calls. Besides, there might not be enough space on the helicopter for all of them.

They have nothing to do now but wait for the helicopter to arrive. The temperature has dropped and a chill has set in. Only the sound of static over the radio interrupts the silence.

"It's Sung and Lal going out," he says to Murph.

"I know."

The distant hum of the helicopter crescendos over the fields. Travelling fast and low, the chopper is incongruous against the land over which it flies. It circles around their position before banking sharply and setting down within their perimeter. Disoriented by the dust kicked up from the rotor wash, an ethereal figure emerges from the storm yelling something indecipherable.

Callum walks out to meet him. "What?"

"Where are the bodies?"

Callum directs him to his vehicle where Sung and Lal are lying on stretchers. The medic kneels first over Sung, shining a red light over his face, inflected in a grotesque mask. Vaguely human. Only the slow rise and fall of Sung's chest indicates he's still alive, his remaining eye staring up with incomprehension.

The medic motions for them to pick up the stretcher and carry it to the helicopter. He stays back with Murph, who's working on Lal. Once the crew has come back, they pick up Lal and carry him to the helicopter, as well. Callum yells something into Murph's ear, who only shakes her head. They exchange glances with each other as the helicopter slowly unfurls and then lifts off.

All of them watch the chopper fly off as exhaustion settles in. Not tiredness. Something deeper and mechanical. In the vanished light, Murph turns to Callum and asks, "What now?"

# PART V

# HOW TO CONSOLE A CRYING BABY

# CHAPTER FOURTEEN

Rotor wash continues to ring in Callum's ears long after the helicopter leaves his sight. Rooted in place, he senses someone is telling him something important from a place far away. But he can't tell who it is or what they're saying, even when he turns to find Murph yelling at him from a rifle's length away.

After giving his head a shake, he sees she's pointing at the outpost behind them, toward an Afghan soldier who's wandered outside through one of the massive steel gates. An apparition dressed in an army smock over top of basketball shorts that droop past his knees. He might have witnessed the whole medevac. Callum has no idea.

Kamal approaches the soldier and asks if anyone else is inside. The soldier casts his gaze off into the distance, searching for something none of them can see. It takes the soldier a moment before he locks eyes with Kamal. He tilts his head to the side and surveys Kamal up and down as if he, too, is unsure if Kamal is real. Without saying anything, the soldier turns and shuffles back into the outpost, leaving the gates open behind him.

Kamal glances back to where Callum stands. "What are we gonna do, boss?"

Murph frowns at Callum before he realizes they're all waiting for him to make a decision. They managed to get Sung and

Lal out, but the two were in bad shape, Lal especially. Even if the medevac crew manage to stabilize him, would they be able to get him back to a hospital in time? Is there even a hospital they can take him to?

That's all out of his control now. He has eight left. If he can get them into a secure location, then he can figure out their next move. "All right," he says. "Kamal, you come with me. Let's see if anyone else is home. Murph, you get everyone back in our trucks and ready to come inside. If things get hairy, get out of here."

"You got it," she says.

Callum peers around the gate before stepping cautiously inside. Everything is dark, though the outpost opens in the middle to the night sky. After flipping down his NVGs, his eyes take a second to adjust to the ghost light casting green shadows over the interior.

A single-storey dwelling dominates the outpost, possibly the barracks where soldiers once stayed. Now its main door hangs off hinges. Behind the barracks is a shed leaning half erect in the far corner and collapsed on top of a pickup truck. A yawning breach opens up on the back wall next to the shed, as if it was blown apart by an explosion. Coils of concertina wire are strung across the gap, but it's cut unevenly, leaving a narrow path that leads out into the surrounding hills.

They sweep the outpost, searching for any inhabitants, beginning with the barracks. Callum creeps up to one of the windows to peek inside before recoiling, repulsed by the stench of recently burnt garbage. A fire pit dug in the back corner of the room holds trash charred beyond recognition.

Continuing past the barracks, Callum toes aside an empty jerry can and checks inside the garage. Aside from the totalled pickup, the rest of the garage is empty. He pauses briefly at the gap in the back wall before circling back to the front of the outpost. After satisfying himself that the outpost is unoccupied, he sends Kamal back to bring the others inside.

Standing alone in the outpost, Callum recalls that he's been here before. Many years ago. At one point, there would have been an entire Afghan platoon here, one of a string of combat outposts branching out from Kandahar City, west along Highway One to Helmand Province and beyond. At ground zero of a global insurgency.

Now the outpost is just a shell. The soldier who met them outside a few minutes ago has disappeared. No soldiers are up on the ramparts. No one is at the gates. The outpost is abandoned.

When the remaining members of his crew enter the outpost, he marshals their trucks inside the gates, ensuring they can bug out in case they get bumped. He directs Murph to set a rotating watch up on the ramparts and offers to take the first shift, but she tells him to get some rest and that she'll come get him when his turn's up.

Callum mumbles something about needing a minute to catch his breath and stumbles over to the far side of the compound, away from the others. Bracing against a wall, he removes Burnes's satellite phone from his rucksack. With his other hand, he tries to punch out a number, but the phone slips from his hand and smashes to the ground.

Holding a hand up to his face, he can't focus on anything in front of him, so he turns his back to the wall and slumps to the ground, next to the shattered sat phone. Then he clasps his hands together to stop them from vibrating. But it's not just his hands. His entire body trembles.

Alerts flash from somewhere deep in his brainstem that he's dehydrated. If he doesn't get some fluid downrange, he'll go hypothermic as the temperature drops to near freezing. The adrenaline crash and no sleep don't help. But he's been here before. What he's experiencing now is something more than a primal response to stress.

Best to deal with the immediate issue.

He grabs a water bottle from his ruck and drops an electrolyte tab into the bottom. After giving the bottle a vigorous shake, he downs the contents in three gulps before taking a second bottle and doing it all over again.

He leans his head against the wall and lets the fluids go to work. Breathes deeply through his nose and holds the breath as long as he can before releasing a long, slow exhale. Presses his fingers into his carotid artery and waits for his pulse to recede. Tunes in to the soundtrack running though his head.

It's a familiar conversation. His own private communion with the past and the future and whatever it is that comes between. One that he learned long ago to reconcile with the path on which he found himself. The why of killing and dying and living. There aren't any answers to any of it inside his head. These are things that happen. Things he accepted long ago.

There have been many nights like this one. Many mornings, too. A hundred times before. A hundred prior lifetimes. But this is the only one that matters. At least right now.

He has no rank anymore. No command. There's nothing binding them to him other than a contract. Maybe that's all there ever was. He doesn't believe that, though. When you take away the uniform and all the dogshit that comes with it, there has to be something else that keeps them together. Some other reason that brought them here. Something bigger than themselves. Something bigger than him. But something nonetheless.

Even though he put the broken body of one of their brothers on a helicopter that night.

There's no decision to make. He wants to continue forward to find Devon because that's what he came here to do. But he will give them the choice. They can continue on with him or go back.

Even though he already knows what they'll all say.

Sunup. Early morning now. Callum must have drifted off. Murph let him sleep through the night. *Shit!* He shouldn't have left them like that.

It all comes back as he shakes the sleep from his eyes. The ambush. Lal. Sung. And Khan before that. Burnes. Devon. This whole fucking country. Was there anything before this, or did it all start here?

He doesn't have time to rehash that now. It's done and they have to move on.

Murph, Kamal, and JP are camped out between the two remaining trucks. No sign of the others. Murph looks up as he approaches and raises her mug. "You want a java? We can brew some up."

"That would be great. Thanks."

He watches as Murph pours water from a jerry can into a pot at her feet. She places the pot on a stand under which is a small camping stove, then turns a valve on the stove, releasing a hiss of gas. Next, she sparks a flame with a lighter from her pocket.

"How come you didn't get me?" Callum asks.

"You needed the sleep," she replies.

By the look of all of them, they needed sleep, too, since they probably didn't get very much.

"Any word about Sung?" Kamal asks as they watch the water begin to boil.

Recalling that he dropped the satellite phone, Callum says, "No, I haven't heard anything yet. Has anything come over the radio?"

"Nope, we haven't heard anything." Murph shakes ground coffee from a tin into the pot of water after she takes the pot off the stove. She stirs the pot with her knife, pours the coffee into a mug, and hands it to Callum. "Who set up the ambush?" she asks Callum.

"I don't know," he answers.

"They had a UAV."

"I know."

"Was it Khan?"

"I don't know. Maybe."

"What does Burnes think?"

"I haven't talked to him yet." He tries sipping from the mug, but the coffee's still too hot.

"Then what's the plan?"

"Unless Burnes tells me otherwise, I'm going to finish the job."

Kamal doesn't say anything and glances over at JP, who hasn't looked up during the whole conversation.

"I know it was a rough night," Callum says, "and not what we expected coming down here. I'll get on the horn and have someone higher pick everyone up."

Kamal doesn't miss a beat. "Nah, we're with you, boss."

"Look, there won't be any questions. I'll make sure you guys get paid."

Kamal jabs JP on the arm. "JP?"

"*C'est ca. Nous sommes avec toi.*"

Callum glances over at Murph. She doesn't have to say anything. He knows she'll stay.

"Reno and Habs are up on watch," Murph tells him. "I think Habs is rattled, but Reno will bring him around."

"Okay then. Let me talk to Burnes. Any idea where he is?"

"Yeah, but you might want to talk to the captain first."

"Who?"

Murph points at a small shack tucked beneath one of the walls by the gates. Was that there when Callum did his sweep the night before? How could he have missed it? But there it is, like a cold sore the morning after a bachelor party.

"There's some dude who calls himself the captain over there," Kamal volunteers. "He poked his head out at first light this morning. Yelled at us in Pashto, then went back inside."

"We've seen a few others floating around, as well," Murph says, "but they haven't paid us any attention."

"Kamal, come with me," Callum says. "We'll pay a visit to this captain." Then he asks Murph, "Can you check on the others? Let them know we can send someone to pick them up?" He places his coffee, which he hasn't touched, on the hood of the truck and walks off with Kamal toward the shed.

Knocking on the shed's door, Callum notices it's riddled with bullet holes. The sound of a television or radio blares from inside. After banging on the door a second time without any response, he barges in.

The dank stench of sweat and curdled milk greets Callum as he steps over an upturned toaster oven. Clumps of plaster have fallen from the ceiling, and rotting wallpaper peels from the walls. A ragged carpet covers the floor inside, its pattern long since faded. Only the grey remains.

A man wearing tattered army fatigues with captain's epaulettes on the shoulders lies on his side, one arm resting on a pillow. The other arm stretches out, flicking pistachios into his mouth. Shells litter the floor around him like spent shell casings.

A young soldier sits cross-legged in the corner, a half-empty bottle of Coke at his feet. A hornet buzzes inside, trying to escape, but the soldier doesn't seem to notice.

Neither looks up when Callum enters the room. They're watching a Bollywood gangster movie on an old TV on top of empty ammo boxes. A gang of heavily armed men surround a house and unleash a wave of bullets at a family cowering inside. Once the carnage is complete, the men climb inside a van and drive off. The captain laughs hysterically while the young soldier stares ahead blankly.

"Ask him if he's in charge," Callum tells Kamal.

After the captain stops laughing, Kamal translates. "He says he's the officer in charge of this outpost."

"Where's the rest of his company?"

Kamal mostly listens while the captain speaks, then he translates. "He says he keeps the wolf from the door."

"What does that mean?"

"I don't know. It's hard to understand him. My Pashto isn't too great."

"All right, tell him we were ambushed last night. Ask him if he's heard anything about it."

Kamal shakes his head. "He says there are many wolves in the hills. Only he can keep them from eating our children."

"Tell him we need a guide. Tell him we can pay."

As Kamal begins to ask him the question, the captain pulls off one of his sandals. Half his foot is missing. He picks at the dead skin on his foot as he tells Kamal a story. The captain's voice becomes thin, even to Callum's ears, as if the man is asleep.

According to the captain, there used to be a man around here who took his donkey past the outpost every day, the animal's panniers loaded down with straw. The man admitted to being a smuggler when he trudged home every night, so the captain had his soldiers search him again and again. They searched his person, sifted the straw, steeped it in water, even burned it from time to time. Meanwhile, the smuggler became visibly wealthier and wealthier. Then he retired and bought a mansion in the city. Years later the captain ran into him in the city and said to the man, "You can tell me now. What were you smuggling when we could never catch you?"

"Donkeys," said the smuggler.

After Kamal finishes the story, the captain launches into a new round of laughing.

Frustrated, Callum asks, "What does all that mean?"

"I don't know, boss."

"Can he help us or not?"

Kamal and the captain begin talking again, but the Afghan officer rambles on despite Kamal's attempts to interrupt him.

"What's he saying now?"

"It's … garbage. I can't understand him."

"This is a waste of time. Forget it." He's starting to sound like Burnes. *Fuck!*

Callum and Kamal get up to leave. The captain waves them off and turns up the volume on the TV.

When they get outside, the young soldier comes out to meet them. He says to Kamal, "My name is Sergeant Shahid. I can help you."

Callum realizes the soldier is much older than he originally seemed. Though his face is youthful, there's a hardness in his eyes. It's always in the eyes.

"Ask him if he knows where we can find Taraki," he tells Kamal.

After Kamal and Shahid talk for some time, Kamal says, "He doesn't know where we can find Taraki, but he knows someone who does."

# CHAPTER FIFTEEN

Habs and Reno drew last watch up on the outpost walls, high off the desert floor. They're above the gates and have a commanding view over the terrain to the south. Only guard towers stationed at the southwest and southeast corners of the outpost have better lines of observation. They're without shelter as the sun bears down on them from the east.

Reno sits with his back to a wall, rifle resting on his lap. The Māori grips the weapon in his hands and releases the magazine before ejecting a round from it that he snatches out of the air. He takes a bore snake from a pouch in his tac vest and pulls it through the rifle's barrel, then places a few drops of lubricant in the chamber and works the action back and forth until it runs free. After wiping away the oil and dust from the weapon with a rag, he places the magazine back on, loads a fresh round into the chamber by cocking the rifle, then sets it back across his lap.

Habs observes the ritual unfold through eyes that feel as if they're wrapped in sandpaper. His tongue feels like a dried piece of jerky, probing for moisture in the parched recesses of his mouth. "Fuck me, it's hot."

Reno grunts something that sounds like "Yeah."

He might have said more than that, but Habs can't be sure, so he asks, "Sorry what?"

"Nothing."

Habs rubs his temples. "I've had a killer headache all night and can't think straight."

"Bummer, man," Reno mumbles.

"I thought I took a Tylenol last night, but I think it was the wrong pill."

"How do you know?"

"Because my dick's so hard right now."

"Better make sure you don't let your little head think for your big head then."

"Probably not gonna be a problem around here."

"Nope. Probably not."

Habs tries to think of something clever to say but can't come up with anything. Instead, he turns to stare out over the wasteland beyond. Far in the distance, beneath three mountaintops, lie endless fields of poppies.

For as long as Habs can remember, the most important thing in his life was to come here, to prove his worth, or something like that. He was too young to join the army when things were rocking and rolling. But when he finally got his chance, the ship had already left the station. Everyone had already taken their toys and gone home. The good fight was over.

When he finally arrived at the battalion, he spent the next couple of years guarding lockers and taking pointless course after pointless course. Hazardous waste materials handling. Safe bootlace operator. Coffee machine repair. Shower stall inspector. Just marking time.

But here he is. After all those years, all that work and horseshit, and for what? To sit here on this goddamn rooftop sweating his bag off in case someone starts shooting at them again.

He got off a few rounds last night. Probably didn't hit anything. But at least now he can say he's been here. Done that. Took the hero selfie and put it up on Facebook.

Not that anyone's going to give a shit.

Least of all Reno.

Habs realizes he doesn't know anything about the guy, even though he's been in the man's shadow for the past forty-eight hours. Habs tried to get it out of him on the drive down, but the big guy doesn't say much.

*Fuck it!* Nothing else to do up here. Might as well ask Reno the most important question any soldier can ask another soldier. "You have a girl back home or anything?"

"Nah. The settled life doesn't do it for me. You?"

There was someone once. Habs met her in a Turkish hookah bar in Montreal, a few years ago now after he joined the army. She had a tattoo on the back of her neck. Said it was a water nymph, whatever that is. He thought it was the sexiest thing he ever saw. After the bar closed, they went back to her place, an attic apartment with the toilet next to the kitchen sink. They stayed up all night getting high and listening to weird music. Violins at the apocalypse kind of shit. It was the last happy night he remembers. But he never saw her again, and now he can't even recall her name.

"No man," he tells Reno. "Not anymore." Maybe he should tell the Māori the whole story. Not just about her. Everything. Why he left the army and why he ended up here. But then he realizes he doesn't know the whole story himself. Better to change the subject. "What's your plan after this? What are you gonna do when you go home?"

"Go home?" Reno mutters, as if Habs asked him what he was going to do when he got back to Jupiter. "Nah. This is it for me. Give me my bullets, water, and some baby wipes and I'm okay."

"And hot sauce?"

"Yeah. Gotta get that balance in ya. What about you?"

"I'm gonna open a bar."

"Yeah?"

"And I'm gonna call it Blumpkins."

"Sounds classy."

"Or maybe Peaks and Valleys."

"Peaks and Valleys?"

"It'll be a strip club, but instead of strippers we'll serve chicken strips on club sandwiches."

Habs has used that one before, but Reno doesn't find it funny. Maybe he doesn't get the joke, or maybe it's just not funny.

Instead of having people laugh at him, Habs always tries to get them to laugh with him, a common survival technique for anyone who's grown up with a stutter. It came in handy when he showed up at the battalion. Being the new guy without any combat experience sucked. Having a stutter on top of that made things pretty savage. He figured the best way to get people to look past it was to make them laugh. And at the end of the day, even if they were laughing at him, that was still better than them not seeing him at all.

Truth is, Habs does know what he wants to do when he gets back. He still has to work out the details, but he wants to save up enough cash from this job so he can go back to school. Habs didn't have the best marks coming out of high school, that's for sure. But there are community colleges that might take him on. Pick up a trade or something. Apprentice for a few years as an electrician before starting his own business. Hire a few other guys to work for him. Maybe even recruit some other veterans. Put up a website and everything.

Habs had an uncle who did that, without the veteran part. Said the money was good until he stopped working because he fell off a roof. Now he collects unemployment benefits that he spends smoking j-bones. For the pain, his uncle says.

But Habs doesn't feel like telling Reno about any of that. Then he notices Reno observing something in the distance. Habs turns his attention in the same direction and spots a caravan of Kuchis trundling along the dried-out riverbed of the Arghandab to the west. Obscured at first by a cloud of dust, they emerge into view in a harlequinade of purples, reds, and greens. Mostly men in long wool coats and peak caps, shepherding goats and sheep. But some women, too, riding on the backs of camels or walking with small children in their arms. Together on some ancient migration, following routes seared deep into their forgotten histories.

The whole spectacle takes Habs away from himself to a place that shouldn't exist in this world, or at least his own understanding of it. He tries to imagine himself there, as one of them, instead of on top of this wall, as a part of whatever it is that he's a part of now. What if he spent his whole life with them and never knew anything else? Who would he be? Would he be happy? Would he still be him?

He feels so very small when he comes to that reckoning, until they finally disappear, returning him to the rooftop, leaving only the winds to carve a sea of ripples in the sand beneath a sepia haze.

With the distraction gone, he can't handle the voices in his head and the silence any longer. He says to Reno, "Okay, I have another one for you. Who would you rather be, Shatner or the Hoff?"

"From what decade?"

Before Habs can respond, a gunshot erupts from the guard toward over his shoulder. He flinches and drops for cover. Poking his head over the wall, he scans to see if anyone is still shooting. When it becomes clear that no fire is incoming, he squints up at the guard tower to see a soldier sighting down his rifle in the direction of the departed caravan.

"Hey!" Habs yells at the soldier. The soldier doesn't acknowledge Habs. He draws his gaze away from the rifle and slides back out of view into the shade. "Where the fuck did that guy come from?"

"He's been there all night."

"Weren't you gonna tell me?"

"I thought you knew."

"No, I didn't fucking know." Habs shakes his head. "But … but … but that asshole can't shoot at whoever he wants."

"Let it go, mate."

"No … no, I'm not going to let it go." Habs picks up the rifle that rests by his side and turns toward the guard tower.

"C'mon," Reno says, "why don't you get out of the sun?"

Reno's voice somehow grabs hold of Habs and stops him from going any further. In that moment of hesitation, he feels his headache coming on again. A belt-fed, fully automatic brain-splitter throbbing at the back of his skull. He pulls his canteen from his tac vest and upends it over his head. But the bottle is empty.

Reno hands him a full water bottle and says, "Keep yourself hydrated, mate. Don't be an amateur."

Habs takes the bottle from Reno before emptying its contents down his throat. He feels momentarily revived but also a little ashamed by his outburst. What was he going to do? Get in a gunfight in their own outpost? When he finishes the bottle, he crushes it between his hands and flicks it at the wall facing them. "What the fuck are we doing here?"

"Sentry duty, I guess."

"No, I get that. I mean, with all of this." Habs gestures toward the guard tower and then out toward the fields below.

"With all of what?"

"The mission. Or job. Whatever it is."

"Finish it. What else would we do?"

"What about Sung?"

"What about him."

"Wasn't he your friend?"

"Look, mate, you want out. No worries. I'll talk to the boss and we'll get you out of here." Reno gets up from his seat and lumbers off. He climbs down a ladder off the roof, leaving Habs alone.

Even though he downed the bottle of water Reno gave him, Habs's headache has settled in full force, detonating with each pulse behind his right eye. He presses the palms of his hands over his eyes and tries to swallow. But there isn't any moisture in his mouth, only the taste of dust and the reek of burning garbage. A wave of nausea rolls over him, making him retch.

But when he closes his eyes, he can only see Sung's face, half of it peeled away, one good eye staring up at him incomprehensibly. He keels over and starts dry-heaving, but nothing comes up. It takes him a couple of minutes before his vision clears.

What's he doing here? He wants to go home. Not that he has any home to go back to. But this isn't where he wants to be and it isn't where he wants to die. *Fuck that and fuck this place.*

Habs places an arm against the wall to steady himself, but his hand slips and he bashes his forehead against the wall. He lies face down for some time on the rampart. Slowly, his vision begins to fade before suddenly the whole world turns black.

Habs comes to when a block of ice is pressed against the back of his neck. At first, he thinks he must be dreaming because nothing in this world could ever feel that good. After blinking the sand out of his eyes, he squints and finds Reno kneeling over him. Then he remembers where he is.

"C'mon, mate, let's get you off the roof." The giant Māori's hand engulfs Habs's shoulder and rolls him onto his back. Reno helps him up into a sitting position and hands him another bottle of water, but Habs sucks down the contents too fast and starts coughing most of it up.

Lifting Habs up by the armpits as if he's a child, Reno slings him over his shoulder in a fireman-carry position. He carries Habs off the roof, down the ladder, and back to the gates where he places him gently in the back of one of the trucks.

The air-conditioning unit pumps refrigerated air into the truck. Reno places a rolled-up blanket behind Habs's head in place of a pillow and puts a full water bottle next to him.

"I'm sorry if I said anything wrong," Habs says.

"It's okay."

"You know, about Sung."

"I know."

"I hope he's gonna be okay."

"Me, too."

Reno turns to leave the truck, but before he does, Habs says, "I want to stay."

The Māori pauses for a moment and pats Habs on the leg. "Get some rest."

Habs's second-last thought before passing out is that he hopes he doesn't have to get up anytime soon. His last thought is that he better not be making a mistake by staying.

# CHAPTER SIXTEEN

Murph grabs the coffee mug that Callum left on the hood of their truck and dumps the contents into her own mug. It's still too hot to drink, but no point in letting it go to waste.

She had JP and Kamal erect a tarp between the two trucks to offer them a bit of shade, not that it makes any difference. Her T-shirt is so sweat-drenched that she could ring it out and brew another pot of coffee. Maybe the company would give her a bonus for saving water. Bunch of cheap-ass dickwads.

JP sits cross-legged facing her with his back to the other truck. Normally, he would be on his feet whenever they had downtime — shadow boxing or doing burpees or some other crazy shit, training for his next fight. Now all he can manage is to flick tiny pebbles into an empty cup at his feet.

This is Murph's first job with JP. But they've known each other for a while. Kamal, who she's been pals with for years, introduced them at a bar in Phuket while Murph was there on some R and R with Elise. They all come from a tight community where reputations count for everything. When Kamal hyped up JP, that was enough for Murph, even though his face was freshly mangled from his last fight in Bangkok.

Over beers and some whiskey and then something else the locals had on tap, she asked them both to join her on this job. For Kamal, it was a homecoming. And JP had done a couple of tours in Afghanistan with the Van Doos back in the day. They didn't need much convincing.

She got to know JP over the coming weeks. He's definitely the strong, silent type, happy to let Kamal do his talking for him. This is different, though. His silence has a deeper edge to it. But it's not anything Murph hasn't dealt with many times before. Too many times.

Her French is crap, but she might as well give it a shot. *"Ça va?"*

*"Oui, bien,"* JP responds.

*"Le guerre est une putain."*

*"Oui."*

That's about all she's got.

She picks up a few of the pebbles that lie at her feet and tosses one at the cup by JP. The first one bounces off the rim, but she manages to sink the second one. "When's your next fight?"

"Don't know."

"I bet Kamal's trying to get something lined up."

JP nods.

"He says you're the next Georges St-Pierre."

JP shakes his head.

"He says you're going to be in the UFC someday."

*"Oui?"*

"Yeah, that's what he said. I think he's full of shit, though."

*"Pourquoi?"*

"I saw the tape after your last fight in Bangkok. You didn't come out of that one looking too pretty."

JP chuckles.

"I don't see you winning the next one, either, sitting around on your ass and turning into a milk bag." She gives that one some space to breathe, lets him chew on it a little bit. He's already up on his feet before she can get the next words out, rummaging around in the back of his truck for the punching bag.

"*Je vais chercher Ash,*" she tells him. "*Où est-il?*"

"*Je ne sais pas.*"

"Okay."

That went better than she thought it would. JP was the warm-up, though. Now she has to deal with the main event.

Ash disappeared somewhere in the night before she had a chance to check on him. She planned for him to take a shift up on the walls with her to give them a chance to hash things out. But when she went to grab him, he wasn't around. And no one else knew where he went. She let it go, giving him time to clear his head.

Murph took the shift by herself, which isn't something she'd have allowed any of the others to do. But JP and Kamal came down. Reno and Habs were up after her. And she wanted to give Callum some time to figure out their next moves and deal with Burnes.

She almost dozed off up there. The only thing that kept her awake was the torrent of coffee that kept her vibrating at a frequency audible only to dogs. In a moment of delusion, she considered asking Sung to hook her up to an IV bag to replenish her fluids. Until she had a flashback of Sung lying on a stretcher in the back of the helicopter, which jolted her awake.

Not her fault. She did what she could. She gave him chest compressions until her arms went numb, keeping him alive long enough to get him off the ground. What happens to him next is out of her hands. She needs to focus on keeping the rest of the team together and moving forward.

Ash couldn't have gone very far. She did a sweep of the outpost after they settled in last night, which didn't take long, since the whole place looks a lot bigger on the outside than it is inside. Aside from the main barracks and the captain's bunkhouse, there aren't too many other places where Ash could be hiding. Unless the outpost has some secret spot she can't see.

Ash does know a thing or two about secrets.

She starts her search at the abandoned barracks where the main door hangs loosely from its hinges. When she tugs on the door, it barely moves. Gripping the door's edge with both hands, she yanks it open, sending it crashing to the ground. As the sound clangs around the outpost, she glances around to see if anyone notices. After the echo recedes, she steps inside.

Murph covers her nose with the crook of her arm to stop from gagging at the stench of vinegar and rotting plants. Although daylight invades the entrance to the barracks, she can't see any deeper inside. She clicks on the flashlight on her rifle, scattering spores of dust as she shines the light around the space in front of her. A long corridor unfolds down the centre of the barracks with many rooms branching off on either side. Most of the doors are open, revealing rooms strewn with trash and overturned army cots. Only one door at the very end of the corridor is closed.

She moves to the closed door and jangles the handle, but it doesn't budge. Slamming her shoulder into the door, she tries to force it open. The door remains locked. She bangs on the door and calls out "Ash," but no one responds.

Murph walks back out of the barracks and stands momentarily in the shade of the building, surveying the rest of the compound. There aren't many other places where Ash could have gone. Reno and Habs are still up on the roof, and she didn't see Ash go up there. Kamal and Callum are still in with the captain. It's unlikely he'd be in with them. Could he have left somehow? She recalls the gap in the back wall that someone tried to block with concertina wire. Maybe he's gone back there for some reason.

The concertina wire lies in a tangle across the gap, not properly staked in. She doesn't want to slice up her gloves, so she attaches a carabiner to one end of the tangled wire, weaves together three strands of paracord, and runs the improvised rope through the carabiner, using it as a hook to pull on the wire. It takes her three attempts at different points of the wire before she opens a passage wide enough to slip through without getting snagged.

Beyond the gap in the wall lies a narrow path that curves around the cliff face, leading away from the outpost. Desiccated scrub brush lines the path as sharp as the concertina wire, slowing her progress. Faded scraps of cloth, small trinkets, broken pieces of mirror cling to the branches. At the end of the path, she arrives at a small building, possibly a schoolhouse at one time. She calls out, "Ash, you in there?

Murph pauses, uneasily, at the silence, glances back down the path toward the outpost. He can't have come all this way. Shaking her head, she steps inside.

Broken chairs and desks are scattered around the room. Pieces of a chalkboard sprinkle the floor. Moss breaks through a crack in the wall, and withered vines snake along the floor. Dust covers everything, choking the room of all light and air. Only a table stands empty at one end like an altar.

"Ash?"

Behind the table is a door partially ajar, emitting a faint glow from inside. She steps tentatively toward the door but doesn't call out. When she passes through the door, opium musk crawls into her nostrils, making her eyes water.

She blinks away the tears and becomes aware of her surroundings. An oil lamp sputters on a thin reed carpet. A gaunt man draws from a ceramic pipe at the carpet's centre, the pebble at its core bubbling before sputtering out. Other men sit on the floor in a circle around the pipe, dark faces pale against the rosy flame.

When her eyes finally adjust to the light, she spies Ash sitting in the circle, so grey he'd disappear if he turned sideways. "What the fuck?" she mutters, barely a whisper.

Murph rushes over and grabs him by the arm, knocking over the pipe as she crosses the room. "We're getting the fuck out of here."

The man smoking the pipe takes no notice of her presence. He turns back to recentre the pipe as Murph drags Ash from the room.

When they step outside, Murph throws Ash against the wall. "What the fuck was that?"

"Why are we weigh'd upon with heaviness, and utterly consumed with sharp distress, while all things else have rest from weariness?"

"Enough of your bullshit." Murph slugs him in the face, a solid right hook to the jaw, folding him in half and sending him sprawling to the ground. She glowers over him until she realizes he isn't moving. Reaching down, she pulls him up by the collar and slaps him on the face until he comes to.

"All right, all right," he says, shielding his face from any further blows. When he senses no more are incoming, he shakes free of her grasp and slides back down the wall, rubbing his jaw. "Fuck, Murph."

"No, fuck you, asshole." She turns to head back down the path, leaving Ash behind, but she only makes it a few steps before demanding, "What the fuck's wrong with you?"

Ash shrugs with his hands but otherwise doesn't say anything.

"C'mon, I'm sending you back. We'll call in another helicopter to pick you up."

"Can't you leave me here?" Murph quickly steps toward him before Ash raises his hands in defence. "Okay, okay, it was a joke." When she doesn't laugh, Ash says with a wry smile, "It would be cheaper than paying for my airfare."

When she doesn't move any further, he pats a spot on the ground next to him. She rolls her eyes at the sky before walking over to sit next to him. When she settles in, he says, "You been training with JP or what?"

Murph rubs the knuckles on her right hand. "That boy couldn't handle me."

"No doubt."

They sit in silence for a moment before Murph says, "Talk to me, dickhead."

He inhales deeply and opens his hands, palms up, to the sky. "What do you want me to say? I've called in air support from spectre gunships at two thousand metres into villages that never had electricity. I saw a boy blow himself up at a checkpoint when he didn't know how to use his suicide vest. I had to pick up the pieces of my best friend and put him in a body bag. I'm too soft for this world."

"That's your excuse for smoking that shit?"

"In my defence, I haven't smoked any yet. Before you showed up, that is."

"You're not getting an apology."

"Not looking for one."

She nods. "This place isn't the entire world, you know."

"I know, but it used to be the only place left that made any sense."

"Then what are you still doing here?"

He leans forward, gazes out over the scorched fields below them, shrugs, then leans back. "I don't know. What about you? Why are you still here?"

"I get bored easy."

"You have Elise now."

"Yeah, I guess I do."

"You should be home with her."

"I know. Told her this would be the last one."

"Is it?"

"Yes. No. I don't know. Maybe …" An image of Elise is seared in her memory as clear as an aurora. She smiles at the remembering, then returns to the reality of having to convince a junkie to help them track down an Afghan warlord. She picks up a handful of sand at her side and lets it run out between her fingers. Sighing, she says, "Shit wasn't so good for me growing up. Not sure I ever told you that. All I remember is being angry all the time. There was probably even a reason at some point but … then I found this. Only family I ever had."

Neither of them say anything, sitting in silence the way friends do when they don't need to speak to each other. For Murph, it's not about understanding. It's taken her a long time to accept that some people are a certain way and there's no sense in pushing back against that. She's not there yet with Ash, though.

Before Murph gets up to leave, she says, "You know that shit you're always going on about? The crisis of modernity and how the silly machinery is all broken?"

"Yeah."

"I think you're right."

"I know I am."

"Well, I don't care. I'm going to finish this job and then I'm going home to Elise. You can come with me or stay. It's up to you." She reaches out her hand and leaves it there while Ash stares off into the distance. With a sigh, he grabs her hand. She lifts him up, and they walk together down the path back to the outpost.

# CHAPTER SEVENTEEN

Callum and Kamal lead Shahid away from the captain's hut into the far corner of the outpost by the crumpled shed. Shahid relaxes visibly the farther away he gets from the captain. Then he opens up about everything except for how to get to Taraki.

Shahid can speak a few words of English but not enough to get his story across, which means Kamal has to translate everything, drawing out the conversation a lot longer than it needs to. It doesn't help that Shahid wants to rant about how fucked up everything got after the Americans left.

As if it was all Callum's fault.

Callum grows increasingly impatient, pushing Kamal to get something useful out of Shahid. But the more frustrated Callum becomes, the more adamant Shahid gets about telling his own story first. Eventually, Callum gives up, and they let him talk.

"I'm a sergeant, or at least I was," Shahid says, "before everything went to shit. We haven't been paid for months. At least not by the government." He pulls a pack of cigarettes from his pocket and offers one to Kamal and Callum, who both refuse. "At one point there was an entire *kandak* stationed between this outpost and several others farther to the west and south. Five hundred soldiers. Maybe more." Shahid lights a cigarette and draws deeply before exhaling a thick cloud of smoke. "You're

Canadian?" Shahid asks, pointing at Callum, the cigarette dangling between his fingers.

Callum nods.

"I can tell. I remember the Canadians. They were good to work with. Treated us well. Always gave us supplies, fuel, food, whenever we needed it. Except every six months —" he snaps his fingers "— there would be a new group of Canadians. I remember one time, one of your commanders marching us out to the helipad to give a big speech. All the troops lined up, fifty degrees outside. He said we were going to win the war in six weeks. Halfway through the speech, one of your soldiers thundered in. *Bam!* Flat on his face. The commander got in his helicopter and flew off to wherever." Shahid makes a helicopter noise and shakes his hand in the air.

"The Canadians left and the Americans came in with the same speeches and parades. In time, the Americans went away, too. Once the Americans were gone, the government in Kabul sucked everything back to Kandahar City. They used one of your terms, centre of gravity. Eventually, they abandoned Kandahar City, for the most part.

"The desertions from the *kandak* started off as a trickle. Some soldiers went back home, wherever that was, or started families out in the villages. Some disappeared and never said why. As our numbers dwindled, the trickle became a flood, and the ones who stayed were often the worst."

"Why did you stay?" asks Kamal.

"You're a Tajik from the north?" Shahid says.

"Yes."

"I'm from the north, too. Outside Kabul. I'm Pashtun, though. We should probably hate each other."

Kamal chuckles. "No, we're good. I served with lots of Pash-tuns, some of them good friends."

"You were in the army?"

"Yes. Mostly out east in Gardez."

"I spent some time there, too. We probably know some of the same assholes."

"It's a small army. Why did you end up down here?"

"My brother was posted here a couple of years ago. I asked to be posted down here after I made sergeant." Shahid finishes his cigarette and flicks it away. It explodes on the ground in a hail of sparks. "At first, things were good. We were never posted to the same base. But we managed to link up every couple of days on resupply runs or on leave to the city. Life was good. Or at least as good as it could be living in this dump."

Shahid pulls a second cigarette from the pack but doesn't light it right away. "I don't know when, but my brother got hooked on opium. That shit's everywhere, hard not to. I saw what it did to my brother and my friends, though. I didn't touch the stuff, except for some *naswar* out on patrol to keep me awake." Shahid lights the cigarette and pulls it to his lips. "My father found out that my brother was a drug addict. He refused to let us come home, said no son of his would use drugs. I stayed, hoping my brother would get clean, but he didn't."

Shahid glances at the cigarette. "There was a mutiny here at the outpost because we weren't getting paid. But by that point, there was no discipline, no chain of command. Even though I was a sergeant, I didn't have any power. Only the officers did."

The cigarette smoulders next to his fingers, a line of ash forming along its length. "One night a private stabbed our commander in the chest thirteen times with a rusty bayonet while the commander was sleeping." Shahid mimics thrusting a bayonet with the hand that holds the cigarette, sending ash flying off. "Then he started wearing the commander's epaulets and demanded everyone call him captain."

"That greaseball?" Kamal gestures toward the hut.

Shahid nods. "Pretty soon we became like a band of goons and criminals. We set up roadblocks and robbed the locals. Or ran patrols through the villages and took whatever we could. I tried to get them to stop, but they didn't listen to me anymore. I stayed out of it and tried to look after my brother as best as I could."

"Where's your brother now?" asks Kamal.

Shahid lowers his head and holds out his hands, palms up. "I don't know."

Callum says to Kamal, "Ask him about Taraki. Ask him if he knows where to find the guy."

Kamal asks and Shahid says, "I don't know where Taraki is, either."

Callum throws his head back in frustration and looks up at the sky but doesn't say anything.

Shahid says something, and Kamal translates. "But he does know someone who does."

"Okay," Callum says. "Who?"

"The Pir."

"The what?"

"The Pir. It's like a religious leader. A Sufi mystic."

"Jesus Christ!"

Kamal grins. "Kinda like that, yeah."

"Where do we find this Pir?"

Kamal asks Shahid, then translates. "The Pir's in a *khanqah*. It's kind of like a mosque. Up in the hills, a couple of kilometres to the south."

"Wonderful. Can he take us there?"

After Kamal and Shahid go back and forth, Kamal says, "Yes, he can take us there. But there's a treatment facility up north by Kabul."

"What does that have to do with the Pir?"

"He says it's very expensive. If we could pay him, he could take his brother there. And then maybe his father would accept them both into their home."

Burnes was carrying most of their cash, presumably so he could bribe Taraki after they ran into him. But all of that went up in smoke. Murph might have a few dollars stashed away in one of her trucks to buy melons or anything else they might need. But probably not enough to send this guy's brother to the Afghan Betty Ford. "Okay," Callum says. "You work out the details with him. But whatever he ends up with is coming out of your bonus."

"You're funny, boss," Kamal says.

Callum was only ninety-percent joking. "I'm going to find Burnes. Go link up with Murph and tell her we're leaving as soon as we can."

Callum finds Burnes alone on the walls away from the others, a pool of tobacco juice the consistency of tar at his feet. "How's your team doing?" Burnes asks.

"They'll be all right."

"Rough night."

"Not the first."

"Didn't seem that way." Burnes spits into the ever-expanding puddle.

"How about Lal?" Callum asks. "Any word?"

"You tell me. My sat phone got blown up in the attack."

Callum doesn't bother to tell Burnes he pulled it out of the wreckage, or that it smashed into pieces when he dropped it. They still have their backup radios for comms. Not that the radios have been particularly reliable.

"He's a tough lad, though," Burnes says. "We've been through worse. I'm not too worried about him. I'm kind of worried about one of your boys, though."

"Which one?"

"Ash. That boy's got a taste for the lotus flower."

"How do you mean?"

Burnes snorts. "Let me tell you, cocaine isn't a drug. I want cocaine like I want a blow job. But opium …" Burnes kisses the tips of his fingers as if sampling macaroni and cheese made with lobster and truffle oil. "That shit messes with the hedonic centres in your brain. Best to stay away if he can."

"I'll let him know." The clues were there, but now it all makes sense. Callum should have picked that up before. Chalk it up to another thing he missed. He'll have to talk to Murph about it and figure out what they're going to do with Ash.

"I'm not going to tell you how to run your team," Burnes says, "but I need to know they're going to be good to finish the job."

"What is the job?"

"You didn't think to ask before now?"

"I thought we were selling insurance."

"Funny man." A slight smile twists Burnes's face. "Close but nah. Cellphones."

"Cellphones?"

"Yeah, cellphones. Those digital crack boxes everyone has in their pockets. Even more addictive than your boy's dope." Burnes mimes using a cellphone in a way that suggests he doesn't know how to use one. "My company was hired by a Chinese telecom. They're trying to expand their network through southern Afghanistan, but they needed someone with experience working in this part of the country. They hired us to set the conditions before they could move in and build their cellphone towers. And that's why we're looking for Taraki. Apparently, he holds the keys to the kingdom in these parts."

"Cellphones," Callum says.

"Almost forty million people in this country and they all want their cellphones. Even if they live on only two dollars a day, we can still charge them a dollar. You do the math."

"Okay."

"What did you think this was about? No wait. Let me guess. You thought we were going to rescue some orphans in a refugee camp from an evil warlord." Burnes chuckles. "I know you, man."

"No, you don't."

"Sure, I do. Why do you think I hired you?"

Callum turns his back to Burnes and leans over the edge of the wall. He could walk away, leave this all behind. Murph could run the team probably better than him. Be done with this place and with Burnes. But that would mean giving up on Devon.

When Callum doesn't say anything, Burnes continues. "Captain Callum King, Meritorious Service Medal. The golden boy. The chosen one. The next in line to inherit the throne. Any of that sound familiar?"

Callum calculates the distance to the ground. Not quite far enough to break Burnes's legs if the man accidentally fell off.

"There were some gaps in the record, though. Some of it was classified and even I couldn't get my grubby little paws on the good stuff."

Callum returns his attention to Burnes.

"I read the trial decision from your court martial. March the guilty bastard in. In the end, they let you off with a conduct unbecoming. But all roads lead to a dishonourable discharge, don't they? I bet that's the part that rubs you the most, isn't it? The dishonourable part. Am I getting warmer?" Burnes squirts a laser of tobacco juice between his top teeth against the wall where it splatters like a bug on the windshield of a Mack truck flying down the highway. "Here's what I don't understand. What was Devon's role? He was only one of your section commanders, but they roped him in, as well. Why?"

Burnes hasn't even finished the sentence before it all flashes back in Callum's memory. The edges are frayed a little, as if someone took a torch to an old photograph, but the pieces are as sharp as ever. The light, the sounds, the grit in his teeth, the static on the radio, the suffocating heat. Moments jumbled together in a jagged collage and imprinted on his psyche.

"Devon got a tipoff from some local that there was a bomb maker in their village," Callum says. "Dev wanted to do a hit on the compound, so I ran it up the chain. They said no. Devon being Devon did it, anyway. When I found out, it was too late." He pauses, gathering his breath. "They walked right into an ambush and got lit up pretty bad. One of Devon's guys was torn in half by a recoilless rifle round, and everyone else in the section had a few scrapes. When their request for a medevac came in over the net, I was the first one on the scene. It was mostly over once we showed up with some armour. By that point, the damage was done."

"You were the fall guy."

"I should've stopped him from going."

"But you didn't know."

"I should've known."

Burnes shakes his head. He spits out another long spool of tobacco juice that arcs over the edge of the wall and disappears out of sight. "And now you're here trying to bring your boy back home in one piece, make up for past mistakes. That's it, isn't it?" He spreads his hands wide as if surveying the vast landscape before him, then pulls the wad of tobacco out of his lip and tosses it over the rampart wall. "Look, you want my story."

Not especially, Callum almost says.

"When I got out of the army, I took a job as a management consultant with some venture capital firm. The boss was a thirty-six-year-old pill job who said 'bro' and 'leverage' a lot. His favourite story was how he made his first million by the time he was twenty-five, moving imaginary piles of money around with other imaginary piles of money." Burnes mimes playing one of those guess-the-ball-under-the-plastic-cup tricks. "Fucking twatknot. Thought he was an A-type because he got upset whenever he lost a game in his ultimate Frisbee league."

Burnes pulls another tin of tobacco from a pocket in his pant leg and snaps the tin between his thumb and forefinger three times. "The Treaty of Westphalia is over. That oath of allegiance you made back when you were a Boy Scout doesn't mean piss anymore. Nation-states are finished. The future is the market-state. Instead of politicians and parliaments, now the world's run by hedge fund managers and venture capitalists."

He reaches into the tin and pinches out a dip that he stuffs back into his lip. "Don't listen to the twee liberals, old boy, with their reasonableness and deference. The elevator's crashing to the earth and they're asking everyone to be polite to each other as if it'll make any fucking difference. The sooner you hoist that aboard, the better off you'll be."

Callum doesn't need a sermon from Burnes. He figured all that out a long time ago. None of that matters now. The only important thing is to bring Devon home. Not that it would give him absolution for what happened. Nothing ever will. Nor does he deserve it. But maybe bringing Devon back will give him some small measure of peace, and that might be enough.

"Let's avoid paralysis by analysis here," Burnes says. "This shithole redlined long before we got here. Let's finish the job."

"We will."

"You fucking better. We're paying you enough. I'm still waiting on another linkup point with Taraki. When that comes in, let's roll."

Callum debates not telling Burnes about Shahid. "We've already got that covered. There's an Afghan sergeant here who can lead us to someone who knows Taraki."

"Who?"

"A Pir."

"A what?"

"He's some kind of mystic. Lives in the hills." When Burnes raises an eyebrow, Callum adds, "Taraki might hold the keys to the kingdom, but the Pir gets final say on who gets to go into the next one."

"Okay. Good work."

"Thanks. I'll go brief the team. We step off in an hour."

# PART VI
# WAR IS A CHISEL

# CHAPTER EIGHTEEN

Callum huddles beneath the tarp next to Shahid, a map stretched on the ground between them. Shahid, brow furrowed in concentration, scribbles a series of lines and circles on the map, as if he's a math student solving a complex problem on the chalkboard in front of the class. After pausing to examine his work, Shahid leans back. "Move south, move fast, is the best."

The scribbles are all on the north side of the map.

Callum glances up at Kamal, who shrugs. He tells Kamal, "Ask him if he knows where we're going. Any landmarks. Anything we can look for."

Kamal asks Shahid the questions, gets the answers, then tells Callum, "He knows the *khanaqah* is in the mountains and that it's somewhere to the south. He said he'll know where to go when we get there."

The only mountains within kilometres are down in Khyber Ghar, about ten kilometres to the south. Except they aren't mountains. More like foothills. Callum was there years ago. There weren't any people there then, but maybe that's changed. According to the map, it looks as if there's a small cluster of dwellings on the west face of the range, which might be a settlement of some sort. Callum has no idea how accurate the map is, though. Could the *khanaqah* be down there?

It's going to be a serious hump, so Shahid better be right. On a straight shot, they could easily do it in under two hours, but Callum wants to stay off the main routes, which means they'll have to cross some shit terrain. It's already past midday and they've blown his time estimate. But if they leave now, they should arrive before last light. They better, because finding this place in the dark could involve some serious ass pain.

As Callum charts out their route on the map, Reno dumps a heap of soiled *perahan tunbans* in front of him. "Will these work?" the Māori asks, holding up one of the shirts for inspection.

The stench of curdled goat milk wafts from the pile. "They should do the trick." Callum was hoping Reno could track down some old Afghan army uniforms, or something else they could use as a disguise. These shirts wouldn't fool anyone up close. But hopefully they should save them a look or two at a distance.

Reno tosses a shirt to Kamal, who recoils after giving it a quick sniff. Then the big guy rips a shirt down each of the seams and pulls it over his head, turning the garment into a poncho. Shahid grins widely while giving Reno a wholehearted thumbs-up.

Callum asks Reno, "How's Habs?"

"He'll be okay. I pumped him full of liquids. He's having a kip now."

"Let's get him up then."

Reno grabs another shirt from the pile before ambling over to the trucks to wake up Habs. The Māori passes by Murph, who hands various pieces of equipment to JP out of the back of their truck.

"Murph," Callum calls over to her.

"Yeah?"

"How do we look?"

"We need a couple more minutes."

"You've got ten."

He can't hear her response, since she's buried in the back of the truck. Probably for the best.

Callum decided to leave behind their two remaining trucks, which wasn't a popular decision. He tasked Murph to divide up all the essential gear, which was almost everything, and hand it out to the team. That means they'll have to leave the trucks locked up at the outpost with the rest of their kit. He sent Kamal to speak with the captain about it, but the man was gone.

They'll probably find the trucks up on cinder blocks when they get back, and their gear for sale on Alibaba.

While finishing his final preparations, Callum spots Ash straggling back, bleary-eyed, to the team. Callum prepares to launch but stands down after exchanging a glance with Murph, who waves him off. He doesn't have time to deal with Ash now, anyway, especially with Burnes pacing at the edge of their little camp, spitting gobs of tobacco on the ground and muttering to myself. Every lap of the camp, Burnes approaches Callum to get them moving, but Callum ignores him. After the fifth or sixth time, Burnes gets the message. They'll leave when Callum says they're ready.

Once they finally get organized, Shahid leads them from the outpost at a quick pace, carrying an AK-47 over his shoulder like a war club. Callum follows close behind, nudging Shahid in the right direction from time to time. The hills loom in front of them like a beacon, so Shahid doesn't need much guidance.

The rest of the team stretches out behind him, Kamal next and JP after that. Reno towers over everyone, and occasionally Callum glimpses Habs in Reno's shadow. Beyond that, he expects to find Burnes and then Ash but can't be sure, since they're too far back. But Murph is in the rear, and he trusts her to shepherd everyone along.

The team makes good time despite the heat, tramping through fields of wheat, golden under the late-afternoon sun. They halt only once for shelter in the shade of an abandoned grape hut. Callum doesn't let them linger; he's impatient to reach the *khanaqah*. Only Burnes, sucking wind from both ends, voices any complaints. Callum pretends he doesn't hear him.

Shahid reaches the end of the field, marked by a waist-high mud wall, and turns to Callum for direction. Callum approaches the wall, beyond which lies open ground covered in loose rocks and sand all the way to the base of the hills. He squints through the scope on his rifle to scan across the hill face from left to right, spotting the structures that show up on the map, about a kilometre distant, but can't make out if anyone's there.

Callum points to the dwellings and says to Shahid, "*Khanaqah?*"

Shahid smiles and gives Callum a thumbs-up.

Once the rest of the team catches up, Callum gives them a minute to hydrate before getting the nod from Murph to press on. He vaults the wall and strides briskly toward the settlement, feeling exposed crossing open ground, but confident the team has his back.

Two hundred metres out from the hills, he motions back to his team to remain in place while he moves forward with Shahid to recce the settlement. Even at this distance, he can tell no one's there.

Approaching the first dwelling, a crude structure made from baked red clay taken from the surrounding hills, Callum peeks through the first open window. Sand fills the room, covering the floor in shallow dunes from wall to wall, reaching up to the ceiling in the back corner and pouring through the doorway. Nothing else is inside.

Callum wanders through the settlement, checking out the other dwellings, but they're all the same, empty except for the sand.

He returns to the first building he inspected and waves in the team.

Burnes is already there, hunched over, hands on his knees, gasping for air. Between laboured breathes, he asks, "Is this it?"

"Doesn't look like it," Callum replies.

"Then what the fuck are we doing here?"

Callum would like to know, as well. Shahid squats in the shade, his AK-47 resting across his knees. Callum points to the empty dwellings. "*Khanaqah*. Pir. Here?"

Shahid shakes his head.

"Then where?"

The sergeant points up into the hills behind them.

"Are you sure?"

Shahid nods vigorously.

"This is dogshit," says Burnes, not quite recovered from his gasping fit. "I knew we shouldn't have trusted this fucking lunch pail."

Callum weighs their options, not that they have any. Burnes clearly doesn't know where they're going, otherwise he'd have taken them there. They don't have any other choice. "We're going."

"Hang on," says Burnes, raising a hand in the air. "Maybe we should hang out here, catch our breath, figure out our next move."

Murph and the rest of the team have joined up with them by that point. Callum asks Murph, "Are we good?"

"We're good."

"All right then. It's going to be dark in a couple of hours and I don't want to get lost in these hills. If we're going to find this place, I'd rather do it now." Callum doesn't give Burnes a chance to respond. He says to Shahid, "Let's go," then sets off through the deserted settlement in search of the *khanaqah*.

Shahid unearths a broken stone path behind the settlement, obscured by sand from the surrounding dunes. He guides them up into the hills, stopping here and there when the path turns faint, to uncover the way ahead. The hills, piled one on top of the other, grow ever higher until the fields below recede in the distance.

At the highest peak, they pass a dead crow along the crest of a ridge, its ribcage exposed like two hands in supplication to the sky. The path twists away from the dead crow and winds down into a hollow between the hills where crude huts made of piled rocks cling to the hillsides like barnacles, each one different than the other.

Callum pauses to survey the scene below. There are dozens of huts, maybe hundreds. It's hard to tell where one ends and the other begins. He can't see anyone from where he stands, at least not out in the open. But people could be inside, hiding or otherwise.

Shahid has charged on ahead and waves Callum after him when he senses Callum hasn't followed. Callum hesitates. Where's Shahid taking them now? Is anyone even here?

Callum waits for the rest of the team to catch up with him on the outlook. They straggle in one by one, exhausted from the hike. He should have let them rest at the base of the hills before pushing on, but he didn't know it was going to be this much of a bag drive to get here, wherever here is.

And it provides him a small measure of satisfaction when Burnes collapses on the ground after being the last to arrive.

Callum gives them a minute to catch their breath and suck back whatever water they have left, then says, "Kamal and JP, come with me. Murph, I want you to post up here with the rest and keep an eye on us."

"You think it's an ambush?" Murph asks.

Callum scans the surrounding hills for signs of life but doesn't find any. "If it is, cover us and we'll fight our way back to you."

"I'm coming." All eyes turn to Burnes in a heap behind them.

"All right," Callum says.

Shahid is already a speck by the time they step off toward the huts below and down the scree-covered slope, which shifts underfoot as they slide down the hill face. No one comes out to meet them, and Shahid has already disappeared by the time they arrive at the huts. Without any clear path through, Callum turns back to Kamal and JP to check if they have any thoughts. Kamal shrugs while JP's eyes dart about as he grips his rifle a little tighter than when they set off. Clearly, they don't have any ideas, either.

Callum picks his way through the maze of huts, some no larger than a mailbox while others are the size of a small barn. Still, there's no sign of any life. He turns a corner and stumbles on a weathered-looking old woman draped in a shawl, standing at the entrance to one of the huts, grim lines etched in the deep corners of her face. She mouths something at him, but no words come out.

"Boss," says Kamal behind him.

Other faces appear in windows and out of doors and around corners. One or two at first, then more and more, until an entire crowd envelopes them.

Callum raises both hands in an open gesture. "Easy." Both to the crowd and to Kamal, as well.

Shahid's head pokes out from behind a hut, and he waves them forward through the crowd. Callum grabs Kamal and JP, and they follow Shahid through the remaining huts a short distance until they arrive at the *khanaqah*, set into the base of a cliff. It's surrounded by a stone wall that conceals everything inside except for three glittering minarets that extend upward at different heights. A thousand pennants line the tops of the wall, each unfurled against a lidded sky. In the centre of the wall is a gate of polished oak inlaid with thick ribbons of iron.

Shahid walks up to the gate and pushes it open. Callum follows, but Shahid raises a hand to stop him and says something to Kamal.

Kamal translates. "You can't go in, boss. Muslims only."

"You're telling me we walked all this fucking way and we can't even go inside?" Burnes roars.

After speaking to Kamal, Shahid disappears inside. Kamal says, "He's going to look for someone who will talk to us."

"Tell him to take his fucking time," Burnes growls.

They all ignore him. Callum asks Kamal and JP, "Can you guys head back and bring in the others? We'll wait here."

"Are you gonna be okay?" Kamal asks.

"Yeah, I think we'll be fine."

The sun dips down over the surrounding hills as they wait for the others to return. Burnes is the first to collapse against the wall. Callum joins him shortly later. They wait in silence, which suits them both just fine.

Callum hears the rest of the team approach before he can see them. "'It was all a dream, I used to read *Word Up!* magazine. Salt-n-Peppa and Heavy D up in the limousine.'" Sounds like Habs.

"Does that kid ever shut up?" asks Burnes as the team comes into view.

Habs grins at Burnes. "What's wrong? Are your syphilis headaches bothering you?"

Burnes pulls himself up off the ground. "What's that, boy?"

"You better sit down," Reno says, ambling in behind Habs.

"And you better put a muzzle on your dog there." Burnes raises himself to his full height in front of Reno but barely reaches his chin.

Callum moves to intercept Burnes. "C'mon, let's go chat."

Burnes shoves Callum away. "What the fuck are we even doing here?"

"When the existence of the market is threatened, it is absolved of all moral commandments," Ash declares. "Profit as an aim sanctifies every means, cunning, treachery, violence, simony, imprisonment, and even death."

Burnes glowers at Ash. "All right there, Chomsky."

"That's not Chomsky."

"You know you're pretty self-righteous for a goddamn mercenary."

"We're soldiers, mate," Reno pipes up.

"Soldiers. I've got more time in a blue rocket than the lot of you do playing soldier. You're all a bunch of fucking amateurs." Burnes storms away through the huts in a different direction than the one they came in on.

"Should we follow him?" Murph asks Callum.

At that moment, Shahid sticks his head out of the gate and tells Kamal that Callum is allowed to enter, but he has to leave his rifle behind.

"No, let Burnes go," Callum says. "He needs a minute to cool off. I'm going with Shahid."

"Are you going by yourself?" Murph asks.

Callum looks over at Shahid, who has already disappeared inside. He turns back to Murph and hands her his rifle. "Yeah."

"Is that a good idea?"

"Probably not. Get some rest. I shouldn't be in there long."

# CHAPTER NINETEEN

A dazzling courtyard of delicate white tiles inlaid in intricate patterns repeating endlessly greets Callum as he enters the *khanaqah*. An arcade lines the courtyard on every side, spaced evenly with marble columns. The mosque occupies the *khanaqah*'s western edge, marked by a golden five-pointed star etched in bronze above its entrance. The remaining buildings are all made of sparkling white stone.

Shahid is nowhere to be seen.

Callum spots a boy, half in shadows, drinking from a copper pail. When the boy notices Callum, he springs to his feet and vanishes into a side door, kicking over the pail in his wake and spilling its contents onto the cobblestone courtyard. The water forms the shadow of a mandala on the ground before dissipating in the heat.

A man steps out of the mosque, jostling prayer beads in his right hand. His crisp white robes pull snugly over his ample midsection. He pauses in mid-thought before noticing Callum, his face lighting up in a warm smile. "Welcome."

"Hello." Callum holds back, unsure if he should offer to shake the man's hand, uncertain if he should even be there at all.

"I am sorry we could not let in all of your party. This is a holy place, you see."

"I think they'll be okay."

"Well, then, what can I do for you?"

"I'm here to speak with the Pir."

"Hmm." He studies Callum intently. "Why don't you and I go inside where it is cooler?" Without waiting for a response, the man strolls across the courtyard and enters a side door. Callum hesitates before following, stopping briefly to right the pail knocked over by the boy.

The room is much larger than it appeared from the outside. White curtains hang from the ceiling, moving listlessly though the windows are shut. The man sits cross-legged on the floor, pouring tea into a cup from a silver pitcher. When the cup is nearly full, he slides it toward a cushion and signals for Callum to join him.

Raising his hand to his heart, the man says, "My name is Aziz, and how do I call you?"

"Callum. Or Cal. Whatever you like."

"It is a pleasure to meet you, Callum. Tell me, friend, why have you come across these hills alone?"

"We're looking for a man. I was told the Pir knows where to find him."

"And why do you need to find him?"

Because they need to find Taraki so that a Chinese telecom company can build cellphone towers across southern Afghanistan. And so Callum can find Devon. When Callum says it all in his head, it sounds so pointless, especially in this place. He doesn't know how to tell Aziz. "The man I'm with …" He hesitates to explain any further, not out of concern, but from a budding knowledge that it doesn't matter. "We need to speak with the Pir."

"I see." Aziz scratches his chin and sips tea. "And you think this man will help you?"

"I don't know. Maybe ..." His voice trails off again as he suddenly feels foolish and out of place, like a child who doesn't belong. He looks down self-consciously at his shirt, starched with salt and rank sweat. His face, hands, and hair are covered in dust, while everything around him is white and pure.

When Callum raises his eyes again, he sees concern softening Aziz's kind face. "I have been most rude. Please come with me and we will get you cleaned up."

Aziz leads him into another room with three wooden chairs spaced evenly around a simple table. A silver bassinette occupies the table next to a folded towel. Aziz takes a seat on one of the chairs and nods toward the bassinette.

Callum approaches the bassinette and gazes into its depths. The water is clear and feels cool to his touch when he plunges his hands in. He cups a handful of water, lifts it to his face, and lets it dribble between his fingers. A weariness flows out with the water as he continues to wash his face, hands, and neck. When he finishes and the water has turned dark, he dries his face and neck with the towel. He could collapse where he stands but takes a seat instead. "Thank you."

"You are most welcome." Aziz smiles gently but is otherwise still.

Callum replaces the towel and sits next to Aziz. "What is this place?"

"It is many things. We call it a *khanaqah*, but it is also a school, a hospice, and a home for many of us."

"You live here?"

"Yes."

"Why?"

"Hmm." Aziz closes his eyes and leans back in his chair. "I was a doctor in Germany. I had a wife and I drove a Mercedes. I drank alcohol and slept with other women. But my life had no meaning. No purpose."

"Did you find it?"

Aziz opens his eyes and gazes directly at him. "Find what?"

"Your purpose."

Aziz chuckles. "Yes, I suppose I have. The Pir's health is not doing so well. So I serve him. I suppose you could say that is my purpose."

"What about your family?"

"They are here, as well."

Callum can't picture Aziz living in one of the huts outside the *khanaqah* with his family, but he doesn't want to ask. "What about the Pir? Has he always been here?"

"No. In fact, I first met him in Peshawar. But he wanted to bring his *ulema*, his congregation, here to his home. Sufis were not allowed here for a very long time. It is becoming safe again, though."

"Why wasn't it safe?"

Aziz removes his wire-framed glasses and cleans them on the hem of his shirt. "Do you know anything about Sufis?"

Callum shakes his head.

"Sufis have always been present in every age of humanity, in every society. Sufis have been poets, princes, and beggars. Sufis have been Christian and Buddhist and followers of other forgotten ways. Sufis discovered evolution before Darwin, created psychoanalysis before Freud, spoke of time and space relativity even before Einstein. Sufis are in this world but not of it. They are the followers of the one true path."

"What does that mean, the one true path?"

"I do not know, but I guess I drank the Kool-Aid, so here I am," Aziz pauses for a moment before breaking out in laughter.

"Can I meet the Pir?"

Aziz's demeanour turns serious. He holds Callum's gaze before saying, "Perhaps. He is in prayers now. But you may be able to observe as long as you don't interrupt. Come with me."

Callum is led out of the room by Aziz and down a long walkway that opens into another open courtyard. His guide gestures to a low bench running along the back wall beneath a stone arch. Callum sits and looks out into the courtyard.

A group of men sit cross-legged on the floor in nine even rows. Some of the men rock back and forth, rhythmically patting their chests. Others sit quietly and don't say anything at all. Still others chant, *"Hu! Hu!"* Tears spill down the face of one man at the back.

Callum knows all these men even though he hasn't met them before. Their stories are very familiar to him. He can see it in the scars on their faces, their missing limbs, in the suffering in their eyes. They're the children of war, soldiers in name only. Boys who grew up without fathers. Boys who were handed a rifle or the trigger to an improvised explosive device by old men who live far away. Boys who had no other choice. And when the old men were finished with them, they were tossed aside like spent shell casings.

And then they ended up here. Because they had no other place to go.

All of them have their eyes turned toward a man who sits by a window where sunlight filters in. The man beneath the window wears long white robes that reach to his ankles and a white turban that rests on his head. His beard, dyed the colour of henna, touches his waist. And though his eyes are cast toward the ground, Callum can see they're a brilliant shade of blue.

He doesn't know how much time passes as he watches them in prayer, each face prostrated to the west in observance of something he can't see, something he can never feel. There's power in that moment, then anxiety, then nothing at all. Maybe just a seed of anger at their piety, now exposed in his eyes as something cruel and unfeeling.

He wants to get up and leave but can't. He's fixed to his seat and through his seat to the earth below. The weight of his life grinds his shoulders, and his vision starts to narrow. It takes all his effort not to collapse on the ground.

A hand reaches out and grasps his own. Callum looks down and sees it's the hand of the man sitting next to him. He glances over at Aziz, who gazes straight ahead, a slight grin on his face.

Callum feels the weight start to lift. He reaches up and wipes the sweat from his brow. The heat in the room is suffocating, but he can breathe again, as if he's been holding his breath and has finally come up for air.

The men finish their prayers and slowly get up to leave the room in ones and twos. Before each man departs, he stops and bows before the Pir while kissing his right hand.

Once they've all left the room, Aziz stands and walks over to the Pir. He bows before the holy man and also kisses his right hand. The two men smile at each other like old friends.

Aziz pulls up a chair next to the Pir, and the two old men talk with their heads nearly together. Callum stands next to them, not knowing what to do, shifting on his feet as he feels the room pressing in on him again. He's about to walk away when Aziz asks, "Do you like ice cream?"

"Excuse me," Callum responds.

"Ice cream. Do you like ice cream? The Pir loves ice cream. I tell him the sugar is not good for his arthritis, but he does not listen to me." Aziz helps the Pir to his feet, and the two men shuffle arm in arm down another walkway. Callum steps in behind them and follows until they enter a kitchen of sorts. The Pir slumps onto a stool while Aziz rummages about in a freezer. When Aziz finally emerges from the freezer, he hands a small tub to the Pir before handing a mini-tub of mint chocolate chip to Callum.

"Do you like mint chocolate?" asks Aziz. "Because we also have chocolate and vanilla. We had strawberry, but that is the Pir's favourite flavour and he took the last one."

The Pir grins mischievously while the little plastic spoon dangles from his teeth.

Leaning against the freezer and digging into his own tub, Aziz says, "The Pir was asking what you and your men were doing here, and I told him you came to be indoctrinated in our ways."

Aziz and the Pir laugh, but Callum can't tell if they're joking.

The Pir says something to Aziz, who then translates. "He can tell you are very weary and have been travelling a long time. He says you and your soldiers can stay here as long you like. Let this be a refuge for you."

"Thank you. Please tell him thank you for me."

Aziz nods but doesn't say anything to the Pir, who sits silently eating his ice cream. Callum doesn't know what to say in response. He has many questions and wants to know so much. What has the Pir seen? What has he done? What does he know? Most importantly, what is Callum supposed to do?

While continuing to observe Callum, the Pir begins to speak. Aziz translates as if they're both saying the same thing. "You are fragmented and lacking certainty. You will not be able to make any decisions that way."

"I don't understand."

"That is your problem, my friend. Like most people, you spend your life asking the wrong question."

"Which is what?"

"What is my purpose?"

"Then what's the right question?"

"What is our purpose?"

Callum still doesn't understand what that means. Sensing Callum's confusion, Aziz says, "There is a shepherd who lives in the hills above the *khanaqah*. His name is Tirich. He will help you see that which you need to see."

"Which is what?"

"The way forward, of course."

The Pir hands his empty ice-cream tub to Aziz, who then tosses it in the garbage. With his other hand, Aziz hauls the Pir to his feet as the two men prepare to leave. Before they do, Callum asks, "Where do I find the shepherd?"

The Pir doesn't turn around but whispers something in Aziz's ear. When he's finished, Aziz says to Callum, "Go back to the courtyard we just left. There is a door there behind where the Pir was sitting. When the sun has gone down, walk out that door and Tirich will be waiting."

What about Taraki? Callum means to ask. But Aziz and the Pir have already retreated from the room, leaving Callum alone. He should follow them, get some answers. That's what Burnes wants. That's the reason he's here, isn't it?

Callum should go back to the others. How long has he been gone? An hour maybe. They should be rested by now. And Burnes has probably cooled off, might even have some ideas about where they can go next.

It's getting late. They probably aren't going anywhere to-night. The Pir said they could bed down inside the *khanaqah*'s walls. They should be able to get topped up on water, too. After a solid rest, they can set off at first light.

He should go back and tell that to Murph.

But who did the Pir want him to see? A shepherd? What's a shepherd going to tell him? Maybe he knows where they can find Taraki. Might as well talk to the guy first. Can't hurt talking to him, can it?

# CHAPTER TWENTY

When the last glimmer of day fades from a window cut high on the courtyard wall, Callum opens the door and steps outside into a completely silent and still night. A soft light from the room behind him illuminates the ground a few paces ahead, but everything beyond that lies in darkness, all the way to heaven, cut by a thin line of red on the horizon.

Callum instinctively reaches for his rifle so he can turn on the flashlight attached to its barrel, but he doesn't have his weapon anymore. He left it with Murph before entering the *khanaqah*. He remembers where he is, what he left behind, and feels exposed in the dark. But he decides against returning to grab the rifle and strides forward away from the light of the *khanaqah*.

As his eyes adjust, he acquires a sense of his surroundings. He stands in a shallow defile that descends for an uncertain distance. With loose stones underfoot, he cautiously makes his way down the natural pathway until he arrives at a wadi running crosswise to the path.

Crouching next to the slow-moving stream, he places his hand, palm down, in the water. Cool to the touch. He pauses to listen for any sound or any other indication of where he should turn next. But the only noise he hears is the soft gurgling from the wadi. No one else is about.

Aziz didn't give him any directions, just that Callum would find the shepherd outside. Did Aziz make a mistake? Why would he send him out here in the dark? Maybe Callum misunderstood him, or perhaps there was some other reason he wanted Callum to leave the *khanaqah*. Callum should go back, find Aziz, and ask him what this is all about. It must be a mistake.

Even better, he should return to Murph and the others so they can figure out their next move, and have something to eat other than ice cream.

As he turns to leave, a faint glow approaches along the wadi line, which coalesces, forming around the shape of an old man carrying a lantern that sways with every step. It casts a warm light ahead to illuminate the dead spaces in his path, between the rocks and down into the crevices The old man makes his way forward gradually one step at a time, the lantern extended high and out in front.

A procession follows in the old man's wake, a small child first and then another before the rest of the throng shuffles along behind. Dozens of them. Men and women. Young and old. Some are dressed in fine robes while others are in rags. One bony young man wears an old army helmet much too large for his head. An old woman has intricate tattoos on her chin and forehead. The procession seems to have no end.

Callum steps aside when the old man with the lantern is a foot away. When Callum peers into the old man's eyes, they are milky white without any pupils. But still the man with the lantern stares straight ahead and continues onward. The rest follow along, streaming around Callum as if he were a rock in the wadi.

Is that the shepherd? Is that who Aziz wanted him to meet?

An unseen hand rests gently on Callum's shoulder from behind, and then another on his back, while another grabs his hand and shirt until he's swept along with the crowd. He resists mildly at first but gives in, curious to see where they're going.

After a short distance, the procession comes to a stop. Callum shoulders his way through to find out why. When he gets to the front, the group has formed a tight circle around the old man with the lantern.

A boy holds a shovel twice his own size. He lifts the shovel high over his head, jams it into the ground, and stomps his sandalled foot on top of the blade, driving the implement deeper into the earth. Digging up a mound of dirt, he dumps it beside the hole. While the others watch, he continues digging until he has opened a pit big enough to lie down inside. When he finishes, he steps back and rests his hands on the shovel's hilt.

Two women with their faces covered in veils step out of the crowd. The first carries a clay jar that she uses to pour a thick, dark liquid into the pit, while the second woman sprinkles barley from a basket, which floats momentarily before sinking below the surface.

A young man marches a goat forward that strains against its leash. The old man hands the lantern to the boy with the shovel before sliding a curved dagger from his belt and slitting the goat's throat. The goat's eyes dart about in terror as black ichor pours from its throat and drains into the pit. No one in the crowd cries out or says anything.

When the goat is finally drained of blood, it topples over next to the brim of the pit. The old man reclaims the lantern from the boy and hobbles off, leaving the lifeless body of the animal behind. The rest of the crowd again follows him, as does Callum.

The old man with the lantern leads them farther into the hills to the entrance of a cave lit only by the lantern and the ghostly light of a crescent moon. The crowd stops, as well, and presses in tightly around the cave's opening. When they all arrive, the old man with the lantern turns and gazes straight at Callum.

Callum doesn't say anything. Compelled, he steps forward and enters the mouth of the cave. As soon as he does, the old man extinguishes the light from the lantern, turning the world black. Callum doesn't hesitate and moves into the cave.

The cave narrows so that the jagged rocks above and all around him scape at his arms and legs. He reaches out to feel the cavern walls so that he can make his way forward without banging into anything. Eventually, he has to crouch so he can carry on, then on his hands and knees, until finally he's flat on his belly, pulling himself along the cavern floor.

He doesn't know how far he crawls until the tunnel finally opens up so that he can stand. Everything is still dark; he can't even see his hand waving in front of his face. Callum reaches out to feel the cavern walls, but nothing is there anymore. He extends his arms in search of the tunnel through which he just crawled but can't find that, either. Panic rises from deep inside him, but then his fingertips graze a soft rock outcropping, damp and covered in viscous slime. With relief, he manages to make out the outline of a rock wall. He places his back against the cave and slides to the ground, pulling his knees tightly to his chest.

Callum calls out his name, which echoes around the chamber. It sounds strange when he hears it repeated back to him, as if it belongs to someone else. He closes his eyes, even though there's no difference, and rests his head on the rock wall behind him.

Callum needs to think, come up with a plan, figure out how they're going to solve this. But whenever he tries to turn his mind forward to the future, he comes up against a wall. Instead, sitting there in the dark, all he can think about is the past. All of the pointless mistakes that led him here.

The court where they held their court martial resembled the conference room of a cheap hotel: faux mahogany tables and second-rate ergonomic chairs that squeaked when they rolled across a brown carpet stained by coffee and cigarette burns. The JAG seal adorned the wood-panelled wall behind the judge's seat, as if that made the whole affair more legitimate.

Devon's trial wrapped up pretty quickly, relatively speaking. Only a couple of months, flash to bang. For Callum, though, it was nearly two years of being marched in and out of that room. Motions and applications and appearances just to hear "procedural matters." Not quite every day, but often enough that he could read the matrix-style code behind the facade, vertical streams of alien characters in black and green that spelled out the lie of his life.

The room was packed in the beginning, mostly with his soldiers, friends, and even some of the senior officers in the battalion. Everyone telling him to "keep your chin up," "you'll get through this," "we've got your back." Until they didn't.

Even some media types showed up in the early days, hanging around on the edges of the courtroom with their notepads and dapper scarves. It wasn't headline news but did generate some clicks: "Rogue army officer leads failed mission." They stopped showing up when they figured out Callum wouldn't talk to them. Or maybe they got bored of the whole thing, like everyone else.

Eventually, the rest of the crowds petered out, as well, until it was just him, the lawyers, and the judge. Penny and his mom, too, most days, sitting together in the front row.

His mom would cough or sigh or drop her keys whenever the lead prosecutor was talking. A hard-angled bastard who would spin about and glare at his mom whenever she did that. The judge kept asking her to be quiet but gave up when he realized she wouldn't listen.

Her diagnosis was terminal at that point, but she didn't tell Callum until after the trial started. When he asked her why, she smiled and told him not to worry about it. She didn't make it through the trial until the end. It was better she didn't.

Penny was the opposite. She didn't move or make a noise the whole time. They got in a big fight the night before the first day of the trial because of his pride and his shame about her being there. He didn't want her to see him like that, and she knew it, which only made things worse. There was no way she was going to miss any of it, though, and he knew that. So there she was the next day and every day after that, and they never spoke about it again.

Penny applied to law school at some point during the trial, which Callum didn't find out about until later. She had talked about it before Timmy had come along, but the trial must have been the thing to push her to get on with it. She was always keen on social justice and fighting for the underdog and probably thought she could have done a better job than Callum's lawyers. Actually, she definitely could have done a better job than his lawyers.

One thing they did agree on without having to say anything was that Timmy shouldn't have been there. Timmy was so young then and didn't understand what was going on. Callum was Timmy's hero, Superman come to life. Seeing Callum at the trial probably wouldn't have changed that. Really, it had more to do with protecting Callum than it did with protecting Timmy.

It was hard to picture Timmy sitting through it all. He was always a quiet boy, shy and happiest when he was alone. But the monotony would have tested even his limits. The whole thing, day after day, bleeding into one. It all became a blur, especially after the initial excitement, if you could call it that, wore off.

Even his cross-examination felt like something rote, automatic. His lawyers tried to talk him out of taking the stand, but he stood his ground, believing he had nothing to hide, that he'd done the right thing. If they all heard him, then maybe they'd believe that, too.

Nearly four days in the box, but it only took four minutes to realize it had nothing to do with the truth, about whether or not he'd done the right thing. It was never about that. He sat there and answered their questions. Yes, sir, no, sir, three bags full, sir.

And it was still another year after that until it was all over.

Callum thought he had grown numb to it all, that this was the way his life would be now, that he would endure their questions and the tedium for the rest of his days. Until the last day came. The day of his sentencing.

The air conditioning wasn't working that day, like many of those final days during the trial. The judge wiped sweat from his forehead with a damp hanky as if mopping up a plate of stew with a crust of bread while he read Callum's sentence.

The blood was pounding in Callum's ears so loud he could barely hear anything else. It was only when the judge got to the end and read those last three words that Callum finally heard what the judge was saying. Discharge with disgrace.

And just like that, it was all gone, everything he ever believed in, everything he ever fought and bled and sacrificed for. They took it all away with three words. One to the head and two to the chest.

He couldn't face Penny after that, couldn't speak to her or look her in the eye, even though she'd been there the entire time. She could live with that, she didn't like it, and called him out on it, but she gave him the space to do what he needed to do.

But there was no way she was going to let him do that to Timmy, to their beautiful boy. Callum tried to shut him out, too, but Penny wouldn't let him. That's what they fought about the most in the weeks after the trial. Neither of them won in the end, though they came to some kind of unspoken truce. Callum would be half of a father and even less of a husband. At least it was something.

It was all so selfish and stupid, and he sees that now sitting alone in a dark cave halfway around the world. He would sit through a thousand more trials to have one chance to go back and make it all right. Callum misses Penny and Timmy more than he ever realized.

Except he's here now, back in the place where it all went wrong. He can't change the past or fix what happened. No one can. But he can find Devon and bring him home. Because if he doesn't, then none of it will have ever mattered.

# PART VII
# INTER ARMA SILENT LEGES

# CHAPTER TWENTY-ONE

The rush of a vacuum, somewhere distant and far away, jolts Callum to his senses, as if he's been entombed in a spaceship hurtling through the universe without anyone at the controls. His head aches, and the back of his throat feels as if someone dragged a wire brush up and down his esophagus a couple of times. At least he knows he's still alive.

After wiping the dust from his eyes, he glimpses a pinprick of light across from him. As he stares at the light, it expands and fills the whole of his vision, like being dropped into the sun. It takes him a minute to recognize the light for what it is: the entrance to the tunnel, his way out.

He crawls back through the tunnel and emerges blinking into the outside world. The blind shepherd has left, and no one else waits for him. It's morning now, and dawn has broken like a fever.

Nothing looks familiar in the daylight. Craggy, hardscrabble terrain extends outward in every direction covered in a fine grey dust like the surface of the moon. Even the sky is robbed of life.

Turning around, he examines the cave. Maybe this is a different entrance than the one he entered the night before. Or was that even last night? He has no sense of time, as if the minutes and seconds between now and before became unspooled from an infinite coil of skelp and pounded flat into a thin sheet of metal so sharp it could slice his existence in half.

Callum can't imagine returning to the cave, not because he doesn't want to, but because the thought itself isn't even conceivable. Like flying an airplane would have been to a caveman. Or walking to the fridge and grabbing a beer would be to a goldfish. Instead, he sets off over the terrain in front of him in search of a path that will take him back to the *khanaqah*.

He comes to the wadi where he first encountered the blind shepherd. The water is still now, barely moving if at all. He kneels next to the waterline, overcome by the desire to gulp back mouthfuls to quench the rawness in his throat. But when he scoops his hand into the water, he pulls up a wad of cud that droops between his fingers before splashing into the wadi.

When he stands back up, he spots the path he travelled the night before, except its on the other side of the wadi. He lets out a deep sigh before reaching to untie his boots and roll the cuffs of his pants up to his knees. Tying the boots together by their laces, he swings them over his shoulder like a pair of boxer's gloves before wading across the wadi. His feet sink into the mire while oily reeds lick his shins. Upon reaching the far bank, he settles on a dry rock and scrapes the muck from his feet, put his boots back on, and meanders for nearly a kilometre back to the *khanaqah*.

The door is locked when he arrives. He tugs gently at first, but it doesn't budge. He bangs on the door, but no one answers. The whitewashed walls are too high and smooth to climb over and run the length of the narrow gully. He'll need to find another way in.

Following the wall along to the far side of the gully, he arrives at a narrow break between the wall and the encroaching hillside, which grants him a purchase so he can clamber on top of a high feature. Surveying the ground below, he realizes there isn't any way to climb over the *khanaqah*'s roof to reach the other side. But there is a route that loops around the *khanaqah* and connects with the village below. He scrambles along the rocky hillside until he finally reaches the village and then backtracks up the path before reaching the rest of his team, scattered outside the *khanaqah*'s gates.

Kamal, providing security in an overwatch position, is the first to notice Callum's approach. "Hey, boss."

Callum tries to respond but can only muster a low growl, since his throat is too parched to form words. Continuing on toward his gear, he yanks a water bottle from his pack and guzzles its contents in three gulps. He empties the bottle over his head, but nothing pours out. Tossing the empty bottle back on his pack, he pats down his bag in search of another one. After he comes up empty, he snatches a bottle out of midair that Murph flips in his direction. While he unscrews the top, she asks, "Late night?"

Downing the bottle, he wipes away the dribble on his chin with the back of his sleeve. "Something like that," he croaks, glancing around to account for the rest of the team. JP is with Kamal. Murph squats on her haunches directly across from him. Habs sits cross-legged, his back resting against the cliff wall, next to a sleeping Reno. Each of the Māori's snores threatens to set off a minor avalanche of rocks lying in wait above them on the cliff face.

"Where's Burnes?" Callum asks Murph.

She brushes the dust from her knees before standing up. "He didn't come back."

"He didn't come back?"

"That's what I said."

"Did you send anyone after him?"

"Was I supposed to?"

Callum doesn't have an answer for that. He vaguely recalls leaving them behind to enter the *khanaqah* last night, or whenever it was. He probably should have done something about Burnes at the time. Now they're going to have to find him. But how are they going to do that?

"We know where he went," Murph says.

Callum gives her a quizzical look as she rummages around in her pack to pull out a map. "Some dude came out of the *khanaqah* last night. I think his name was Aziz. He told us where to find Taraki, which is probably where we'll find Burnes." She unfolds the map on the ground, places four heavy stones on each of the corners, and scans the map for a couple of seconds before locating the *khanaqah*. She traces a line on the map away from the *khanaqah* two kilometres to the west, toward an unnamed built-up area made up of a handful of nondescript buildings. She circles the area. "Here."

"Can't we leave him?" Habs pipes up.

Weariness has set into Habs's face, as if the boy has aged years in the past couple of days. It's a look Callum knows well. When he glances back at Murph, he sees it in her face, as well, though not to the same degree.

He feels it, too. The fatigue. Deeper than he ever has before. Now more than ever, he wants to go home and be done with this place. But if they can get to Burnes, and if Burnes found Taraki, then Devon should be there, too.

Kamal walks up the path toward them while Callum and Murph are still huddled over the map. "What's going on?"

"We're going after Burnes," Habs says.

Kamal spits on the ground, "Fuck that guy. Let's *didi mao*."

Callum doesn't raise his eyes from the map but removes the stones from the corners and begins to fold it back up. "I'm not leaving him."

"He made his choice."

Callum locks eyes with Kamal. "I'm not leaving him."

"This is bullshit." After a second, the wild Tajik stomps off, shaking his head.

Callum asks Murph, "How are we doing for water?"

"Aziz topped us off last night while you were gone." She nods in the direction of the *khanaqah*. "There's something else."

"What?"

"Ash is staying."

"Staying where?"

"There. In the *khanaqah*."

"Like fuck he is."

Murph sighs. "I knew you were going to say that."

"Seriously?"

Murph doesn't say anything.

Callum says, "We're not going to debate this. He isn't staying here."

"He talked to that Aziz dude for a while, you know, when you were doing whatever it was you were doing."

There it is.

"Aziz said he could stay. It's cheaper than rehab."

Ash is a grown man who can make his own decisions, even if they're bat-shit stupid. And this wouldn't be the worst place for Ash to spend a couple of days getting squared away. Aziz is a good man and will look after Ash.

"All right then," Callum says, "let's find Burnes, then we'll come back for Ash."

"Sounds like a plan to me," says Murph.

"Get everyone up. We step off in ten."

It takes the better part of two hours to make their way down from the *khanaqah* through the old stone village and back into the fields below. As they skirt the edge of the hills, three massive satellite dishes come into view in the distance, beyond where Murph marked on her map. Taraki must be there. Devon, too.

Before coming to the satellite dishes, they arrive at a built-up area where a great tower splintered in half stands at the edge. A staircase hangs on the remaining wall, spiralling up toward a rooftop that no longer exists. All that remains beyond the tower are the husks of burned-out buildings, walls blackened with soot, charred roofs, debris scattered on the ground.

A vendor's cart unsettled on a broken wheel leans at the base of the tower, small wooden boxes piled neatly in it. Each box is full of even piles of pistachios, while a single unlit lantern hangs from the cart's post. The vendor sits on a stool next to the cart, chuckling to himself. As they approach, he straightens the *pakula* resting crookedly on his head and starts clucking at them as they pass.

Callum says to Kamal, "Ask him if he knows where we can find Taraki."

After letting the vendor ramble, Kamal tells them, "He says a demon lives in the hills and that the demon comes into the village at night and chews on people's fingers so that when they wake up their fingers are bones like a skeleton."

"Because that isn't fucked up at all," Habs mutters as he passes by the vendor.

A cemetery lies farther along the road, each grave marked by a cairn. They're nestled below tattered pennants that cling to poles, each one bent to the wind. A child sits on top of one of the rock piles. Bandages cover his hands and he's crying, a siren wail that carries over the fields while vultures pluck at his feet.

Callum halts the group at a distance from the boy as Murph grabs Callum's arm. She nods at one of the prayer flags, offset from the others. "We need to stay away from those rocks."

Murph is right. Something's off, but he can't tell what. Old instincts kick in as he surveys the site, searching for markers and a safe path through to the boy.

Habs pulls up behind Callum and says over his shoulder, "We've gotta help him."

The boy has spotted them. His wails grow keener as he tries to wipe the tears from his eyes, the bandages on his hands smearing mud across his face.

Callum reaches across Habs to hold him in place. "Stay here."

Before Callum can take another step, though, Habs says, "Fuck this," and surges toward the boy.

A concussive wave knocks Callum to the ground, followed by a cloud of dust that washes over him, obscuring everything in its path. Opening his eyes in a haze, Callum takes a minute to understand where he is and what happened. He wipes the dust from his ballistic glasses so he can see. Habs lies prone on the ground, his body twisted awkwardly, arms pinned behind him. The kid took most of the blast, shielding Callum and the others from the worst of it.

Crawling over to Habs's side, Callum sees the blood pumping from his face and neck. He can't tell where the wound is because of all the dirt covering Habs's face. The kid's mouth is open in a silent scream. Callum realizes he can't hear anything because of the ringing in his own ears.

He grabs a bandage from his first-aid kit and tries to wipe some of the dirt and blood from Habs's face. Deep wounds gouge the kid's cheek and neck. Callum staunches the flow of blood by pressing the dressing into the wound on his neck, but that doesn't have much effect.

Murph falls in on Habs's other side. She appears to be yelling at Callum, but he points to an ear and shakes his head. Murph turns her attention to Habs and starts checking his body for any other injuries.

While keeping pressure on the bandage pressed into Habs's neck, Callum glances up to survey the damage to the rest of the team. Reno is helping Kamal sit up. They were both farther back and missed most of the blast. JP, slumped against a wall, shaking the dust from his hair and clothes, appears to be otherwise okay.

Through the ringing in his ears, Callum can barely make out Murph shouting at him. He has to look at her mouth to understand what she's saying. "Habs is going to be okay, but we have to get him out of here."

Callum nods in agreement. He yells at JP to come over and give him a hand so he can call in a medevac on the sat. Then he remembers they don't have the phone anymore. They could hump Habs back up to the *khanaqah*, hoping Aziz has a means to call out. Or they could make their way back to the Afghan army outpost, but that's too far away. Habs wouldn't make it.

JP stumbles over to their side before leaning down to assist Murph. When he does, Callum goes over to Reno to make sure Kamal is okay.

Just as Reno gives him the thumbs-up, a group of armed men scream down the trail, at least ten, maybe more, farther back, weapons drawn and aimed at Callum and the others. Callum jumps to his feet, arms raised, putting himself between the attackers and his team. One of the men butt-strokes Callum in the stomach, sending him to his knees. He puts up his hand, pleading with them to listen. A second blow crashes into his temple. His last vision before blacking out is of Habs, silent and unmoving in the dirt.

# CHAPTER TWENTY-TWO

Blood seeps from the gash in Callum's forehead and dribbles along the crater of his eye socket before pooling in the dirt. He reaches up tentatively to probe the wound with his fingertips and winces from the pain as he draws his hand away from his face. The wound is deep and will need stitching. Nothing Sung can't handle. Then he remembers Sung is gone.

His head aches and the vision in his right eye is blurred. He rolls onto his side, grateful to find a patch of shade beneath the hills to rest his eyes. But as he turns his gaze upward, he realizes he's lying in Reno's shadow. The giant Māori stands over him, rifle raised, shouting at a shapeless horde somewhere beyond Callum's sight.

He struggles to his knees but nearly stumbles back onto the ground before Reno reaches out and hauls him to his feet. Only then does his focus click back into place to see a swarm of pissed-off scoobies apocalyptically waving around AK-47s as if someone jammed a bayonet into their nest.

Kamal and JP are up on their feet, forming a trilateral perimeter with Reno while Murph huddles over Habs in the middle, pumping Habs with chest compressions and pleading with him to stay conscious and otherwise ignoring the commotion around her.

Callum pushes down Reno's rifle while attempting to mollify the swarm with his free arm. He yells at them, "Taraki!

Taraki!" The swarm hesitates, momentarily confused. Callum says to Kamal, "Tell them they need to take us to Taraki."

Kamal glances sideways at Callum before dropping his rifle to low-ready and relaying the message. A spokesman for the swarm emerges to exchange words with Kamal, who nods at the swarm leader. "He says the Ferengi is already with Taraki."

"Burnes? Is he talking about Burnes?"

"He doesn't know his name."

"Tell him Taraki wants to see us."

While Kamal continues to converse in harsh tones with the swarm leader, Murph looks up at Callum. "Habs is in rough shape. We need to get him out of here."

"That's gonna be a little tough right now."

"He's going to bleed out. We can't stay here."

"I know, I know." Callum pivots back to Kamal, still in a heated exchange with the swarm leader. "What's going on?"

"They'll take us, but he says they have to take our weapons."

Reno growls, "Not a fucking chance."

A thundering headache threatens to split Callum's skull open again. He's exhausted and can't think straight. How did it come to this? Habs is bleeding out. They're surrounded on all sides. He's not going to lose another one. Not like this. He led them here. Now he needs to figure out a way to get them all home. He turns to Murph. "Can we move him?"

"Not a good idea."

"We don't have any choice. If we get to Taraki, I can get us a medavac. Fellas, hand over your weapons."

"This is bullshit," Reno says before reluctantly putting his rifle on the ground. After he does, Kamal and JP follow suit.

As soon as they've handed over their weapons, Murph and JP hoist Habs onto a collapsible stretcher. Callum and his team then follow their armed escort who bracket them along a footpath for about a kilometre out of the village and into the foothills until they come upon a fortified compound beneath the massive satellite dishes.

A transport truck shuttles out of the compound's main gate, forcing them to the side of the road. When the truck passes, they continue past two guards who wave them through. Inside the compound, there are at least twice as many armed scoobies, mostly loading up Sea Can containers with unmarked boxes. All the workers stop their various activities to eye Callum and his people as they make their way in.

The swarm drops them off in front of a single-storey building at the compound's centre and then melt off to resume whatever jobs they were conducting before. The swarm leader motions for Callum to follow him into the main building. Before trailing him, Callum drops his pack at Murph's feet. "I'll get help."

"From who?" she asks.

"Devon."

"Devon? How do you even know he's in there?"

"I don't. But if he's not, then I'll talk to Taraki."

Murph looks up at him, worry in her eyes.

"Just hold tight and keep Habs alive," Callum says. "I'll get us out of here."

He shadows the man to a room at the back of the building where his escort bangs twice on a door before opening it and motioning him to go inside. Light filters into the room from a window cut in the far wall, faded carpets cover the concrete floor, and black leather sofas surround the largest TV Callum has even seen. Taraki lounges on one of the sofas in a red Adidas track suit, playing video games on the TV. When Taraki notices Callum at the door, he beckons him to enter and sit on one of the couches.

Burnes leans against a wall, arms crossed, and shoots Callum a glance as he sits on a sofa opposite Taraki. Before Callum can say anything, Taraki points toward a mini-fridge next to the TV. "Red Bull?"

"No thanks," says Callum.

"Doritos?" Taraki asks, handing a bowl to Callum from the ottoman in front of the TV. "Sweet chili heat, bro."

"No thanks."

Taraki shrugs, reaches into the bowl, and stuffs a handful of chips into his mouth before resuming his video game.

Callum looks up at Burnes, who doesn't seem amused. "Where's Devon?"

"How the fuck would I know?"

"He's not here?"

"Does it look like he's here?"

No, it doesn't. Devon isn't here. Never was. Callum came all this way and for what? For the belief that if he could find Devon and bring him home, it might help redeem a part of himself that was lost?

A foolish hope.

He knows that now, maybe always did. But it doesn't matter. He came here, chose to do so, and has to live with that decision and the impact it has on the people counting on him. Callum can't walk away from them. Too late for that. Habs will die if he doesn't do something about it. "Habs hit an IED," he tells Burnes.

That draws Burnes's attention. "Is he okay?"

"We need to get him out of here."

"Not gonna happen."

"Why not?"

"We need to wait."

"For what?"

"Not for what, for whom." Burnes uncrosses his arms and walks across the room to peer out the window.

"For whom then?"

"Our competitor."

"Our what?"

"You think this frat boy goat fuck runs the show here?" Burnes nods over his shoulder at Taraki, still sitting on the couch playing video games.

"I don't care. We need to get Habs out of here."

"What are you gonna do? Shoot your way out?" Burnes puts his back against the wall again and slides to the ground. Unclasping his hands in an open shrug, he says, "The best thing we can do is wait."

"We don't have time to wait. Habs will bleed out if we don't get him out of here."

Burnes doesn't say anything, merely turns his gaze upward to stare at the ceiling while drumming a manic rhythm on his knee. Taraki isn't paying attention to either of them.

Callum isn't going to stick around any longer but needs to come up with a plan. Burnes is right. They're going to have to shoot their way out of here past at least twenty of Taraki's goons, plus who knows how many more sulking around the compound. If Callum can get to a rifle, he has a shot at getting everyone out of here.

Just as he's about to flee the room, the distant thrum of a helicopter approaches over the hills. Burnes jumps to his feet to glare outside the window.

"Who are they?" Callum asks.

"My employer hired a rival firm to do the same job. Looks like they got to Taraki first."

"Why did they do that?"

"Hedge their bets. Hire two mercenary groups to achieve the same aim but only pay the one that succeeds. It's the new business of war. You should look it up."

"What does that mean for us?"

"I guess we're going to find out shortly."

Sand blasts through the open window as the helicopter thunders down next to the building. Callum raises his arm to protect his face against the cyclone raging through the room. Shaking off the disorientation, he takes stock of his situation as the swirling storm recedes. Burnes and Taraki stand shoulder to shoulder, peering through the window. Taraki's AK-47 leans against the wall in the corner. Sensing his opportunity, Callum springs toward the rifle but is stopped in his tracks as the door slams open.

Two men wearing green combat fatigues and black face masks force their way inside, one after the other. The first man enters, rifle raised, shouting inaudibly over the rotor wash still reverberating outside. When Callum doesn't react to his commands, the second man jabs a rifle into Callum's sternum, forcing him to flip around and face the wall. With his head turned to the side, Callum catches a glimpse of a third man strolling casually into the room. He shoves Burnes away from the window while gesturing at whoever's flying the helicopter to kill the engine.

The helicopter's engine rings in Callum's ears, so he can't hear the conversation conducted behind him. But he feels the rifle muzzle release from his back, allowing him to turn around to see one of the two green-clad men escort Taraki out of the room.

After they're gone, the man who had his rifle jammed into Callum's back says, "Cal?"

When Callum doesn't respond, the man removes his bala-clava. Callum doesn't recognize him at first, but it quickly settles in that it's Devon.

"Hey, man, what are you doing here?" Devon asks.

After taking a moment to recover from the shock, Callum demands, "What the fuck do you mean what am I doing here? You asked me to come here. Where the fuck have you been?"

The third man interrupts and asks Devon in a Russian accent, "You know this shitass?"

"Yeah. I told you guys about him. We served together in Afghanistan." Devon waves at Callum. "Colonel, this is Callum King. Callum, this is the colonel."

"I don't give any fucks." The colonel turns to Burnes. "You're late."

"We got held up."

"Hmm," mumbles the colonel.

"There was an ambush outside Kandahar City and then we couldn't find Taraki …"

The colonel dismisses Burnes's excuse with a wave of his hand. "The Afghan police will be here shortly to collect you." He spins on his heel and heads toward the door.

"I don't think so. We had a contract."

The colonel spins back and presses his nose into Burnes's face. "Do you know who you are, Burnes?"

"No, who?"

"You know in movies. The pussy henchman. Like security guard in evil villain's layer. And the hero arrives to capture villain. And the hero shoots pussy henchman first before he gets villain. That's who you are. Pussy henchman."

"Is that right?"

As the colonel chuckles at his joke, Burnes draws his Glock and double-taps two rounds into the Russian's chest. Before the colonel hits the deck, Devon swings his rifle around and fires a burst in Burnes's direction. The automatic fire stitches Burnes diagonally across his torso.

Callum launches himself at Devon with a tackle before Devon can get the full burst off as it continues upward to explode into the ceiling, kicking up a cloud of dust. He drives Devon into the wall with as much strength as he can muster. The rifle slips from Devon's grip and skitters along the floor as his breath is knocked out by the impact. Callum tries to get to his feet but is sent tumbling to the ground when Devon sweeps a leg out from under him.

"What the fuck are you doing?" Devon gasps.

"What the fuck am I doing? What the fuck are you doing?" Callum crawls over to Burnes's side to check his vital signs.

"He was gonna shoot me," Devon says defensively, pointing at the motionless Burnes on the ground.

When Callum flips Burnes over onto his back, his eyes stare lifelessly up at the ceiling. He reaches down to feel for a pulse, but the dead man's skin already feels cold to the touch. "I wish he shot you," Callum snaps at Devon.

"Fuck you, man."

"Fuck me? No, fuck you." Callum rolls over onto his back as blood pours down his face. The gash above his eye must have opened up again when he tackled Devon. Pressing the palm of his hand to his forehead, he grabs Burnes's Glock and tucks it into the front of his pants before struggling to his feet. With a grunt, he reaches down to grab Burnes and hoist him off the ground and over his shoulder.

"Where are you going?" Devon asks.

Callum hesitates at the door. He should carry on and leave Devon behind. Forget about him and move on with his life. "I don't hear from you for months and then I get this voice message to come all the way over here. Then nothing. Nothing at all."

"What do you want? An apology?"

"How about an explanation?"

"What can I say? The Russians offered me more money."

"Jesus Christ, you sold us out for that guy?" Callum indicates the lifeless colonel on the ground.

"I actually liked that guy. He was pretty funny. And Burnes was a complete asshole. I didn't owe him shit."

"What about me? You don't think you owed me anything?"

"For what? Because of everything that happened before. Is that what this is? You came over here to save me because you fucked it up last time? Well, guess what, bud? You're too late."

Callum wipes the blood from his forehead and steadies Burnes on his shoulder. "We can sort this out later. Habs hit an IED. We need to get him out of here."

"The kid with the stutter?"

"Yeah, the kid with the stutter."

"It's going to be tough now seeing as your boy just shot the one guy who could have flown us out of here."

Before Callum can respond, the building shakes violently as if someone dropped a joint direction attack munition on the roof. Callum and Devon share a glance, then sprint from the room toward the sound of the explosion.

# CHAPTER TWENTY-THREE

"We need to get out of here, Murph," Reno says.

"I know," she replies.

"Habs isn't going to make it."

"I know."

"Callum isn't coming back, is he?"

"Can you shut the fuck up for a second, please?" Habs's head rests on Murph's lap. Her arms, numb and slick with blood, pump the kid with chest compressions. Reno, to her right, and JP, to her left, plug the remaining holes in Habs with bandages, torn sleeves, and a dank tube sock, whatever they can find to staunch the bleeding.

She needs time to think, to figure out a way to get them out of this mess. But the only thing she can focus on is keeping Habs alive, to keep the compressions going even though she can't feel anything below her shoulders. Reno and JP both offered to switch with her. Each time she refused, her only respite the pauses she takes periodically to check that Habs is still breathing.

Reno's right. They can't go on like this. Habs won't make it unless they get him to a hospital. But how are they going to do that?

Murph already sent Kamal to work on their captors. Out of the corner of her eye, she can see him pleading with one of the men standing guard, impassive behind a pair of Aviator sunglasses. Kamal inches closer, growing more animated, spouting steam like an overheated machine gun. He could easily drop the guard where he stands, but that wouldn't do them any good. Dozens of other Afghans loiter about, each brandishing some version of a semi-automatic rifle. And those are just the scoobies she can see.

They're in a gravel parking lot in front of a building carved out of the surrounding hillside. The cliff face rises steeply on either side to their north and south. The eastern passage, where they first entered, is blocked by Hesco barriers and a front gate. Murph can't see the western passage because it's blocked by a maze of Sea Cans, but assumes it's the same.

Taraki's men are everywhere, scurrying about, loading and unloading trucks, smoking and joking. Even if they could take them all out, then what? Where would they go? They could take one of the trucks lying around, drive back to the Afghan army outpost, call in a medevac. But who would she call?

And where the hell's Callum? He said he was going to get them out of this. She believed him, but where is he? Reno's right. Maybe he isn't coming back.

Her thoughts are interrupted by the sound of a helicopter that swoops in low over the surrounding cliffs and lands behind the main building, out of Murph's sight. Before the rotor wash fully dies down, three men in green combat fatigues approach the building's main entrance from around the side.

They don't look like Afghans.

"Who's that?" Reno asks.

"No idea, but it might be our way out of here."

A pebble sails over Murph's shoulder and ricochets off Reno's chest. Absorbed in patching up Habs, Reno doesn't notice at first until a second stone, larger than the first, smashes into the side of his head. Murph snaps around to scan the boulder field behind them and spots Ash peeking out from behind one of the large rocks.

"What's Ash doing here?" grumbles Reno, rubbing his head.

"Keep it quiet," Murph hisses, glancing up at the guard to see if he noticed.

Murph checks back at Ash, who gestures for them to join him. He must have found a way through the surrounding cliffs to reach the camp. But there's at least two car-lane widths between Ash and them. Even if their guard doesn't see them get up and carry Habs across the open ground, there's a good chance someone else will spot them. Then it will be open season.

"Take over for me," Murph tells Reno. She surveys their surroundings, finally noticing everything for the first time. Most of the activity appears to be over in a loading area by the main building and at each of the gates. Other than that, it doesn't look as if anyone has eyes directly on them except for the one guard.

A row of transport trucks are parked next to the main building. If she can get to one of the trucks, then she might be able to ram the gate with it, draw everyone's attention away so her men can get to the helicopter, assuming the keys are in the truck, no one sees her, and she doesn't get shot up before getting to the truck. It's their only chance to get Habs out of there.

"This is what we're going to do," she tells Reno and JP. "I'm going to grab one of those trucks over there and create a diversion. When I do that, I want you guys to grab Habs and get to the helicopter."

"Too late." Reno points at the boulder field behind them where Ash was hiding. When Murph glances back, she spots him skirting low to the ground behind the boulders before emerging in a dead sprint toward the trucks.

"Shit!" she says. Ash must have thought of the same plan.

After making it over to the trucks, Ash disappears from view around the far side. Murph can see the driver's door open as Ash climbs inside, head peering above the truck's dashboard as he frantically searches the cab for keys or anything else to start the truck.

Murph starts to think about whatever distraction she can make when the truck's engine spurts into life, belching a cloud of noxious smoke. From behind Reno, their guard yells, "Hey!"

"Oh, shit!" says Murph.

The guard swings his rifle around and aims at the truck, which lurches forward a few centimetres as Ash navigates the vehicle's ancient transmission system. Before the guard fires off any rounds, Kamal slams him to the ground and wrestles the rifle away. When the guard refuses to remain in place, Kamal butt-strokes him in the head, leaving him unconscious on the ground.

"All right, let's go." Murph helps JP and Reno lift Habs off the ground. With Kamal taking point, they move toward the helicopter, which has finally shut off its engine.

As Kamal rounds a corner, he nearly stumbles over one of Taraki's goons leaning against the wall, a cigarette dangling from his lips, an AK-47 at his feet. Kamal yells at him to throw his hands up. Putting his fingers to his lips, the man emits a high-pitched whistle, drawing the attention of his mates, who arrive within second, all carrying rifles.

Before Kamal and the others can respond, the truck slams into the building, taking out the crew that just arrived on the scene, mashing their bodies against the wall in a blood-spattered collage of legs and arms.

Murph sprints toward the truck and climbs onto the cab to find Ash dazed inside. A fresh wound has opened up on his forehead, oozing blood over his face. She pulls him from the cab and to the ground. "What the fuck are you doing here?"

"I saw the explosion back at the *khanaqah*. Figured you guys could use some help."

"Thanks for the rescue," she says, genuinely happy to see him. "Can you walk?"

"Yeah. Help me up."

Kamal appears over Murph's shoulder to help Ash to his feet. "Good to see you, pal." He hands rifles to Murph and Ash, having liberated them from the wreckage. "We've got to move."

Not exactly according to plan, but Ash bought them some time, even though Murph can already hear a commotion swarming towards them.

"All right," Murph says to the others as they huddle around. "Kamal, you stay on point. I'll follow you. Reno and JP, you guys have Habs. And, Ash, cover us from the back. We make our way to the helicopter and get the fuck out of here. Everybody good with that?"

"What about Callum?" Kamal asks.

*Shit!* They'll have to get him. Murph says, "Let's get Habs on the helicopter first and make sure we can even fly the thing out of here. Once we do that, I'll go back and get Callum. Let's hope we don't attract any more attention to ourselves."

They all acknowledge grimly, but she senses something new in their faces, something that wasn't there before. An edge. And the hope they can finally escape this mess.

Kamal leads them through the wreckage to the side of the building, checking around a corner before stepping forward into the open. A squad vectors onto their position from less than a hundred metres away. Kamal sends a burst in their direction to keep their heads down before motioning to Murph and the others to sprint forward to cover.

With the new group of scoobies blocking the direct route to the helicopter, Murph scans for another way forward. They could backtrack and loop around the building from the other side, or they can pick their way through the maze of Sea Cans to their front. It's hard to tell from her position if there's even a route through the Sea Cans, but at least it should give them some cover.

"C'mon, Murph!" shouts Kamal through a fresh burst of his AK-47.

"Cover us," she says to him as she leads the others at a low sprint. Once they make it into cover, she yells at Kamal to join them while she snaps off a few suppressing rounds.

After Kamal rejoins them in a huff, Murph retakes the lead as they dart through the Sea Cans stacked two or three high in places, unsure whether or not someone will pop out behind a corner and light them up.

They come across the helicopter on a pad in the middle of the Sea Can village. Murph hears commotion all around but doesn't see anyone. Cautiously, she steps into the open but jumps back when a burst of machine-gun fire rakes the ground in front of her.

Kamal and Ash lay down covering fire as she darts toward the helicopter. The side cargo door is open. Murph climbs inside and walks to the cockpit where the pilot is dozing, reeking of rotten potatoes. She jams a rifle into his shoulder to wake him up, but he doesn't budge. When she yells in his face, he finally wakes up.

"You need to take us out of here!" Murph shouts at him.

"No speak English," says the pilot as he roots around in his flight suit to pull out a flask and take a swig.

"C'mon, let's get out of here!" Ash cries from the back as he tumbles into the helicopter with the others behind him.

"The pilot doesn't speak English," Murph tells him.

"Bullshit." Ash stumbles his way into the cockpit. "Asshole, fly us out of here."

The pilot shrugs, tucks the flask into his jumpsuit, and begins flicking various switches on the helicopter's ancient console.

"No, wait," Murph says. "I have to go back for Callum."

"We're not going to make it out of here if you go back for him," Ash insists.

"We're not leaving without him."

A ring of scoobies appears outside the helicopter and forms a circle around the cockpit, their weapons pointed at the pilot, who panics and starts flicking the control panel with greater urgency, causing the helicopter blades to whirl to life overhead.

Murph glares at the pilot. "Hang on! We're not leaving yet."

The pilot doesn't respond and gradually pulls back on the control, lifting the helicopter off the ground. As the chopper begins to rise, a hail of bullets slams into the aircraft, sending Murph and Ash crashing back out of the cockpit as the helicopter banks away.

Murph regains her feet and hollers at the pilot, "Stop! We have to go back!"

A blast shatters apart the rear of the helicopter, sending it into a tailspin until it crashes into the ground and knocks Murph unconscious.

# CHAPTER TWENTY-FOUR

Callum trails behind Devon with Burnes's dead weight draped over his shoulder. Gunfire echoes down the corridor, distant but growing louder as they draw closer to its source. Devon disappears out of Callum's sight when he rounds a corner. The gunfire wanes and all becomes silent, the only sound Callum's heartbeat thundering in his ears.

Devon jumps out ahead. "Hurry up, old man."

When Callum catches up, he finds Devon waiting by the entrance where Callum first came in.

While doing a press check on his rifle, Devon says, "You're going to have to leave him here."

"We're not leaving him."

"And how the fuck are we going to fight through all of that while you're wearing a dead guy like a rucksack?"

Callum shifts Burnes to his other shoulder and nearly drops him in the process. Devon's right. Who knows what they'll find on the other side of that door. He can always come back for Burnes once they clear the area. Callum puts the body down against the wall, just inside the door, then kneels in front of the corpse and says, "You were a prick, but you deserved better than this." He reaches out and props himself up, using Burnes's shoulder.

Devon glues his ear to the door. The gunfire has fallen silent. He smirks at Callum. "Just like old times."

Callum take a deep breath before following Devon outside. A truck is smashed into the building, its front end crumpled like a hollow-point bullet that found its target. That must be the crash that set this whole thing off. Callum checks the cab, but no one's there. No sign of Murph or any of the others.

He duckwalks behind Devon along the side of the truck. Reaching the end, he peeks around the corner. A trail of bodies and shell casings lead away through the maze of Sea Cans. They follow the trail until they stumble on the body of the other Russian, slumped against the back of a pickup truck with a chunk of his skull missing.

"Looks like he tried to head off in a hurry," Devon comments.

"Wasn't that your buddy?"

"Who? Olaf? No, that guy was a dick. He owed me money."

Shouting draws their attention away from the dead Russian. It's somewhere deeper within the labyrinth. They track the sound and arrive at a makeshift helicopter pad with a Russian Hind attack helicopter looming in its centre, a ten-thousand-kilo behemoth bristling with bad intentions.

Scoobies surround the chopper in a semicircle. Taraki, in the middle, barks orders at them while pointing his pistol at the cockpit. Callum follows the line of sight along Taraki's pistol into the cockpit. Murph stands behind the helicopter's pilot, an AK-47 pointed at the man's head.

"Is that Murph?" whispers Devon.

"Yeah."

"What are we gonna do?"

Callum can't see the rest of his team, either inside the helicopter or anywhere else. They must be with Murph, somewhere farther back. He can negotiate something with Taraki, get all the parties to walk away from this mess before it gets worse. He just needs to get between Taraki and the helicopter. Before he does, Taraki's crew opens up with a full salvo.

With a deep, mechanical hum, the chopper's propeller whirls to life, gradually at first, then with increasing velocity. Undaunted, Taraki's men continue to pour fire at the cockpit. Although the cockpit is capable of withstanding small-arms fire, it will only be a matter of time until their rounds breach the hull and hit one of Callum's people inside.

He'll need to draw Taraki's fire, to give the helicopter enough time to escape, but he isn't going to shoot Taraki's men in the back. He yells at them to get their attention, but no one can hear him over the noise of the helicopter and the automatic gunfire. When that doesn't work, he steps out from behind cover and fires a round into the leg of the man standing next to Taraki, who looks down, dumbfounded. When he turns around, Callum stands there with his rifle aimed at him.

With a roar, the helicopter climbs into the sky and banks to the north. Taraki and his men forget about Callum and turn back to the disappearing aircraft. A rocket flies out of a nearby compound and explodes into the helicopter's back rotor, launching the chopper into a tailspin before crashing into the hills.

Callum doesn't wait to watch the crash. He grabs Devon by the arm, and they both take off in a dead sprint while Taraki and his men are distracted. They barely make it behind cover before a barrage of rifle fire clangs into the Sea Cans at their backs.

Surveying the terrain ahead between their location and the crash site, Callum spies a lone hut at the base of the hill four hundred metres away. From there, it's a straight shot up the hill to reach the crash. He says to Devon, "Cover me. I'll take the first bound to that hut."

"Rog."

"Three, two, one." Devon leans around the corner to spray a burst at Taraki's men while Callum dashes across the open ground to the hut, stray rounds kicking up dirt at his feet. When he arrives at the hut, he motions Devon to join him. As Callum snaps off a few rounds, Devon crumples to the dirt before picking himself up and staggering to Callum's position.

"Are you all right?" Callum yells over the din of incoming fire.

"I got tagged." Devon pulls his hand away from the small of his back. It's covered in blood.

"Let me see."

Devon swats Callum's hand away. "Fuck off! You get up to the crash. I'll cover you."

Callum checks in the direction from where they came but can't see any of Taraki's men. "All right." He takes a deep breath, counts to three, and scurries up the hill toward the crash.

He's almost there when his right leg collapses underneath him. It takes a second to register before he realizes that a round has pierced his leg. Wincing through his teeth, he clamps a hand over the wound to stop the flow of blood. Rolling onto his back, he spots a scoobie's head over a wall in front of the compound. He aims down the barrel of his rifle before sniping off a round. Callum can't tell if he hit him, but the man's head disappears.

Callum doesn't have time to deal with the wound steadily gushing blood down his leg. The round mustn't have hit an artery, otherwise it would be pumping a lot more blood. He needs to get to the crash site. Then he can deal with the wound, as long as he doesn't pass out first.

Struggling to his feet, he limps toward the fallen helicopter. Pieces of it litter the approach. One of the rotor wings is lodged in the ground, the blade projecting into the air. Bits of fuselage are scattered about, slick with jet fuel, burning his nostrils every time he inhales. The cockpit and cabin have rolled onto their sides, with the top of the helicopter facing downhill. He advances from the far side of the hill to give him cover from any fire from below, then waves Devon in.

After Devon limps his way to the helicopter, he grabs Callum. "Go get Murph and the others. I'll hold them off." When Callum pauses for a beat, Devon adds, "I'm good."

Callum gets to the cockpit, bangs on the windshield, and yells, "Hey!" The pilot is slumped over the aircraft's controls and doesn't respond. He peers deeper into the chopper, but smoke obscures the view. Pulling on the door of the cabin, he hollers, "Hey, Murph!"

When he doesn't get any response, he steps into the gloomy interior, lit only by sparking wires hanging in a tangled jumble. In the dimness, he hears moaning. He attempts to pull himself into the helicopter through the open door, but something obstructs his path. It feels like a heavy sandbag, but he can't make it out at first. Reaching down, he realizes it's a man. Reno!

"Jesus Christ, Reno!" He tries to find the Māori's face, feeling where he thinks the man's neck would be to check for a pulse, but it's like sticking his hand into a bog. When he pulls his hand away, it's covered with bloody mulch.

Callum drags Reno out of the helicopter by the arms, the dead-weight of the Māori's body causing problems. It takes him a while to get Reno fully outside the helicopter. In the light, he can see that the body has been completely crushed above the shoulders.

Callum doesn't take any more time to survey the scene and heads back into the helicopter. "Murph?" he says again. "Kamal?" He hears moaning once more from somewhere deeper in the helicopter. The smoke and darkness obscure his vision, so he moves toward the sound by feeling his way. Toward the front of the helicopter, he discovers another body lodged awkwardly into a small space. Callum can't make out who it is at first, but it isn't the body that was moaning. He nudges the inert body but gets no response.

Another body is lodged behind the first one, groaning louder now. He yanks hard to get to the trapped man. When he does, the person cries out in pain. "Ash, is that you?" He can tell by the moans that it is. "Jesus, what are you doing here?" When Ash doesn't say anything, Callum says, "I'm going to get you out of here." He reaches down and tries to pull him out. The moaning becomes a high-pitched wail until Ash passes out. Callum pulls him to his chest in order to move him back down the helicopter. As he does, bullets slam into the side of the chopper in a new round of fire.

Callum leaves Ash inside the helicopter door and crawls to the far end by the cockpit to find Devon slumped over, eyes closed. Callum slaps him awake. "Hey, I need you to hang in there, pal."

Devon bolts awake, tightly gripping his rifle. "I'm good, I'm good."

He's losing a lot of blood, but Callum doesn't have anything to plug him up. He checks around the front of the helicopter and spots two scoobies trying to flank their position. They've crept up behind a series of low rocks two hundred metres away. He manages to pick one off with a burst from his rifle, but the other ducks out of sight before Callum can tag him. Heavy machine-gun fire from the buildings to the south lands just in front of the helicopter, forcing him back down under cover.

Blood from the wound in his leg gushes out in a heavier flow. He takes a tourniquet from his first-aid pouch and slides it over his leg, cinching the knob to staunch the flow of blood. When he thinks it can't get any tighter, he gives it another twist with a grimace. The blood slows to a trickle, and he limps back to check on Devon, whose eyes are barely open. He says, "I need you to stay with me, man. Ash and the others are in the helicopter. I'm going to bring you up to them, okay?"

Devon mutters something incoherent. Callum hauls him to his feet and carries him over to where he left Ash. When they get to the entrance of the helicopter, Ash has pulled another body from the wreckage. It takes Callum a second to realize it's Murph, her face covered in blood and smoke. Ash leans over her, giving her chest compressions. Callum asks, "What about Habs and Kamal? Are they still in there?"

Ash doesn't look up, just shakes his head. "They're still in there. They didn't make it."

"We need to get out of here. Can you move?"

"I think both of my legs are broken. I'll cover you guys. Just get Murph out of here."

Callum glances at the hills above them. He'd have to carry Murph on his back about five hundred metres before they could get into a defensible position. And then he'd have to come back for Devon and Ash. And then what? Where would they go? Even on two good legs without anyone shooting at them, the prospects don't seem great.

"No, we're going to have to fight it out here." He inserts a fresh magazine into his rifle and charges a new round into the chamber. "I figure Taraki only has five or six dudes left. You stay here with Murph. I'll hold them off."

"We were going to wait for you," Ash says between chest compressions.

"Okay."

"It was my idea. We were going to take the helicopter hostage, trade one of their guys for you."

"Okay."

"I fucked it up. I fucked everything up." Ash pauses to glance up at Callum with bloodshot eyes before turning back to Murph.

"You did good, Ash. You came back. You did good."

Callum doesn't know what else to say but wants to make it right. The only way he can now is to fight their way out. He crawls along the side of the helicopter, back to the cockpit. He can't see anyone at the rocks where they were previously shooting. There's no sign of Taraki's men anywhere. He edges out a little farther to look south into the compound below.

Squinting through his scope, he makes out a lone individual on top of the roof of one of the buildings. The man gestures to the east and yells into the courtyard below. Callum scans along the infil route to the east where there's a dust cloud approaching their position. It takes him some time to make out three pickup trucks driving toward Taraki's compound, each full of armed men in the back. As they get closer, Callum sees they're wearing Afghan police uniforms.

Gunfire erupts from the compound below at the incoming Afghan police. The lead pickup is hit by a flurry of bullets and swerves off the road and into a ditch. The remaining two vehicles continue through the fusillade. The trucks pull up behind a couple of walls, and the Afghan police dismount behind cover. They return fire into the compound in front of them. A furious gunfight ensues, with the Afghan police bounding under cover and firing at the entrance to the compound. One policeman waits at the edge of the compound before throwing a grenade over the wall. He shouts at his colleagues to take cover before an explosion goes off inside. The policemen stream into the compound, out of Callum's sight. Bursts of gunfire can be heard inside as the policemen clear from room to room. A short while later, two of Taraki's men escape through a rear exit and make their way up the hills in the opposite direction of what's left of the helicopter.

Now's their chance. With Taraki occupied, maybe he can get Devon and the others into a secure position and figure out their next move from there.

Callum runs back to check on Devon, whose eyes are only open in half slits. Ash is in no better shape and has stopped working on Murph. But he manages to raise his head as

Callum says, "The Afghan police are here. Sit tight. We're —"
His words are interrupted by an explosion that tears apart the
rest of the downed helicopter, sending Callum flying through
the air to land on his back. His last image is of the blue sky
above before he passes out.

# PART VIII
# THE THANE OF CRUMBS

# CHAPTER TWENTY-FIVE

Ocean air chases sleep from his room. The taste of salt fills his senses as he lies naked on the bed, blinking at the ceiling fan that spins around and around and around. He rises slowly and makes his way to a low sink to splash water on his face, avoiding the grey recess of his eyes in the mirror. Pulling on shorts and a T-shirt draped over a chair in the corner, he walks out of the small bungalow and down a path to the beach.

Water splashes over his feet, then up to his shins and knees as he wades into the surf until the waves lap at the hem of his shirt. He stands there and gazes out over the swell. Sunlight lances through the low-hanging clouds, unsettling the vast solitude.

Two children play in the surf farther along the beach. They take turns body-surfing on a broken board someone has discarded, laughing and splashing each other as the waves roll in, silver-skinned naiads unseen by the world around them.

Fishermen cast their nets far out in the bay, competing for space between speedboats ferrying in new hordes of backpackers from the main island. Their destination is the jetty that pokes out from the centre of the beach like a bony finger, beckoning them in where they disgorge into the cafés and bars just opening, already filling up with hungover partiers from the night before.

He can't remember how many days he's been on the island. Weeks maybe. He can't recall how he ended up here, just that he has. And every morning is the same. He walks down to the water and stands in this spot. The children play in the waves. The speedboats race in. The cafés open, and he wonders how it all came to be.

Reluctantly, he leaves the ocean behind and makes his way back up the path in search of coffee. Hoping to create some distance from the incoming hordes, he seeks out one of the more secluded cafés farther along the beach. The main path, which circles the island, is lightly trafficked at this end of the beach. Cars aren't permitted here, so backpackers get around on the occasional rickshaw or bicycle. For the most part, though, people just walk. Only the occasional local is this far south on the island at this time in the early morning, so he has the path mostly to himself.

He settles on an empty café except for a young and curated-looking couple. Australian probably. They scroll through their phones, only stopping periodically to take selfies, occasionally of each other but most often of themselves. They're like two brightly plumed and exotic birds plucking gnats from their feathers before preening for their mates.

The bartender approaches when he grabs a seat at the bar. Bob Marley wails from the speakers. Music franca at every bar in the tropics catering to this lot. "Hello, stranger," the bartender says as she pours him a cup of coffee without him asking.

The smell from the steaming cup snaps him awake. Although the mug is still piping hot, he takes a sip and feels instantly invigorated. "Thanks."

She smiles faintly as she watches him drink from the cup, her eyes as dark as the wine-coloured sea. "You have walked by my bar for many days now, but this is the first time you have come in."

He doesn't remember seeing the bar before but nods while holding the cup in front of his face between his hands, but doesn't say anything.

As she leans over the bar, a gold necklace with a *C* pendant on it falls from her shirt where it dangles from her fine neck. She clasps her hands together intently next to his. "What brings you to my island?"

"This is your island?"

"As much as anyone else's, yes."

"I guess I'm just completely lost."

"Then you have come to the right place."

With effort, he breaks away from her gaze so he can take in his surroundings. The bar is carved out of the rainforest itself, leaving him unsure where one ends and the other begins. Ebony, teak, and scented sandalwood trees grow all around. Wild rattan vines hang from the ceiling and wrap around the bar and beneath the tables and back out into the trees. The whole place smells of citrus and brittle pine.

"Where is your wife?" she asks, pulling him back in while she traces the tattoo on his ring finger with her own.

He tries to remember where she is but can't. He isn't even sure he has a wife. That part of his mind is blank. Shaking his head, he says, "I don't know."

Removing his hand from beneath hers, he returns to survey the golden bay outside the bar, where gulls circle over the skiffs returning with their morning catch that will be served in the bars later that day. The scene is somehow familiar, but he's not sure how. Some memories still linger, like climbing to the top of the bluff hand in hand to watch the sunset over the ocean. But he can't picture her face. Or even remember her name. All of it has been erased.

"Are you still eager to leave and return to your home?" she asks.

"Excuse me," he says.

"I can see it in your face. You are thinking of home right now, are you not?"

"You ask a lot of questions."

"Does that bother you?"

"Yes." He takes a long sip of coffee. "No."

"Can you tell me a story?" she asks.

He shrugs. "I don't know any stories."

"Sure you do. You know many great stories. You even played a role in some of them." Before he can respond, her hand shoots out and regains hold of his. Although he tries to pull it back, he can't break her grasp. "I know a story about a boy who liked to play soldier with his many friends. They all gave each other clever names. And then the boy grew up to be a man of many exploits. And he wanted everyone to know this about him, that he was special and did many things. But nobody cared. So he ran away and no one ever saw him again."

She lets go of his hand and releases a strange laugh that unsettles the surrounding rainforest. When her eyes return to his, they have a playful glint in them, but something darker, as well.

"Thanks for the coffee." He places a crumpled bill from his pocket on the bar and gets up to leave.

"Come find me later, my unhappy friend," she calls after him. "I have more stories I can tell you."

Outside the bar, the path curves away to the south, skirting along the beach line where the island is mostly uninhabited. The path going north leads to the busier part of the island where the beach is crowded with bars, hostels, and dive shops. He can already hear the *thump-thump-thump* of bass playing from a nearby café, so he decides to spend more time alone and turns south.

Away from the noise, the island is mostly quiet. The dense rainforest looms over his right shoulder. Deep shadows fade into the trees where the light doesn't touch. The few noises are an occasional twerp from an undetected animal or squawk from an unseen bird.

He walks as long as he can, not knowing where he is or where he's going, figuring he must have arrived at the western side of the island, away from the buzz and action. Settling in the shade of a massive tree down on the sand, he looks out over the sea, devoid of all life and sound all the way to the horizon. At least on the surface.

Stretching out in the sand beneath the trees arcing over his head, he catches glimpses of bright sky through the waving canopy. Another memory comes to him. Of a woman. His wife perhaps. They were in a place similar to this one. And she was happy. But she wasn't able to sit still and enjoy the moment with him. She wanted to be off somewhere, wild and restless and free, exploring the jungle and the reef and each one of the little bars lining that beach.

They were here once long ago and were supposed to come back but didn't for reasons he can't remember. Maybe he did once, but not anymore. All of the dishonoured promises. His mostly. The debts he left behind for her to carry.

He closes his eyes and tries to remember, to fill in the rest. But when he fixes his mind on the outline of where she would fit, he can't. As if she's standing in front of the sun and is obscured by the light. Or maybe she is the light. With a sigh, he opens his eyes and looks back over the water.

A small dinghy putters along the beach from the north and pulls up onto the beach. Two feral ditch pigs in tank tops and oversized board shorts pile out of the boat and haul the dinghy onto the sand. One man tries to conceal the boat in the shrubs beneath palm fronds, while the other tosses burlap sack after burlap sack out of the back of the dinghy.

The two work in practised silence, though not too efficiently. The man concealing the boat has to constantly rearrange the coverage of the fronds, which keep sliding off the dinghy, leaving the boat exposed in various places like a balding man combing the few remaining strands of hair over his bald head. While he hustles around in a hopeless attempt to cover up the vessel, his companion takes periodic breaks when the other isn't watching. Once the boat is eventually covered up to the first fellow's satisfaction, the two men throw the sacks over their shoulders and make their way up the path.

They nearly trip over Callum, who's been sitting in silence watching them the whole time. *"Oi!"* says the frond-layer, after recovering from the shock of finding Callum. "You see all that?"

When Callum looks at them and doesn't respond, the other man says, "Okay then. You don't see anything, right?"

"I want fifty percent," Callum says.

"Of what?" asks the frond-layer.

"Whatever's in the bags."

The two men glance at each other, not sure what to say.

"You look like a right-hard fucker, so we don't want any troubles, yah?" the slacker says, his rough-cut dreads whipping back and forth beneath a greasy bandana as he shakes his head.

"I'm just fucking with you," Callum says while the two men laugh nervously at each other. "Seventy-five percent."

"Look, we still have twenty kilos back at the other island. We'll give you a half of that. Just give us a hand bringing this lot up."

"Twenty kilos of what?"

"Mushrooms."

"Mushrooms?"

"Yeah, mate, magic fucking mushrooms. You know, to make the magic boom-boom drink. Why else would you come to this island?"

"I heard the scuba diving's good."

"That's a joke, isn't it?"

"No."

"Well, bugger off then."

"Hang on a sec." The frond-layer grabs his buddy by the arm and hauls him off for a private conversation. When they return, he says, "Look, I'm Scotty and that's Charlie. You wanna make a few bucks?"

"Doing what?"

"It's a little complicated, but we work for this chick …"

"Her name's Crystal," Charlie chimes in.

The bartender. Callum says, "I think I met her earlier."

Charlie laughs. "Oh, I bet she likes you."

"Knock it off, right?" Scotty says, whacking Charlie across the back of the head. "Why don't you come find us later and we'll fill you in then? We'll be at the Teegarden."

"Thanks. I'll keep that in mind."

Charlie gives Callum a thumbs-up before he lopes off after Scotty into the forest. One of the bags over his shoulder splits open at the bottom, spilling out a trail of mushrooms. Callum calls out to warn them of the spill, but they're already too far away by that point. Probably for the best, though, since he doesn't want to get involved in whatever they're mixed up in. And strangely enough, seeing all those mushrooms reminds him that he's rather hungry.

He gets up from the sand and continues around to the northern part of the island where bars begin to sprout out of the brush. They're not quite as established as their competitors on the east side, but he still encounters the odd backpacker he hoped to avoid. He decides to cut inland away from the beach. The island is much less developed here, since this is where the locals tend to live in shacks huddled together.

Some way down a path hacked out of the rainforest he comes upon a little hut, set off to the side beneath the canopy. A low bar made of roughly cut teak with three high stools tucked underneath occupies the front of the hut. A wizened man sits on one of the stools smoking a cheroot. When he sees Callum approach, he yells at someone back in the hut. A portly woman walks out and waves for him to sit at the bar. She pours him a glass of juice from a plastic jug on the bar before turning back inside.

While she rattles around, the man rests an elbow on the teak bar, observing Callum through smoke rings that he blows from his spliff. Woodfire smoke pillows out of a chimney from the hut, and the sweet smell of curry wafts in his direction. He's already salivating by the time the portly woman strides out with a bamboo bowl stuffed with rice, vegetables, and thick-cut chunks of whitefish, all slathered under a heavy yellow sauce that pools off the spoon when he raises it to his lips.

When he finishes the meal, the man reaches over and hands him the cheroot. Callum hesitates momentarily before taking the spliff. He draws the pungent smoke deep into his lungs and exhales slowly, letting the smoke drift up before dissipating in the air. Callum smiles at the man before taking a second drag, which leads to a coughing fit, sending the old man into a fit of laughter.

The woman scolds the man for laughing and pours Callum another glass of juice, which he chugs down to quench the fire burning in his throat. Gratefully, he peels a wad of bills from his roll and hands them to the woman. When she refuses, he leaves them under the empty juice glass. With a genuine smile, he claps the man on the back and gets up from his stool. Unsure whether from the meal or the smoke, he feels curiously enlightened. Tired of being alone, he figures it's time to end his solitude and goes in search of people.

# CHAPTER TWENTY–SIX

An islander, off to serve Bintang beers at one of the island's many bars, passes Callum as he works his way back toward the beach. And then another islander appears, quiet and sprite-like, out of the rainforest. Soon the trickle of islanders moving in the same direction becomes a stream, as they pour from their shacks hidden behind the trees.

Callum is in imposter in their home. But aside from the odd curious glance or impish chuckle, they pay him little attention. Perhaps, then, he isn't an imposter. Maybe that's just the way he sees himself. Maybe he's something less. Something not imposing at all.

He wants to stop them, to turn back the tide. He reaches out to a passing boy, as if the boy were a rock in a swift-flowing river. But the boy slips through his grasp, and Callum finds himself swept up in their current and carried away toward the beach.

When they emerge from the forest, nighttime has already begun to fall. Glass lanterns hanging by copper wires from the trees flicker to life. The lanterns, in many different shapes and sizes, cast kaleidoscopic colours onto the ground and the darkening trees, and already the beach alights with backpackers in the early stages of intoxicated revelry.

His buzz from earlier has begun to fade, diminishing any appetite he might have had to dive into the frenzy unfolding in front of him. He considers returning into the forest. But when he looks back, he can't make out the path he just came through, as if the forest has closed in on itself. Resignedly, he turns south to head back to the little cabin on the beach, which should give him some measure of refuge from the alcohol-fuelled hordes.

Electronic tribal music blasts from the bars lining the path on either side, creating a cacophony as they compete to draw in as many of the backpackers as they can, who spill out into the path, choking the way forward as Callum makes his way along the beach.

He arrives at a circle of onlookers formed around a shirtless man twirling fire *pois* that whip around in a tight arc. The fire twirler's eyes follow the imperceptible path of the *pois*, as if he's managed to slow down time to a pulse only he can see. Callum jostles his way around the outside of the circle but is stopped by a woman whose face is painted completely blue. She hands him a clay stein with a bright smile but is clearly disappointed when he politely declines the offer and continues onward.

Eventually, the crowd thins. He picks up his pace and avoids making eye contact with anyone in his way until he narrowly avoids a puddle of vomit in the middle of the path. As he steps around the puddle, he collides with a man bent at the waist, spewing all over the ground. The man curses Callum in German while wiping his mouth with the back of a hand.

Callum mutters a half-hearted apology to the man. When he turns around, he finds himself facing the bar he was in that morning. Crystal's bar. The urge to go inside is irresistible, though he knows it would be a mistake. He wills himself to turn away and walk home, but he can't move and feels rooted in place.

Two deeply tanned young women giggle as they pass by him arm in arm. The taller of the two reaches out and tugs on Callum's T-shirt, pulling him inside after them. Without offering any resistance, he follows.

Although the bar isn't as crowded as some of the others farther up the beach, most of the tables are taken except for one or two at the back. Callum shouts at his two new companions something about grabbing drinks at the bar, but they can't hear him over the music. The taller one gives him a bright smile in acknowledgement before following her friend, who has joined a table of wild-looking fairies.

Already forgotten, Callum shoulders his way through the crowd lined up two deep along the entire front of the bar. Three bartenders hustle to mix drinks and pour beers for their thirsty patrons. But none of them are Crystal.

Callum cranes his head in every direction, hoping to catch a glimpse of her somewhere. Maybe she's in a backroom or serving a customer. He gives up after a minute or two when it becomes clear she isn't there. As he prepares to leave, one of the bartenders slams a Bintang down in front of him. Callum isn't sure if it's meant for him at first. When he realizes it is, he reaches into his pocket to grab some cash for the bar, but the bartender shakes his head and refuses to accept any money.

With a shrug, Callum raises a silent toast before taking a swig. After pulling the bottle from his lips, he spies his two prior companions who have clearly forgotten him, dancing together on top of one of the tables, their limbs and bodies writhing in rhythm to the jungle music. Rising toward ecstasy, they draw in an audience that congregates around them.

Mesmerized by their performance, Callum loses all sense of place and time until a hand claps him on the back, breaking the spell. Glancing over his shoulder, he sees Charlie's face with a wicked grin. Or maybe it's Scotty. He can't remember which one is which. Either way he feels vaguely annoyed by the disturbance.

Charlie mouths something at Callum, who shakes his head and points at his ear, indicating he can't hear him. Charlie leans in closer, his breath smelling like bong water, and yells, "We've been looking for you."

Callum shouts back, "Why?"

"We need your help."

"I just want to enjoy my beer, man."

Charlie grabs the beer bottle from Callum and gives it a little shake. Indicating his displeasure after discovering there's nothing left in the bottle, Charlie blindly tosses the empty over his shoulder where it shatters above the bar, raining shards of glass on the bartenders.

As the bartenders recover from the impact, Scotty lunges over the bar and grabs a bottle of tequila in each hand. Spinning around in victory, he raises the two bottles high above his head to a chorus of cheers and proceeds to pour tall shots into the outstretched cups of his new friends.

The first bartender to recover hops up on the bar, swinging a baseball bat in Scotty's direction. Scotty dodges the first blow but blocks the second with one of the bottles of tequila, which explodes, sending a fresh wave of glass and tequila into the crowd.

Charlie dashes forward and yanks the bartender's foot out from underneath him, toppling him off the bar. As a second bartender emerges to flick a beer bottle at Charlie's head, he ducks the incoming projectile, allowing the bottle to sail undetected into the mob.

After dusting shards of glass from his hair and shirt, Callum springs toward Charlie and puts him in a headlock. With Charlie under one arm, he grabs Scotty by the scuff of his shirt and begins to haul them both out of the bar. Before he makes it more than two steps, Callum collapses to one knee after a stool splinters into pieces over his back. Once he regains his senses, he checks back over his shoulder where an angry islander points down at him, spittle foaming at the edge of the man's lips.

Callum rises to confront the angry islander, intending to diffuse the situation. Unpersuaded, the islander launches a wild right hook. Callum narrowly eludes the blow, sending the islander crashing into a nearby table. Two backpackers seated at the table gaze distraughtly at their freshly spilled beer. But their dismay quickly turns to thoughts of vengeance as they muscle the soggy islander off the shattered table. Another bartender somersaults off the bar in a kamikaze like attack, landing squarely on top of the trio, who all collapse onto the floor in a heap.

The entire bar erupts into a melee of frenzied limbs and heat-seeking beer bottles, any distinction between friend and foe meaningless. Callum spots Charlie and Scotty, both on top of the bar. Scotty is still pouring shots of tequila, while Charlie shouts directions like an army colonel issuing orders on top of a hill being overrun. Wading through the haze, Callum fights his way to the bar where he manages to drag Charlie and Scotty from the bar so they can beat their retreat.

When they finally make their way outside, they sprint down the street past crowds of bemused spectators. They all pull up when they're far enough away and bend over gasping for air.

"That was fucking mental," Charlie says before heaving into the bushes.

"What the fuck!" Callum says as he begins to walk away.

"C'mon, we owe you a drink." Scotty hurries after Callum and puts his arm around Callum's shoulder.

Shrugging out of Scotty's embrace, Callum says, "Not a chance."

After Callum makes it a couple of metres from them, Scotty calls out, "Crystal wants to see you, mate."

Callum pauses mid-stride. These morons incited a riot, but he does want to see Crystal again. Glancing back at them, he sees they're both waiting there like two idiot puppy dogs.

When neither of them move, Callum finally motions as if to say, "After you." They bound forward, elbowing each other out of the way, eager to lead Callum off to meet Crystal, even though he knows it's a bad idea.

Scotty and Charlie take him to a clearing away from the beach, set deeper into the surrounding rainforest. Blissed-out backpackers lounge in hammocks or on massive bean bag chairs, sewn together from brightly coloured scraps of cloth. The strange kaleidoscopic lanterns set among the trees cast light all about, keeping the jungle's darkness at bay. It isn't a bar and no one is in charge, the vibe definitely more mellow than the last establishment he was in.

Callum pauses at the clearing's edge, searching the crowd for Crystal. When he turns to leave without finding any sign, Charlie grabs him by the arm and drags him onto a nearby couch. Offering only mild resistance as he settles into the couch, Callum asks, "You want to tell me what that was all about?"

"Bit of a misunderstanding that," Scotty says.

Charlie follows up by adding, "We got a bit carried away there."

Charlie and Scotty exchange glances before Scotty says, "It's complicated."

"There's a war going on," Charlie contributes.

"Between Crystal and that lot back at the bar," Scotty says.

"Over what?" Callum asks.

"What are wars usually about."

"All right, then, what does she want with me?"

"W don't know," Charlie says.

"She didn't tell us," Scotty chips in.

Looking around, Callum asks, "So where is she?"

"She'll be here later."

Callum attempts to rise from the couch but falls back after Charlie latches onto his arm and tugs him down.

Scotty raises a hand to catch the eye of a server who appears from a curtain hanging between two trees. "Just relax, mate. Have a drink with us."

The server approaches the trio and sets a tray in front of them on top of a tree stump. Three earthware mugs balance on top of the tray.

Scotty leans over with his elbows on the edge of the tree stump and runs the long, curved nail of his trigger finger along the rim of one of the mugs. He grins at Callum and says, "*Carpe scrotum*," before guzzling down the contents of the mug and slamming it back on the table.

Charlie slides a mug in front of Callum. "What do you say, cabbage?"

Callum peers into the dark elixir, so thick it barely moves when he swirls it around in the mug. "What is it?"

"Black magic." Charlie raises his mug in a silent cheer.

He should get up. Walk away. Leave this place and never come back.

He should go home.

But where's home?

Callum closes his eyes and tries to picture it but can't. The image slips away from his grasp like a minnow in the shallows, leaving him floundering in the current.

Maybe this will help him remember.

Callum raises the mug to his lips and takes a sip. The bitter taste scrapes along his tongue, causing him to gag on the after-taste. It takes Callum a minute to get the whole brew down. When he finally does, he says, "That was fucking awful."

"It's better on toast with some vegemite," Charlie says.

"What now?" asks Callum.

"We wait," Scotty says.

Charlie has pulled the hood of his sweatshirt over his head and shadow-boxes in his seat, like in a video game. Left-right-left-right. Jab-jab-cross-uppercut. *A-B-A-B*.

Callum opens his mouth, but no words come out. He can see the letters in his mind. Black letters on a white page. But he can't say anything so he just nods.

"You can hear your voice in your head, can't you?" Scotty says.

Callum nods in response.

"Not just your own voice, but everyone you've ever met. They speak to you, don't they? The living and the dead."

Callum eyes Scotty. His shaved, tanned head stretches out under the torchlight and elongates until he looks like some kind of alien sex panther.

"I met a man once," Scotty says. "He called himself the Thane of Crumbs. Said fire was our first secret but that we let it burn too long until all the young were dead and heaven curled in at the edge."

Charlie gets up before retching in the bushes and stumbling off toward the bathroom while Scotty laughs, a deep guttural sound. "The devil whispers, mate, but will you follow?"

Callum tries to speak but still can't. Suddenly, a progress bar flashes on the screen in front of him, filling slowly at first until it speeds toward the end. He doesn't want to be in this place any more, so he gets up from the bench, leaving Scotty behind, muttering incomprehensibly to himself.

The path narrows to a single point beyond the beach. Light and sound diminish, buffered by the jungle canopy. Out of the belly of some mechanical beast, away from the hum and the noise and the electricity, along a jetty, reaching out across the water, falling away over the edge into night.

Stars drop into the ocean like pennies thrown down a well. Slowly at first, one by one, emptying the night sky with increasing velocity until vertigo sets in and Callum has to close his eyes to stop from spinning.

But when he opens his eyes, only darkness remains.

He can feel his self unwinding, his centre spinning away. Thought, experience, being. A sudden recission. I'm not here. This isn't happening.

And then a single red light appears, pulsing somewhere in the distance, a beacon or a signal. He stares at the red dot until it grows into the size of a great red sun. The light expands further still until it fills the whole of his vision. Warm. Inviting. Enveloping.

He swims along in the current of the red light toward its source, certain he must arrive at a place where nothing fades and everything goes on and on. A place where he'll finally be free of himself.

Arriving at two heavy wooden doors, he steps through into an ancient church. Everything inside is stone and light. Nothing else. Just silence. As he moves barefoot down the aisle, his feet glide along shallow dunes of sand as fine as snow. An elderly woman sits in the front pew, not moving or saying anything. She stares up at a massive olive tree that grows out of the altar, reaching up into the light. He pauses at her shoulder and follows her gaze to the top of the tree. She turns to face him and says, "Climb."

Grabbing the lowest branch, he scales up through the tree's many limbs. Up and up, he climbs until he can no longer see the ground or the woman below. He continues on to the very top of the tree, its leaves brushing against the ceiling of the church. When he finds a trapdoor that swings inward when pushed, he pulls himself through into a room of darkness.

The red light returns, blinking in the distance, guiding Callum forward. The floor moves underneath him, swirling and shifting, as he steps forward. The shapes coalesce into human forms, into bodies that writhe and merge into one another, an infinite tangle of limbs and boughs that move out of his way as he lurches toward the red light beaming down upon him from the top of a great tower.

When he arrives at the base of the tower, Calypso is there, sitting on a great throne, a riot queen who commands the light and the dark. She smiles sweetly at him. "My unhappy friend. Do not waste any more of your life on this island." Callum climbs onto her lap like a small child, closes his eyes, and sleeps.

# PART IX
# EULOGY VIRTUES

# CHAPTER TWENTY-SEVEN

"All right, let's get started. For the record, the time is 0832. The speaker is Major Tom Alcinous from the Directorate of Defence Counsel Services. Sir, could you please state and spell your name?"

The windowless office is white. White walls. White ceiling. White floor. White stacks of paper stacked evenly on the white desk. The computer white. The major's hands and teeth white. Everything except for the major's eyes, which are black and fastidious, poised eagerly behind wire-rimmed glasses.

"What am I doing here?" Callum asks.

"You've been charged pursuant to sections 130 and 132 of the National Defence Act."

"I'm not military anymore. The NDA doesn't apply to me."

"It's the only way we could get you out of Afghanistan. Someone had to convince the Afghan government you're still serving. Hence, me and well ... all of this." The major waves his hand at the piles of paper on the desk. His eyes disappear as he returns his gaze to the computer where the screen reflects brightly on the mirror of his glasses. "And you have friends in high places, my friend."

Callum looks down at a mark of ash on his palm. He can see in that mark everything he's ever held. A knife. A letter. An empty glass. An entire history that weighs no more than that dull stain. He spits on his palm to wipe it all away. "Where's my team?"

The major's fingers pause above the keyboard. "How much do you remember?"

Just splinters of memories. None of them fit together. He woke up in a room. Kind of like this one. His eyes pressed tightly together, resisting the light. People speaking. They wouldn't stop, but he couldn't understand them. They wouldn't tell him where he was. They wouldn't listen to him. He tried. Then needles jabbed into his arm. He tried to pull them out, but they held him down until he couldn't see or hear anything. Just pain. The only thing he could feel. The only thing he wanted to feel.

He just shakes his head.

"The report we heard was that the Afghan police had to scrape you off a hill somewhere in the Panjwai. You spent the next couple of days in a hospital in Kabul before we even found out. Apparently, you were pretty banged up. And then it took us a while to pull you out."

"What about ... was there anybody else?"

"There were no survivors, at least that we know of. I'm sorry."

His vision peels away at the edges and collapses inward to a point so far and distant he can't see the end. The darkness sucks in everything, every breath and fibre of his being.

"Do you need a minute?"

"You should have left me there."

"That wasn't going to happen. Despite your crimes, you're still a citizen of this country. On that basis, the Government of

Canada, and apparently a few others with significant resources, went to great lengths to ensure you were tried according to the laws of this country."

"What do you want?"

"Why were you there?"

"Does it matter?"

"I guess not. The charges, such as they are, don't mean anything. We had to draft them up for diplomatic purposes, though I'm sure that whatever payments were made had the more persuasive effect."

"Then what am I doing here?"

"Well, we can't quite let you go, at least not yet. The wheels of justice grind slowly and all of that."

"This has nothing to do with justice."

"That's one way of looking at it." The major removes his glasses so he can rub the bridge of his nose before returning them to his face. He leans over the table and steeples his fingers. "You know, I remember your first trial. I was brand-new to the directorate. Don't worry. I didn't have anything to do with your case. But it was bullshit. Everyone knew it. But we had our orders, didn't we? I guess you had your orders, too, but you didn't listen to them."

Callum doesn't say anything and lets the major continue.

"I always wanted to ask you about what actually happened. And then this." The major gestures with both hands toward the computer screen. "I see your name again. Like a ghost. Ten years later. I didn't believe it. None of us did. And there are still a few of us around from those days. Captain, Retired, Callum King. Can you believe it? I guess the bigger question, and probably the more interesting one, is why would you ever go back?"

Had he ever stopped to ask himself that question? Of course, he had. It was to bring Devon home. But was that it? Was that all? What about redemption? Revenge? Renewal? There were a hundred other reasons, but none of them were ever the answer, at least not the right one.

"I was an important man," Callum says. "Not the most important. I wasn't the chief of the defence staff or anything. But people respected me. They asked for my opinion. My son worshipped me. My wife loved me. And then it changed when you took it all away."

The major leans back in his chair with a sigh and crosses his arms on his chest. "You reckon that's our fault, do you?"

"Can I go now?"

"Afraid not. I still have to write up my report, which has to go through the chain for approval. Who knows how long that's going to take? You know how it goes." The major types a few last keystrokes into the computer before removing a thumb drive and placing it squarely on top of the stack of papers on his desk. "I suggest you make yourself comfortable. You could be here a while."

After the major leaves, a young corporal in military police uniform pokes his head in the door. "Sir, could you come with me?" He escorts Callum down the hall. Not in handcuffs or chains. Not to a cell. Just back to the room he came from earlier. A simple room with a single desk and a narrow bed, a closet in the corner, mostly empty except for an old blanket folded on the top shelf. He's spent days of his life in rooms like this one. Weeks. Months even. The exact same room as every other dorm room in every barracks in the country.

They never locked the door when they left. There were no bars on the windows. He could have walked out of the door and off the base any day, and nobody would have stopped him. But where would he go?

That's not the point though, is it? There are places he could go. But the only other place he wants to go is back to that hill with Devon and Murph and Kamal and the rest. To die in their place. He knows that chance is gone. So he'll wait here, though he's not sure why.

The MPs check in on him periodically. At first, he was a real curiosity, a mystery no one understood. Who was this guy? What did he do? Why were they even looking after him? One or two of them tried to get it out of him, asked him if he wanted to go outside for a walk or watch some TV in the lounge. But they never got very far. Eventually, they stopped asking and the novelty wore off. Still, they came by every day to drop off food or fresh laundry, sometimes even a newspaper they thought he might read. Instead, the food piles up on their trays, mostly uneaten. And the laundry remains unused by the door.

He's not a prisoner. This isn't a jail. He's not going to stand trial. But he wants to. More than anything. He wants to stand in the witness box and say all the things he didn't say the last time. He wants to tell his story so everyone will know about the things he's done. He wants to stand in front of the world and say the names of all the soldiers he's lost. And he wants everyone to know it was all his fault. But no one knows, no one cares.

He's just a bureaucratic headache, the subject of some memo no one ever reads but that ends up passed from colonel to bored-ass colonel. They all scribble their minutes in the margins and write "ACK" over the top of their neat little signature blocks. Thirty years of service condensed into a rank and made-up position.

He waits alone in that room with dreams that come fitfully during the night and again during the day. They all bleed into one another so that he's not sure which is which.

He dreams he stands in a large hall between pillars of stone that are chipped and crumbling and he's soaking wet even though the floor's covered in sand. Three other men wait in the room. They speak a different language, but he can understand what they're saying. They came to the room looking for something. One searches for inspiration, the other for recognition, and the sad one longs for happiness.

But mostly he dreams of Penny.

One of the guards brought him a letter the first day he was here. It was from Penny. It started with nothing. No "Dear Callum" or "Hi." That was as far as he ever got. The letter remained in its envelope beneath his pillow, radiating sorrow and infecting his dreams with remorse.

Penny wanted to live in a world without monsters, where nothing bad ever happened. But that was a world where he didn't have to exist. And he was afraid that if he read that letter, that if he acknowledged her at this point in time, he would know she was always right, that he never had to exist at all. And he would embrace all the pain he could muster just so he never has to face that terrible thought.

Penny came on the third day. He didn't know it then until she told him much later. But they wouldn't let her see him at first. Probably for no good reason other than her visit required thirteen levels of approval. Because they didn't know what they were going to do with him.

It's not until many days later, after first meeting with the major, that a young MP pokes his head in Callum's room and says, "Sir, there's someone here to see you." Callum doesn't understand why they still call him sir. He doesn't know how to respond, so he mumbles something that sounds like okay while the MP stands awkwardly in the doorway. Eventually, he follows the MP down the hall into the lounge. The room is dark and no one is there. He leaves the light off and approaches the window to watch cars pass by on the street below.

Backlit by light from the hall, Penny's image appears in the window as negative space. The same vision of her he's had every night since he saw her last. He remains at the window, afraid her image will disappear if he turns around or even says her name. She, too, stays distant in the doorway, not moving or saying anything.

Penny is the first to break the deadlock. She crosses the floor to sit on a low bench by the window. With her feet crossed at her ankles and her hands clasped in her lap, she looks up at his face in profile. He has to dig his fingernails into his palms to stop his hands from shaking.

His eyes drift down from the window and settle on her hands tightly clasped in her lap. He keeps them there, unable to meet her gaze. "How are you?" she asks.

His voice catches in his throat before he answers, "I'm okay."
The lines around her eyes soften momentarily.

"How are you?" he asks.

"Okay."

"How's Timmy?"

She nods before blowing out a sigh. "He's good." She reaches out her hand and weaves her fingers through his.

He can't hide the shame and grief anymore. It all pours out of him like a burst dam. "I couldn't bring him home, Penny. I couldn't bring any of them home." He led soldiers to their deaths. Left his wife. Allowed his son to grow up without a father. What kind of a man is he? He wants to say that all to her. He wants her absolution. Her forgiveness. But she knows. She always did. And he did it all, anyway.

Penny doesn't move or say anything, lets it all come out of him. She sits and watches in silence. When he finishes sobbing, she says, "I spoke with someone named Tina from the company you were with. They're going to get you out of here."

"And where would I go?"

"That's up to you. You have to decide. But you can't stay here."

"Can I come home, Penny?"

She drops her hand back in her lap and looks away from him for the first time since she sat down beside him. "No, not yet." She gazes back up at him. "You need to see Timmy first. He's pissed at you. And he doesn't understand what happened. You need to get his permission first."

"Okay." He wipes the snot from his face with the back of a sleeve. "Okay," he says a second time, this time with more certainty.

"I have to go now."

She gets up to leave. Before she reaches the door, he says, "Penny …"

"Yeah?"

"Do you remember when we were young and we believed anything was possible?"

"Yes."

"I want to believe that again."

"That's still what Timmy believes." She looks back at him. "Take care of yourself." Then she's gone.

He sits alone in the room for a long time after she leaves, waiting for the MP to come back and get him. But he doesn't. No one does. They've all forgotten about him.

But for the first time since he can remember, he knows what he has to do. He lies back down on the couch beside him, stares up at the ceiling, and finally sleeps without dreaming.

# CHAPTER TWENTY-EIGHT

A nameless MP shakes Callum awake. "Sir, the major wants to see you." Sunlight leaks into the room around and underneath the blind that someone must have drawn in the night. What time is it? Noon maybe? He didn't mean to sleep in this long. But he feels refreshed. More so than he has in days.

"Can I go for a piss first?"

"The major said he wants to see you." The MP hovers over Callum expectantly.

"All right then." Callum swings his legs down from the bench and cants his head to the side to work out a crick in his neck. He follows the MP down the hall and back to the same room where he met Major Alcinous before. The major keeps his eyes fixed on the computer monitor in front of him and waves at the empty chair near his desk.

After Callum sits in the chair, the major says, "Well, I guess you're free to go, but before you do, we need a few signatures." He slides a file folder across the desk to Callum.

While the major leans back in his chair, Callum opens the folder and pulls out a stack of legal-looking documents. As Callum flips through them, the major says, "That first one there is a waiver of liability. Then a non-disclosure agreement. And finally, a release. They basically say that you're not going to sue the government and that you're going to keep your mouth shut."

Callum has seen all this before in one form or another. Heretofore and thereafter and all that dogshit language lawyers use to confuse mouth-breathers like him. Why can't they just speak normally?

The major says, "You're welcome to get a lawyer to look at them for you, but ... well, it's not going to make a difference. You need to sign them."

"That's it then?"

"What were you expecting? A trial and media coverage just like last time?"

Callum flops the folder down on the table. He flips to the last page, grabs a pen sitting next to the computer, and signs by the note that says "sign here." Then he slides the stack of paper back toward the major. "Can I get some money for the bus?"

The major checks the last page to confirm the signature is there and returns the papers to their folder. Then he hands an envelope to Callum marked "Privileged and Confidential" across the seal. "This is from your former employer, or whatever they are. It should help you with the bus fare." He slides his chair back from the desk and prepares to rise. Before he stands up fully, he says, "I would say, stay out of trouble. But my job is boring. I wouldn't be too fussed if I see your name across my desk again." With a curt nod, the major leaves the room with the folder tucked under his arm.

A cheque slides from the envelope and drifts to the floor like a dead leaf. Callum watches the cheque fall before turning to the letter. The paper is weighty, as if written on ancient papyrus. The name of some corporate lawyer is etched at the top: Esq. JD Asshole. "Thank you for your service with the company.

This letter is to notify you of your termination. Please find enclosed payment in consideration of your severance. I trust the foregoing is satisfactory. Sincerely yours, Asshole Esq."

He picks the cheque up off the ground. It will help with the bus fare, if he had a goddamn bank card to cash it with. Crumpling up the Dead Sea Scrolls, he tosses them in the garbage, then folds the cheque in half, puts it in his pocket, and walks out.

They provided him with old army PT gear: grey sweatpants and sweatshirt two sizes too big; a pair of no-name white sneakers that barely fit his feet; and wool socks, green gitch, and an extra-small T-shirt. That's it. He doesn't have anything else. No bag. No wallet. Not even any ID.

He checks the hall to see if any of the MPs are there. But no one is around. What are the chances? He finally wants to talk to one of them and they're gone. He tries to take the elevator to the ground floor, but the light doesn't turn on when he presses the button and he can't hear any movement inside the shaft. He takes the stairs instead.

The ground floor is silent and abandoned, as well. When he comes to the main entrance leading outside, he pauses for a moment before opening the double doors, uncertain what he should do. With a deep breath, he pushes them open and steps outside.

Snow falls from grey skies the colour of a smeared windowpane. He pulls the hood of his sweatshirt up over his head and plunges his hands deep into his pockets. Bounding down the stone steps two at a time, he jogs past the abandoned guard shack and continues away from the base without looking back.

He can't recall how far it is to his father's residence, or even where it is exactly. Ten kilometres east maybe. But he needs to go there first. To see his father.

Callum sets off at a slow trot and is already winded by the time he reaches the corner. And he can already feel hot spots forming on his heels. But he keeps running, anyway, and doesn't stop.

He doesn't recognize the city at first. Everything looks strange and unfamiliar. It moves and hums in ways he doesn't understand. He draws the strings on his hood even tighter to block out the distractions all around him. And slowly, as he bends his head into the wind, the way ahead comes into focus.

When he arrives at his father's building, he collapses on the ground into a deep pile of snow next to the entrance. He gulps down great mouthfuls of frigid air deep into his lungs before exhaling tiny storm clouds of moisture into the air. Cold from the snow seeps through his clothes and numbs his skin.

"Sir, do you need help?" asks a concerned soccer mom who happens upon him.

Callum sighs. "Why does everyone keep calling me that?"

"Should I get a nurse?"

"I'll be okay, thanks."

It's weird being back. He still feels guilt over sticking his old man here. But they didn't have much of a choice after his mom passed away. Especially after Larry fell off a cliff. They found him at the bottom of a gulley behind his property with a broken leg and an empty bottle of whiskey after not hearing from him for a couple of days. After that, Larry was sucked down a gravity well of prescription pain meds and conspiracy theories from the Dark Web. That's when Callum sent him here. With the rest of the inmates.

Penny offered to look after him, and she would have without a second thought. That definitely would have been Larry's preference. But he wouldn't wish that on his worst enemy.

How long has it been since he's been back to see his dad? Months maybe. Before he left. Whenever that was. Not sure what he's going to find, he reluctantly rolls off the snowbank and brushes away the snow that collected on his body. He walks through the sliding doors and up to the front desk where a considerable-looking nurse eyes the Rorschach blot forming on his chest from the melted snow and sweat.

"I'm here to see Larry," Callum says.

"Who?"

"Larry King."

"Ah, yes, Larry King."

"Yeah, that's my dad."

"That always gives us a laugh."

"I'm sure it does for him, as well."

Chuckling to herself, she slides a clipboard toward Callum across the counter. "Sign here, love." She points to an empty slot on an empty sign-in sheet.

"Where can I find him?" Callum asks.

"He's on the fifth floor."

Before he turns to leave, he asks, "How is he?"

"Hmm. Your father's a prickly peach, isn't he? Especially after his accident."

"What accident?"

"It's probably best you see for yourself, love." She smiles up at him warmly and grabs the clipboard from the counter.

He checks to see if there's an emergency exit he can escape through, but the elevator is right next to the front desk and the nurse is still smiling up at him. He presses the up button and waits for the elevator to arrive without looking back at the nurse.

The elevator opens to a lounge. An ancient television plays a black-and-white movie with the volume turned down low. Two old men sit around a Formica table. One of them sleeps with his chin burrowing into his chest, while the other spoons thick soup from a plastic bowl. He asks the nurse on duty where he can find his father. She nods toward the window before returning to her computer.

That can't be him. Callum almost spins around to leave, but the old man turns his head slightly, as if he knows someone's watching him. He walks over to the old man and sits at his side. "Dad …" The old man turns to look at Callum. The eyelid of his left eye droops like burnt candle wax, and the left side of his mouth turns down in a permanent frown.

"Dad," he says again.

The old man's face turns toward him as his right eye blinks multiple times. *"Rrrrr,"* Larry groans out of the right side of his mouth. *"Rrrrr,"* he moans again with more force.

"Hi, Dad. Can I get you anything? Do you want water? Or a coffee? I'm dying for a good coffee."

Larry reaches out with his claw-like hand and places it on Callum's knee. His father's right eye keeps blinking. But there's something like a smile that creeps across his lips. "I'm home now, Dad."

"*Rrrrr,*" Larry groans.

"Yeah, I'm home now." He places a hand on his father's shoulder. Larry's right hand reaches out to Callum and pulls him in for an embrace. Callum extends both of his arms and pulls his father in close. He smells stale like a discount loaf of bread the grocery stores put out on the shelf that no one ever buys. But it's right and good to be here with him again.

"*Rrrrr.*"

"Penny came to see me last night."

"*Rrrrr.*"

"Yeah, she's a good woman."

"*Rrrr.*"

"I haven't seen Timmy yet, though."

"*Rrrrr.*" Larry thumps his chest with his right hand. "*Rrrrr.*"

"He's got the fire in him, does he?"

Larry shakes his head, spittle dribbling down his chin. "*Rrrr.*"

"Of course, he does. He's our boy, isn't he?"

Larry reaches out again and slaps Callum on the leg a couple of times.

"All right, Dad, I'll go see Timmy. I'll come back tomorrow, okay?"

The old man acknowledges by nodding.

"I'll come and see you tomorrow." Callum leans over and kisses his father on the forehead.

They're two old soldiers who went away to fight wars in far-off places started by fat men for petty reasons. But they never questioned or challenged the why. Because the why never mattered to them. Nor did it for the boys they ran away with.

From broken homes and boring lives. But for Timmy it would be different. He had to make sure of that.

Callum leaves his father alone by the window and thanks the nurse on the way out. He takes the elevator back to the ground floor and waves to the lady at the front desk, checking the clock above the counter. Should be enough time for him to get to Timmy's school before he gets out for the day.

It only takes him ten minutes to jog to the nearby school. By the time he arrives, students are already streaming out of the exits. He worries he might have missed Timmy. Or even if he hasn't, how will Timmy react? Maybe he doesn't even want to see his dad. Maybe he should have asked Penny first if there was a good time he could stop by their place. Their place. It's still his, too, he realizes.

As he contemplates leaving, he spots Timmy bounding down the steps by himself, his backpack slung over one shoulder and a basketball under his other arm. "Timmy!" he yells, but Timmy doesn't respond. He shouts his son's name a second time, stopping Timmy in his tracks.

Timmy eyes his father at a distance and adjusts the backpack over his shoulder. "Dad?"

"Hi, son."

"You're back."

"Yeah, I just got back. A couple of days ago."

"I know."

"Right," Callum says. "I'm going to grab a java. You want to join me for one?"

Timmy looks uncertain at first, but then says, "I don't drink coffee. But, yeah, sure. I have basketball practice tonight, though, so I can't stay too long."

"No worries. I think there's a place a block over. We'll get you back for basketball practice."

They walk in silence for most of the block before Callum asks, "How are you doing?"

"I'm okay."

"Your mom says you're doing good."

"You saw Mom?" Timmy asks, his voice perking up.

"Yeah, she came by to see me last night." Callum holds the door open at the coffee shop and lets Timmy enter first. His son orders a hot chocolate, and Callum asks for a coffee. They get to the cash register before Callum remembers he doesn't have any cash on him. "Sorry, son, but I don't suppose you have any money on you?"

Timmy doesn't visibly react. He pulls out his debit card from his wallet and taps it on the machine. They grab their drinks from the counter and slide into a booth. Timmy slumps down in his seat and wrestles with a straw from his hot chocolate. "You know Mom got you home, right?"

"What?"

"Well, it wasn't her personally. It's not like she went over there herself. She got someone at her firm to call in some favours."

"Oh, yeah?"

"Yeah. She wouldn't tell me herself. I had to ask one of the guys she works with." He adds, "the guy is a complete asshole."

"Is that right?"

"About what? The guy being an asshole or Mom getting you home?"

"Mom getting me home."

"Yeah. Crazy, eh?" Timmy stares at the bandages on his father's hands, noticing them for the first time. "What happened over there?"

Callum removes his hands from the table. "Things didn't work out like we wanted them to."

"Okay."

He wants to tell Timmy everything but doesn't know where to start. How do you tell your child about all the mistakes you made in your life, especially when your child already knows.

"I'm sorry, son."

"For what?"

"I'm sorry I left you alone."

"What about Mom?"

"I'm sorry I left her, too."

"Then you're coming home, right?"

There's so much he could say, so much he should say. Why do the truest things always remain unsaid? "Not yet, bud. I can't go home just yet."

"But you aren't going back, right?"

He doesn't know what the answer is. But he knows what he has to tell him. "No, I'm not going back." Saying it, though, makes it real. He reaches across the table with his good hand to place it over Timmy's as his son wipes tears from his eyes. "No, I'm not going back."

# ABOUT THE AUTHOR

**Andrew Paterson** is a former infantry officer who served with the Canadian Army and deployed to Afghanistan in 2010 as a Platoon Commander. He now lives in Ottawa with his wife and two sons.